***

Mickey D's

It was that day when I learned that McDonalds wasn't just a place to go to get a bite to eat; no, it was much more. Much, much more. So much more that I would have laughed myself to death had I traveled back in time and told the me from the day before.

It all started when I finally managed to get the guts to talk to October. I'd had a crush on her all year—senior year of high school—and it was about time that I got up the courage to ask her out. I wasn't a socially anxious kid, by any means, but I did have quite a bit of anxiety around the subject of her and talking to her.

She was cute. Real cute. About half a foot shorter than me, with long brown hair that she sometimes wore up in a braid; nice, pretty eyes; a body that wasn't too fancy but had just the right amount of girly-ness. It wasn't just her looks that I was attracted to, though. She was smart, could hold her own in a conversation about abstract topics—though I had only learned that through eavesdropping—and was, as far as I could tell, a kind and caring girl. Love sure was strange in how it distorted my perceptions of her, and even though I had rose-colored glasses on, I knew to keep myself at least somewhat sane.

I tapped her on the shoulder when class was over. My stomach was boiling over, and my shoulders were trembling. *Keep it together,* I told myself.

"Hey, October. Can I talk to you?"

"Sure, Max," said October, putting her books back in her bag.

"When everyone is gone," I said, regretting it instantly after I saw the look on her face. It was a look not of confusion, not of disgust, but of resolution. It was so far from what I had expected that I didn't know what to do—I regretted its effect on me. Of course, anything she did was bound to have an effect on me.

October seemed to think for a minute, then nodded. "Only ten minutes, because I have to get to work." She met my gaze and smiled. Real maturely. "Sure."

Yes! went my heart. *Keep it together,* said my brain.

Some of the kids in the room—most of them October's friends—watched us as they left. The teacher also eyed me before he left through the door. Then, all was silent. There was no one left in the room.

I took a deep breath.

"I like you, October. In a romantic fashion."

October didn't seem surprised. But, she didn't answer how I would have expected. "Come with me," she said, picking up her backpack and getting out of her seat. "We're going to go get some burgers."

"Burgers?" I repeated, too confused to say anything else. I quickly grabbed my backpack—a little too fast—and followed her out of the room. We walked through the hall until we left the school building. Then, we left the campus, walking along fifth street until we came to a McDonalds restaurant.

"Is this where you work?" I said, as we stepped into the burger joint. The smell of oil and flavoring and hamburgers being grilled filled my nose, as well as the smell of cheap cleaner and cheaper plastic. The place was decorated in garish reds and yellows that I had once learned were designed to get people hungry, get them in, and get them out. Color psychology—it's what red and yellow do to your brain. I could feel it working.

October walked up to the counter, still having said nothing since we left the school.

"Hey, Toby," said the guy behind the counter. "What are you going to have?"

"Two Giant Robots," said October.

The guy behind the counter grinned. "Who's the tagalong?"

October grinned back. "My new boyfriend, Fry. Get your nose out before I punch it bloody."

Whoa, I thought. *Not what I expected.* Then my brain wrapped around what had just happened. *Wait, what?* Still processing. *Boyfriend? Punch?* A pause. *Boy—Boyfriend?*

I reached out towards October. "Hey, October—"

She cut me off with a wave. "No talking. Just watch."

Fry opened a panel on the counter to reveal a high-tech operations hub that looked like it had been taken from the set of a military thriller. He punched in some numbers real fast-like, and then he flipped open a glass box like this was come cliché action flick, shoved a key into a keyhole, turned it, and then punched a big red button.

A surprisingly normal tone played over the loudspeakers. "McDonalds will now be closing for an emergency cleaning operation. All customers are to vacate immediately."

I stood in the center of the waiting area, still too confused to process what was happening. The customers willingly obliged the command that had come over the loudspeaker, filing out of the room, taking their dinners with them, until it was only me, October, Fry, and the workers in the back, who were still running around as if there were more orders to process. It took me a moment to realize that they weren't working with food equipment—it was more like the bridge of an aircraft carrier, with radars, buttons flashing, green everywhere, a holographic projection of the city where the deep fryers once were.

Where did it all come from? My mind asked. *Where did the food equipment go?* Though, I was barely sane enough at the moment to even register words.

October placed her hand on my shoulder. "I like you. In a romantic way." She said it forcefully, though not without tenderness.

That's nice, I thought, still unable to process my feelings on the matter. On a whim, I placed my hand on October's shoulder.

She raised one eyebrow, took my hand, and dropped it down so that we were holding hands while staring at the high-tech techno-fever happening in front of my eyes like a metal ballet. Fry just stood there, smiling with an awful smile that told me he knew what kind of loop-de-loops my mind was turning in the moment.

Have I said how much it was to process yet? Yeah, it was a lot to process.

October raised her free hand up as if to say: "Look at this. It's amazing, isn't it?"

"You're amazing," I said, too fast to stop it coming out of my mouth.

Fry laughed, until October glared at him, and then she kissed me on the lips, though she had to pull me down to do so.

Things were happening fast. Were they? Hell if I knew, really. I was still reeling over the fact that Star Trek suddenly appeared in the middle of my local burger joint.

"So, ah," I said, after disengaging. "What's this all, like, for?"

October motioned with her hand. "You'll see." She let go of my hand and walked around the corner, appearing a couple seconds later behind the counter. She donned an apron that I could now see was bulky because it was bulletproof—I had always thought that they only hired fat people or something at this place. It seems that I was wrong. October met my gaze, grinned, and then she saluted, at attention, to the others who were also in the room. There were three others besides Fry, the ones who had been operating the food equipment before, but who were now operating the radar and the sonar and the big thing with lots of antenna on it and whatever else was shoved into that cramped, linoleum-floored space. A chair appeared out of the ground, the equipment moving to make space for it. October sat in it, placing both hands on the armrests, where she gripped two joysticks. She met my gaze again and grinned even larger, which I didn't think was possible.

"Routine patrol launch now operational," she said. "The XO is on the deck. Launching bot, checklist operations all green."

The walls around me began to move. Seams in the wall opened up to reveal shining metal arms and gears and pistons like the inside of a Michael Bay movie. If this was a movie, the camera would be panning. But it wasn't a movie. It was real. It was all happening around me so fast—I still hadn't even gotten it into my head about October.

Suddenly, October's face changed. "Over the counter," She said, holding my gaze. "Now."

Without thinking I obeyed, vaulting over the counter in what I imagined was a cool fashion as the floor opened out around me and the roof folded up to become a chest—the chest of a giant robot. The kitchen was raised up like an elevator and placed right in the center of the whole shebang, whatever it was supposed to be, with the gears and the metal bits and the gaudy red and yellow colors all coming together to form an outline, the silhouette of a figure. It was a giant robot.

Holy shit.

I could see our school, across the road, from over the rooftops of the surrounding stores. For some reason, the people walking by on the street did not seem to notice the fact that the local McDonalds had just turned into a giant robot. That was the first sign that I had gotten my wits back—it was the first real question I had. Until then, I had been taking everything in with too much stun soup to be able to ask critical questions.

I looked at October. "Hey, what you said about me being your boyfriend—"

"Quiet," said October, waving her hand at me. "Load guns two and three with salad rounds. Load gun one with a Big Mac piercing round." She paused, her face determined, totally adult, not at all looking like an expression that a senior in high school would wear. She looked mature. Like a real captain—and that was when it really hit me.

Holy shit. This is really happening.

I covered my temples with my hands and knelt down on the linoleum.

"Get up," said October, leaning out of her seat to touch me on the shoulder. "I'm showing you this for a reason. Though, things may get a little rough."

"Why is that?" I asked.

October's gaze looked far away, as if she was lost deep in thought. "King is here. I thought it would be okay to activate if we only did it for a little while, but it seems like King got wind of this." She paused, seeming to suddenly realize something. "It's almost as if... He knew before it happened." She eyed me suspiciously. "Are you—" She shook her head, putting her fingers to her temples. "Never mind. You can't be, there's no way, I know you're a bad actor." She took a deep breath, flexing her fingers around the controls which I assumed were for the giant robot that I was now in the center of, as if this were an anime from the eighties or something. Like Gundam. That was a fun show.

But I had a feeling that this wouldn't be fun.

"They take over entire neighborhoods," said October, her gaze still far off. She paused, looking around at the monitor that I now noticed wasn't a window. "Startup sequence finished. Give me a location on the target."

"Two miles South-Southeast," said one of the guys at the machines—they were all guys.

"It looks like it really is King," said Fry. "I'm getting a message. Patching it through—he must be here for an audit. I think we caught him right when he was here. Maybe that's why he noticed our little setup."

October seemed convinced, and the look of suspicion left her face. She gripped the controls and began to move them. The robot took a few steps, practiced ones, telling of great skill that shouldn't have been achievable by a senior in high school. The thing felt like it handled like a tank, but it was managed lightly, elegantly, the world passing by with little much more than a shake here and there. I wondered why we weren't tearing up the buildings and concrete and cars and asphalt around us, but I quickly dropped the matter as my mind was already too full. We probably were tearing up the concrete but from what I saw that wasn't much of a problem compared to everything else.

A little box opened up on the monitors displaying the outside world, and a face that was obviously the face of a bad guy appeared, grinning.

"Ah, October. How nice to see you react to my audit, in this simple little town. Do you really want to go up against me right now, in your damaged state? Are you really coming back for a rematch when I so clearly beat you last time?" He paused, still grinning. "The North side is mine. You will lose, not only your place among the Franchises, but your life as well."

"The Franchises have nothing to do with our fight," said October. "They left you long ago."

"Things have changed, October," said the man, who I assumed to be King. He really did look evil. I didn't want to judge a book by its cover, so to speak, but every warning bell in my body was going off. The guy just had to be a bad guy. He laughed. "The Franchises support me. They will unite behind the banner of my corporation because we have the power to win. We are the ones who will control this continent. America is ours for the taking, and there is nothing you can do to stop us."

"You're wrong," said October, as she punched a button, cutting off the feed. She swept her hand through the air. "Fire Big Mac round!"

The giant robot raised its left arm, responding to October's touch, and a blast came out of its hand. A shot of bright orange arced through the sky and hit—no, it couldn't be, but it had to be—another giant robot, this time in the color scheme of Burger King. Blue and white.

Burger King. Oh, how I hated that place, ever since I found a toenail in my bun. That was not a fun memory, considering that my burger was half-finished before I noticed it. I wasn't a picky eater when it came to restaurant brands, and I really didn't bear that much ill will, but it all came flashing back to me when I saw that blue and white robot in the distance.

The Big Mac round—*Seriously? Big Mac round?*—smashed into the side of the enemy robot with enough force to send it reeling. However, it weathered the strike and stood back up, coming towards us as a speed that I thought was way, way too fast for something its size. Apparently, I was wrong. The cars on the street swerved to avoid it, but then they continued on their way as if nothing had happened. Something was seriously wrong with the world. There had to be an explanation for that.

But, I was in the middle of a giant robot that had been a McDonalds restaurant just a couple of minutes ago. The world was obviously a lot different than I thought it would be.

"Load another Big Mac round in tube three," said October, handling her controls. She piloted the McDonald's bot behind a church, knelt it down, and extended a periscope above the roof. The Burger King bot stopped, surveying the surroundings.

"I know you're there," came the voice of King.

"I know I blocked that guy!" said October.

"Commander," said one of the operators, "Our jamming technology isn't working. I think he must have some sort of technology that's getting him through. I can't tell what it is, but it's powerful."

October moved the robot through the downtown area, stepping on cars, grabbing a false front and using it as a shield as an explosive round rocketed through the air and detonated close enough that my bones shivered.

"You can't hide forever!" said King, his voice deep, gravely, and so obviously bad-guy that it was comical. "The Franchises will rule you out! Your store will be removed from the roster, and I will control this land!"

"That's what this is about?" I said, with enough surprise to surprise October.

October looked like I had just asked the stupidest question ever. "Is there anything more important than this in the world?"

"Than what?" I asked.

"Food!" said October. "The right to feed Americans!" She maneuvered the McDonalds bot cleverly enough to avoid a harpoon that looked way too dangerous to be functional. The harpoon embedded itself in the middle of a Lowes sign. October made a dive for the strip mall in which the Lowes was situated, getting behind the long, oblong box of a Walmart superstore. The Burger King bot stalked us, getting closer.

And then, October made a pounce, rocketing over the Walmart with a literal rocket that somehow was strapped to the McDonald bot's back, slamming into the Burger King bot. The Burger King bot whipped its fist around, impacting our bot, toppling us over so that we crushed a row of parked cars. October maneuvered her hands around the controls faster than I could track and the McDonald's bot kicked the Burger King bot in the chest, pushing it backwards into the side of the Walmart Superstore. The roofing collapsed and sparks shot up into the air from the several telephone poles that the bot had gotten tangled into. October seemed to sense the opportunity and grabbed the wires, pulling, and then she chest-bumped the Burger King bot. The Burger King bot tumbled, laying waste to more of the Walmart building, destroying a neighboring Starbucks. The sign tilted at a precarious angle. October grabbed it with both hands and lifted it up in a motion to stab the Burger King bot. The Burger King bot blocked it with a cross of its arms and then fired a round from a hidden cannon in its stomach. The smoke obscured everything around us. We rocketed backwards, spinning, a smoking hole in one of our legs.

When had I started thinking of it as us? Was I one of them?

A solid knock in the side jolted me out of my reverie. I hit the wall and slid onto the linoleum, looking dimly up at everything that was happening.

"Hold on," said October, noticing my predicament. "This will be over soon."

I noticed that everyone else had some sort of equipment that kept them steady as the robot moved. Even though there were shocks, they were much less powerful than they should have been given the circumstances, and so I postulated that there was some sort of high-tech gyroscopic shock-absorbing system in place. Otherwise, we would never be able to fight like this.

October was obviously tired, even though the fight had only lasted perhaps five minutes so far. Her knuckles were white, and she had almost chewed a hole in her lip. The other people in the cockpit kitchen were no better. Fry was the only one who looked to be holding it together.

I had seen him at school before, but only in passing. My mind wandered as the world fuzzed, then blurred, and then everything was silent. The battle was over. The Burger King bot stood above us, wounded but triumphant. The right arm of the McDonald's bot hung uselessly at its side, and the right leg trembled where the Burger King bot's stomach cannon had impacted it.

October slumped down from her chair. "That—that was tough." She cracked her knuckles, a slight smile reappearing on her face. "But we did it. We didn't lose that bad."

I thought it was strange, but I didn't comment. This King guy was obviously a level higher than October, high as her level was. He had to be, for her to be glad about only losing a little.

The return to the corner between fifth and main was strange. We trekked past enough destruction to fill a kaiju movie, but no one seemed to notice—and then I saw a swarm of helicopters, of trucks and cranes, hundreds of people everywhere in uniform black suits. The McDonalds bot settled back down in its corner, and the whole robot began to disassemble itself, slowly at first, and then faster as beams of metal reassembled over my head, as chairs flipped out of the ground and as light fixtures turned from gears back into their original shapes. After only a minute, the restaurant was normal again. The instant the last bit of metal slipped behind the walls, several men in suits walked through the doors.

October got up to greet them. One of them flashed a badge.

"Franchise Auditor Collins. Your battle has been recorded as a 30% loss in quarterly profits, duly noted."

October huffed, putting her hands on her hips. "Can't you cut me some slack? They had a world-class pilot with them."

"Sorry," said Auditor Collins. "I'm just doing my job."

The sound of construction came from outside. Through some of the smashed windows, I could see the destruction we wreaked being repaired, fast enough that I could see the change visually. By the time I had registered what was happening, it was all finished. Even the paint scratches on the McDonalds restaurant that had come from the battle were gone, after only five minutes.

When the auditors left, October came over to me and put her hand on my shoulder. "Sorry you had to see that. We weren't planning to have a battle this early in the month." She paused. "I just wanted to show you something cool."

My jaw dropped. Finally, it dropped, after everything that had happened, and it was at the stupidest thing ever. "Cool? You call that cool? What the hell just happened? Did I step into a crazy dream or something?"

October grabbed me forcefully and kissed me. For a long time. I didn't kiss back, mostly because I had no idea what to do in the situation. When I was almost recovered and was almost enjoying the experience she pulled back and looked me in the eye. "Does that feel like a dream to you?"

"Er, yeah," I said, truthfully, regretting having said it immediately.

October laughed, long and hard. Her calm, pretty demeanor that she always had at school came back as if it had never disappeared in the first place. Gone was the forceful, lusty captain of the giant robot. Back was the kind girl who was always willing to share her notes, who had a soft voice and kept to herself in school, though she had no lack of friends.

She smiled. "I like you too, Max. In a romantic way."

"If that wasn't already obvious," I said, really starting to doubt my own feelings.

What was I getting myself into?

Holy shit! What am I getting myself into! My mind was blank. And, I think that was for the best.

What would happen tomorrow? Would she ignore it? Everything that happened? Would it be as if it had been a normal "I like you" conversation? What was I in for?.

Setting myself, in the middle of the McDonalds restaurant, I tried my best to pretend that it had all been a dream. Little did I know that it had only just started.

2

* * *

Papers, Please

The day after I told October I liked her was strange. In the morning, I came to school, unsure of how to act around her—had she really done those things? Had she really kissed me, forcefully, and said that she liked me? I had a hard time believing that the girl that I knew from school would act like she did—was there some sort of mistake? Had someone given me a drug that I didn't know about?

But she was waiting there, in the front lot of the school, where the flagpole was. I had a clear vision of the McDonalds down the street from where I stood. There she was, leaning against a wall, looking my way. When she spotted me, she waved. I waved back. It felt strange. Why was this girl even noticing me? All I did was tell her that I liked her. Wouldn't that normally drive girls away? It always had, in the past—even if I had been their friend, once I let the beans spill, they were gone. I feel strange to say it, but up until the day before, I had never gone out with a girl, never kissed a girl. Sure, I had liked plenty of them.

Maybe I'm just strange like that.

October walked up to me and gave me a quick peck on the cheek. It was a surprise, almost to the point that I tensed up. So she really liked me. I felt a little weird, but overall, happy. Just happy to be alive.

October looked down at her feet for a moment in a previously characteristic but now uncharacteristic fashion—she was being bashful. It was a surprise after how she had acted in the pilot's seat of that giant robot. She had been so commanding then, and in the moments after. It was almost as if she was a different girl.

I started walking towards the school building. Crowds of high-schoolers surrounded us, chattering away, parking bicycles, doing their thing. The school bell rang the five-minute mark, a single low tone that lasted for around five seconds and sped up the activity around us. October walked beside me, not saying anything.

We entered the building. Students flowed all around us. I wanted to say something. Anything. But I couldn't. I couldn't gather up the courage to speak. She was silent. I caught her glancing at me, but when I met her eyes, she looked away.

"Sorry," she said, finally.

I thought she was apologizing for yesterday, until I saw her hand pointing down a fork in the hall.

"Ah," I said. So she had her first class that way. I might have known that before, but I had taken extreme care to not learn too much about her, as that would have been stalkerish and probably not healthy for me. It was a moot point now.

Class was long. I couldn't stop thinking about the day before, couldn't pay attention, and yet every time I looked at the clock it was as if no time had passed at all. But finally, the time came when I could meet October in class, in Biology. I sat down next to her when I came into the room. Seating at my school has usually been voluntary, especially for seniors—it's one of the perks we get for being so mature. Like we're mature at all, but hey, who can complain.

October smiled at me when I sat down. "How was your day?" she asked.

I sigh. "Crazy. Hectic. Slow."

October frowned. "That's bad."

There was an awkward silence.

"About yesterday—" I said, before October cut me off.

"Do you want to go somewhere after school?" she said.

I blinked in surprise for a moment. "Er, does it have to do with what happened yesterday?"

October's expression became coy. It was cute, but at the same time, it really freaked me out. I think I might have been traumatized by the experience the day before, because I was starting to get some flashbacks. Was my life in danger then? I don't know. All I know was that it was scary.

October frowned. "You don't look so good."

Is this really a good idea? My mind said. *Do you really like her enough to get involved in something crazy like this?*

Yes, my heart said. *Hell if you do, hell if you don't,* said my brain. I agreed with my brain. Pick your poison, so to speak.

I picked. "Yeah, sure," I said. "I'll go with you after school."

October smiled, a genuine expression that could not possibly have been faked. For that reason, the suspicion that it had been faked came to me, almost on a whim, but not quite.

I'm still confused. Yep, just confused. I decided to go with the flow.

"Where are you going to take me?" I asked.

October put her finger on her lips. "It's a secret."

The bell to begin class rang. The teacher got up from his desk and the lecture began.

We were learning about the Krebs cycle. It was AP Bio I was in, the one designed for the test at the end of the year that had the potential to get you out of college hours. I think I had a pretty good handle on the subject, and so I let my thoughts wander during class, occasionally letting my eyes wander as well. Several times I glanced at October and found her looking back at me as well. Each time our eyes would meet for a moment and then part.

Typical high school romance. I started to get angry with myself for not handling it better. I didn't want any of this cheesy stuff. Sure, it was fun, but I knew if I didn't find some common interests between us we would soon drift apart.

And then there was the place October had promised to take me. The second half of class was filled with trepidation as I felt the clock ticking closer and closer to the end of the school day. Images from the day before flashed through my mind. The Burger King bot. Falling against the linoleum. The high-tech weaponry, the feeling that I was about to die. I don't know how October handled it so well.

Class ended. The teacher left. October gathered her things and looked down at me from where she was standing. I was still packing, but soon, I finished, and the two of us left the room without saying anything.

On the way to wherever we were going, I turned to October, wanting to talk, unable to. Finally, I spoke.

"Do you like video games?" I asked.

October shook her head. "No," she said. She smiled at me. "Do you?"

"Yes," I said. I was about to go on a tangent about my favorite video game when I realized that it probably wouldn't be that interesting. At least to her.

There was another long, awkward silence. I looked at October again. "Do you like anime?"

"What's that?" asked October, an interested look on her face. "Are those... Wait, I know! Those Chinese cartoons, right?"

"Japanese," I said. "They're Japanese."

Had she been someone other than my girlfriend—was she my girlfriend yet? I didn't know, but she had called me her boyfriend—I would have ranted about that. It really bothers me when people do that. I guess I'm just your average weeb in that respect.

More silence. Then, I pulled out my last card. "Do you like reading?" I said.

October's smile brightened. "Yes, I do!" She sounded excited, whereas before she had sounded politely interested.

I used to do a lot of reading, back when I was in elementary and middle school. I read some pretty big, adult books back then. Oliver Twist unabridged, Pillars of the Earth, The Lord of Rings trilogy. So I had a lot to talk about.

"What's your favorite book?" I asked.

"The Hitchhiker's Guide to the Galaxy," said October. "It's the best."

I lit up. Finally. Something we had in common. "I love that book too," I said. "Have you read all of the sequels?"

October nodded her head vigorously. "All of them, multiple times." She fell silent, seeming to go into contemplation. "I thought that kind of stuff was kind of stupid until I got hired."

Here we go. She's opening up.

"Go on," I said.

There was a small silence, more of a springboard than a stoppage. October looked pensive.

"At first I thought it was all a load of bull," she said. "A guy in a suit came to me one day when I was alone at home and said I had talent that would allow me to protect the world. He said he was with McDonalds." She laughed. "I mean, McDonalds? Seriously?"

"I know, right?" I said.

We had long since left the school campus, and were now heading past the McDonalds that October worked at. Where we were going, I didn't know, but at the same time I had an inkling of what it was going to be about. I had the feeling that October wasn't prefacing with an autobiographic bit just for the fun of it.

"That was when I was in seventh grade," she said. "Most Franchise bot pilots are scouted at that age."

"I see," I said. I was interested. Real interested. However, I wasn't sure how to show it—I decided that the best choice would just be to listen.

October's pace slowed down, and then stopped, as we approached a crosswalk. A jogger came up next to us and did that running-in-place thing that joggers always do at crosswalks.

October played with a strand of her hair. "At first, I was terrible. I couldn't hold my own to save my life. But then, I found a teacher who just clicked with me. I don't know how, I don't know why, but after I found him I rose to the top of the chain pretty fast. That's why I'm a pilot now. Most people wash out of the program. I'm one of the few people who didn't."

"Are there any other people at our school that know about this?" I asked.

"Yeah, there are," said October. "Plenty of them. Once you get into the scene you'll start recognizing them, but most of the time we tend to keep to ourselves."

"Yeah, I never see you hang out with Fry at school."

October elbowed me in the ribs—it was a friendly gesture. Her bashful personality was starting to melt away, beginning to be replaced with the personality I had seen yesterday after school.

I did have some questions.

"Why didn't people seem to notice that there were two giant burger bots fighting each other over their heads?" I asked. Obviously, there was a huge reason for that. I prepared myself for the most stupid answer possible.

"Have you watched Men in Black?" asked October.

"Yeah," I said, knowing where this was going. "You mean, they literally erase the memory of an entire town on a monthly basis?"

"Hell," said October, "There could be hundreds of incidents like this that happen every day and we could just be forgetting it. I have a strong reason to believe that clothing outlets do the same thing fast food restaurants do, though I have no proof and only assume that because there's no reason why it wouldn't happen. In the case of clothing outlets, we're the bystanders."

"What about the people that get killed?" I asked.

October looked to be deep in thought for a moment. "It's part of the job."

There was a long silence after that, during which we walked through the crowded downtown part of the city, with little Mexican restaurants and pawn shops crowded together between dirty fences and side-parked vehicles. That's what Benton, California looks like. A place where drugs are probably sold in abundance, a place that isn't as bad as the streets of skid row in LA, but is a lot worse than, say, nice little Irvine just north along the freeway.

October stopped at a small office that had no sign, instead sporting the faded sun-etched shadow of the shop that had preceded it, where there had once probably been neon letters. "Quicken Loans," it read. Ha, nice place she was taking me, this girl, October. I was getting in deep. Maybe even over my head.

There was a metal grating behind the glass front door, the metal being scratched with its paint peeling off, the glass etched with graffiti. October pushed the doorbell—I had no time to wonder why there was a doorbell for a business like this—and a high-tech panel popped out of the wall. October entered a passcode, palmed a hand reader, looked into an optical sensor, and spoke two words.

"October Autumn."

I had always been curious about why her parents had given her the name October when her last name was Autumn. Not that I could complain, having a name like Max Biggs, as if I was a B movie star or something. I had the idea that my parents would get along well with hers.

The door opened, the gate folding aside, the door opening automatically. October stepped through, grabbing my hand. We both entered at the same time. The door slid shut behind us.

It was cold. Very cold. I didn't know what to think at first, as my eyes adjusted, and then I saw a desk. That was it. Just a desk. White walls, no windows, a single door in the back, a long desk that cut the room in half behind which sat a man in a suit who looked very similar to the Franchise auditor who had come in to talk with October the day before, after the battle.

"Welcome, October," said the man behind the desk. A classic greeting. Nothing wrong with it, but it sounded so stereotypical that I couldn't help but laugh a little on the inside. It was just what a man in a black suit should have said in the situation.

October walked up to the desk and pointed at me, while still maintaining eye contact with the man. "He needs to fill out some paperwork," she said.

"Wait, paperwork?" I said, walking up next to October. "Is that what this is about?"

"What else would it be about?" said October. She put her hands on her hips and frowned at me. Her personality from yesterday during the battle seemed to be returning. Was it just school that made her shy?

I looked around the room, still unable to find any clues that would lead me to a conclusion about the situation I was in. I looked back at October.

"I'll fill it out. I think I have an idea about what it is."

The man behind the counter smiled, wolfishly, and then plopped a solid stack of paper several inches high down on the countertop. I stared at it for a moment, uncomprehending.

Finally, I managed to speak. "All of this?"

"All of it," said October. "You want to stay with me, right?"

"Er, yeah," I said, unsure of what to say. "Yeah, I do."

October pulled up a chair and sat down in it, folding her hands behind her head and looking at me. "So, do the paperwork. Doing it will make you an official member of the team at the McDonalds on fifth and main. Store number 12346, to be exact."

"I see," I said. "No online application?"

My attempt at deadpan humor did not go as I wanted it to go. I smiled sheepishly. "Fine. I'll do it." I picked up a pen, sat down next to October, and spent the next two hours filling out forms that asked about pretty much everything that had ever been related to the concept of me. It was a monster, and if this were a cheesy parody video game, I'm sure the papers would have risen up from the desk and played the part of a mini-boss. Which I would have then defeated with spells of fire.

When the paperwork was finished, October clapped her hands together and grabbed me by the arm, pulling me up as she pulled herself up. She held onto my hand and looked me in the eyes. Her nose came up to about my shoulder, which meant that I had to look a little bit downwards to see her.

She smiled. "You're coming with me."

We walked out of the building and onto the street. The world seemed different, somehow. Like it was pulsating, flashing, like everything was tinged with psychedelic madness. I presumed that it was most likely because I had just spent the past two hours staring at small print and tiny letterboxes and forced myself to stop thinking about it.

It worked, and I ended up thinking about October. She confused me, to say the least. I took a good, long look at her and tried to sort my feelings out. Did I really want to get involved with her?

"What are you thinking about?" asked October, keeping her eyes on the horizon, invisible though it was through the bustle of downtown.

The question surprised me. Though it was a perfectly normal question, it wasn't one that I had a ready answer for, at least not one that I wanted to share. My thoughts were private, and feeling for the first time that I was obligated to share them was a little bit scary. So, I thought about it.

After a while—perhaps a minute—I spoke. "I'm a little confused," I said. "I don't know where this is going, and I feel like I'm the protagonist of an anime."

October laughed. "I know the feeling. Or rather, I knew it. Once you get into the gritty reality of being a McDonalds pilot the adventurous part fades away." She paused. "Also, I'll say now that you won't be able to back out of this for the next four years. Franchises are like the military in that way. You serve a term of enlistment and you can't get out of it unless you're injured in combat and honorably discharged."

"I read that in the contract," I said, though the impact of the decision I had made had yet to really hit me over the face like I knew it would. I stayed silent for a minute.

"So where are we going now?"

"We're meeting the crew, and then we're going to go on a date."

"Ah," I said. "Wait, a date?"

October laughed. It was a little awkward listening to her because of my own state of mind, but I bore with her. She looked up at me, making eye contact. "Yeah, probably to the mall or something."

"You like shopping?" I asked.

October shook her head. "No, well, yes, as much as any other girl, but there's a great Barnes and Noble at the mall."

"I see," I said, not at all surprised. "Why don't you just go to the library?"

"Because..." Said October. "Because I don't like the atmosphere. It's too academic. I like the feel of the bookstore, and it even has a coffee shop. The library doesn't have a coffee shop." She began to skip, just a little bit, which made her seem younger and more carefree than I had imagined her to be. She got a couple of steps ahead of me, turned around, and stood in front of me.

I stopped.

"Can I hold your hand?" said October.

"Sure," I said, as a jolt went through my body. *Ah, so this is what it feels like to be in love.* Or, perhaps it was something similar.

October came back to my side and took my hand. Her hand—it was shaking. I almost mentioned it, but then realized that it probably wouldn't have been beneficial. Instead, I took it as a sign that things were perhaps going better than I thought they were.

We reached the corner of fifth and main, where October's McDonalds was situated. October let go of my hand and reached for the door—and then she froze. A look of surprise crossed her face, and then fear, and then resignation, and then resolution. The muscles in her jaw stood out.

Without looking at me, she spoke. "Sorry about this, Max, but we're probably going to have to miss a couple months of school."

I was too stunned to say anything. I could only stand there, uncomprehending, as October sighed deeply and pushed the door open.

A man in a suit—much different from the auditor in terms of presence but still the same in terms of fashion—walked up to October. He flashed a badge.

"Franchise military resource department, Dan Brown. I'm here to talk about an expedition."

October saluted. "October Autumn, ready to deploy, sir."

The military officer faced me. "I presume you are the new team member?" He waited for a second, almost enough time for me to nod. "We can't afford to train you at the moment. You're going to be doing a lot of on-the-job learning." He looked me up and down, and then turned to October. "Teach this team member to salute," he said, and then he started walking towards the door. "I've left the documents for deployment in the break room." He paused, door open in his hands, and looked back for a moment. His face—it was afraid. "Capitalism help us all." Then, he was gone.

"What was that all about?" I asked, a little confused, to say the least.

October shook her head. "We're deploying." Her voice sounded dull, listless.

"Where?" I asked.

"I don't know," said October. "Though I'm sure it will probably be somewhere in Xen."

"Xen? Where's that? Somewhere in Kansas?"

"It's another dimension."

I paused. "I know I was joking, but you didn't have to take it that far." Waited for the punch line.

October looked serious. Deadly serious. I had the feeling, in the pit of my stomach, that she wasn't kidding.

"Seriously?" I asked.

"Seriously," said October.

I could tell. She wasn't kidding. We really were going to go fight in a different dimension in a giant robot made out of a McDonalds robot.

Oh, the craziness of love. What had I gotten myself into?

3

* * *

Communist Space Orcs

The portal was slated to open at exactly 10:00 pm our time. It was an hour after I had learned that I would be fighting in a different dimension in a robot made out of a giant McDonalds, and I was having a really, really tough time.

Despite how the brand was thought of—at least at this restaurant—being a team member required a whole lot of physical skill, dexterity, and stamina. Or so I had been told. And so, I was being tested, pushed to the limits of my endurance so they could see what kind of a physical specimen I was.

I was in it for the long run. Only now was I realizing this. My parents wouldn't miss me—their memories would be manipulated so that when I came back it would be as if I had been there the whole time—but I was certain that I would miss them, and in the middle of my tenth set of fifty push-ups the reality finally hit me, it finally dawned on me that I had entered a world that was much, much different than the world I had once known.

When the testing was over, October walked up to me and wrapped her arms around me—a sudden move, one that I didn't expect, and one that I wasn't sure how to take. I could see Fry and some of the other crew members watching, unreadable expressions on their faces.

"I'm so glad that you're going to be here with me," said October.

Her words confused me. How could she be this attached to me already? Did I do something special?

Well, it wasn't that I couldn't understand it. Just that it felt strange. In fact, I wanted to do the same thing—and I did, I hugged her back. We were going somewhere and I wasn't sure how it would turn out. There were a lot of variables involved, most of which I couldn't see. That fact alone made me more scared than anything else had ever done.

But I was in it—I had filled out the paperwork. Whatever was going to happen, I would be a part of it, whether I liked it or not. This was going to be my life for the next few months.

I pulled away from October for a moment and examined her really closely for what I later realized was the first time. She was a girl, she was cute, but more than that, she smelled a little bit like coconut. That was what I noticed.

She saw me looking at and smiled. Then, she stepped back and posed in a slightly ridiculous fashion that was at once girly and adult. Her smile grew wider until it became a grin.

"How do you like it?" She said.

This was too much. I was getting embarrassed. I rubbed the back of my head and looked down at my feet. "Fine. You're very pretty."

Fry walked up behind me and slapped me on the back. "Hey now, we have work to do. And, we need to introduce you to the rest of the crew." He pulled me across the floor of the restaurant, through the bathroom hallway, and into the employees only area. October followed us.

The three people who I had seen operating the machinery yesterday afternoon were sitting around the break room table eating jelly beans and talking. When I came into the room, they all fell silent. One of them, a tall blonde guy with medium-serious acne got up and approached me. He extended his hand.

"October's boyfriend. Nice to meet you. My name is Kyle."

I shook his hand. It was a strong handshake, a little too strong. He grinned and let go, and then motioned to the other people around the table, an older man with silver hair and glasses, and a young African-American kid who looked to be no older than sixteen.

"That's George," said Kyle, pointing to the older man.

George nodded in response.

The black kid got up and shook my hand. "My name is Andrew," he said. "Nice to meet you."

"That's all of us at twelve three forty-six," said Kyle. "We're glad to have you aboard. Sorry you had to get hired right before we went out on deployment."

I shook my head. "It's my own fault for getting involved at this time."

Kyle grinned. "Because you asked out October, right?" He slapped me on the back. "I've been hearing about you for a long time from her. She thinks you're cute."

October leaned against the wall and crossed her arms. "A lot cuter than you, Kyle," she said, her voice at once venomous and jovial.

Kyle laughed. "I'm not cute," said Kyle, "But I am handsome." He ran his hand through his blonde hair, which was neither short nor long, covering his ears but just barely. It was a motion that fit his frame and his stature. I was sure that he intended it that way—he seemed a lot smarter and more conscious than he initially appeared.

I looked at George, and then at Andrew, and both of them acknowledged me with a nod.

October took me by the hand and dragged me to the door. "Let's let the crew finish their rest break in peace," she said. "You have some selection to do."

"Nice to meet you, Max," said Kyle, with a slight bit of teasing in his voice. "I hope we become good friends."

"Yeah," said October, "Get too close to him and your nether bits are going to mysteriously disappear in the night."

Kyle, Fry, and Andrew laughed together, while George watched with mirth in his eyes, though he did not join them.

October led me out of the break room and into the kitchen, through an employees-only door. She brought me to a small, metallic machine that looked half like a pasta strainer and half like a football helmet.

"Put this on," she said, lifting up the helmet part of it. Some wires attached to its underside pulled up with it, locked into the wall, where there was a readout panel that spat strings of numbers out underneath a graph that looked like an EKG reading but could have been anything. She waited for a second, watching the screen, and then she held the helmet out to me. "Here," she said, her eyes still on the screen. "Put this on."

I reached for the helmet, took it in both hands, and then lifted it over my head. With just the slightest amount of trepidation, I put it on. It slid past my hair and locked into place with a click.

October pressed some buttons and turned some knobs and then she frowned. "I'm not getting much—wait—" She paused. The screen looked the same to me as it did before. "Seriously?" said October, peering closer at the screen. She pressed some more buttons, turned some more knobs. The screen beeped once. October looked at me with an expression that was at once full of awe and disbelief.

"What?" I said, a little put off by her reaction to whatever was going on. "Why are you staring at me?"

"Your stats," she said. "They're ridiculously high."

"What, my physical exam?" I said. "I thought I failed miserably."

"You did," said October. "Or, well, you failed just about as miserably as a senior in high school with little history with physical activity should have on a professional-level military-grade fitness exam." She paused, looking at the screen one more time. "But that's not what I'm talking about. I'm talking your potentials. I wouldn't be surprised if you had the most powerful potentials this side of the Atlantic Ocean." She paused again, looking a little deflated. "But, they're only in one skill."

"Oh?" I said. "And what is this strangely RPG-like category I excel in?"

"It's not an RPG skill, though you could say they're related. I'm talking your potentials. That's what they're called."

"So tell me. Stop beating around the bush."

"Let's just say that you'd make a very, very good sniper, because the name of the skill won't matter to you."

"Try me."

"Alpha-dexterity. You have a very high Alpha-dexterity, as well as a ridiculously high Type Two Motor Coordination stat."

"Er, yeah, those names mean nothing to me."

"The thing is, both of those skills are crucial to the job of a sniper. With a little bit of practice, you'd be the best sniper in, in I don't even know anymore." October was starting to get excited, I could see it in her eyes. "I mean, I thought you were special, but this—this proves beyond a doubt that I was right about you. My intuition was correct." She paused, watching me for a moment. "In case you were wondering, that's not the only reason why I think you're special."

"I wasn't wondering."

"Oh," said October, looking a little disappointed.

"But I'm glad you think that way," I said, trying to cover myself.

October frowned, not in a bad way, and then she poked me in the stomach. "I'll requisition a rifle for you before we move out." She smiled, turned around, seemed to think better of it, turned towards me, and gave me a peck on the cheek.

When she pulled back, I put my hand to where her lips had contacted my skin. A weird feeling came over me. "Thanks," I said, not knowing why I said it.

"You're welcome," said October, before she turned around and headed into the break room.

I stood there, alone, the helmet still on my head, probably looking like a total idiot.

"Alpha-dexterity, eh?" I said, to myself. "I wonder..."

The kitchen seemed a lot bigger when there wasn't anyone inside. I ran my hand along some of the metal fixings and wondered how they were able to prepare food when most of the space was taken up by equipment that looked a far cry from what would have been used to prepare food. Or, it could have been the opposite. I didn't trust my judgement on what was used for food prep in a fast food kitchen like this. That blade-looking thingy, it could have been an antenna, or it could have been a chopper, or it could have been both. The walls started to feel claustrophobic, the linoleum started to shine brightly, too brightly for my eyes, and I felt a little wobbly, a remnant from the physical exam. Deciding to take a rest, I sat down on an open counter and looked around myself.

This was it. This was where I was going to spend the next few months, according to what I had heard. Where was I going? What kind of a place was Xen? Who would I be fighting?

An old couple came up to the glass door, knocked, found it locked, and walked off. I'm sure they just wanted a late afternoon snack, seeing as this place was a McDonalds, after all. I wondered if it was good for their business to be closed at such a time, if their purported primary business really was their primary business after all. For all I knew, the money that supported them could have come from the sale of all this expensive-looking high-tech technology to the military, and the food was only a front to hide the real deal. You never know, and considering what was happening to me in the moment, I was prepared to believe anything.

After about half an hour Fry came out of the break room with a mop and a bucket on wheels and began to clean the floors of the kitchen.

"Do you need some help?" I asked.

Fry shook his head, stretching his arms above his shoulders before plunging in with the mop. "No," he said, not facing me. "This is the job I get paid for. You're going to be on the fryers, as far as I know, and so you'll be cleaning your fair share of grease off of metal surfaces."

"What else do you do?" I asked. "What are your, your, uh, potentials?"

Fry shrugged. "I'm an all-rounder. When we're on the ground in suits I carry the mortar rounds. Kyle is the squad machine gunner, and Andrew is the technician. George is just a rifleman to fill everything out." He paused. "I heard you're going to be a sniper."

"I guess so," I said. "Though I haven't learned anything yet."

"Oh, you will," said Fry. "Though you're probably going to use a rifle for much of this next campaign until they can train you properly. Snipers are a beast to handle."

"What, you don't have some sort of auto-learning device that automatically teaches me to be a sniper?"

"If we did, that would be convenient," said Fry, starting to mop up around my feet. "But we don't. You'll have to learn the old fashioned way. I'm sure you'll get plenty of time to shoot on the range between battles."

"Have you been deployed before?" I asked.

"Yeah, two times," said Fry. "Lost a couple of friends, got hit once in the arm." He pulled up his sleeve. "Beam rifle grazed me, an inch to the left and I would have lost my right arm. All I'd have left is a cauterized stump."

There was a long, skinny burn running straight across the middle of his upper right arm. It was white, now, but it must have once been bright red.

"Beam rifle?" I asked, my head finally snapping out of the stupor seeing the scar had put it in.

Fry grinned. "Oh, that's the least of what's out there. It was a Saith sniper, wasn't even aiming for me."

"Saith?"

"Spider-like insectoid with brains equal to any human and an exoskeleton as hard as rolled steel."

"Wow."

"I know. Wait until you see a rhinoderon." Fry paused. "Well, no, you won't see one, because those are in the jungles of Rez and we're going to Xen."

"Is Rez another dimension, like Xen?"

"No, Rez is a planet orbiting a star some thousand light-years away, I forget the name, goddamned thing was hot as hell, though. Xen is another dimension. I'm not too sure about the details, but it's supposed to be a rather small one, just a big flat piece of land sitting in a pocket in hyperspace. No connection to this dimension."

"I don't think I'll ever look at a McDonalds commercial the same way again."

Fry looked at me, his face dead serious. "You're going to get bored joking about that real quick."

I paused, my eyes locked on his. After a long while, Fry turned around and continued to mop the linoleum floor. When he was finished with the kitchen he went through the employee doors and started mopping the eatery floor.

I watched him, for a lack of better things to do. The consoles and readouts and buttons around me beeped, filling the room with an ambient noise that wasn't so different than what a kitchen would sound like, only it wasn't a kitchen. It was a high-tech cockpit for what had to be a multi-million-dollar superweapon disguised as a restaurant. I mean, considering the cost of a tank, the robot I was in had to be exponentially more expensive. I wouldn't be surprised if the cost was in the billions. The craft certainly looked complicated enough to rival a nuclear submarine in terms of complexity and technology, and those were supposed to cost billions of dollars.

And it was all run by a bunch of part-timers, most of whom were high-school students. There had to be some sort of auto-training machine. Either that, or the controls were really simple.

I looked at a panel to my right. Surprisingly, I could almost immediately tell what it did—it was a pressure readout that gave the level of joint flexibility and pressure in the hydraulic system. Good to know that the McDonalds super-robot worked on conventional principles.

Wait, why did I understand that? I looked at the panel again. Why did everything make sense to me?

I was reminded of the feeling of psychedelic off-ness that I had felt immediately after finishing the stacks of paperwork earlier that day. Did that have to do with what I was experiencing? I walked around the machine some more, reading other screens, understanding it all, down to the smallest detail. It was as if I had spent years in college learning everything—I even knew the theory behind everything, though I couldn't put it into words.

I looked over the counter and caught Fry's attention with a wave.

"Yes?" he said, walking over to the counter.

I pointed to the machinery. "Why do I understand this?"

"You filled out your paperwork, right?"

"Yeah," I said.

"Then you should know this stuff. It's pretty basic."

"I thought you said there was no magical learning device."

"There's no device that will give you the fine-tuned muscular development you need to operate equipment on the scale of a sniper rifle. Making you learn stuff is easy. You probably know pretty much everything there is to know about this job already."

"I, er—" I had an overwhelming feeling. "I knew that."

"I know," said Fry. "Now, can I get back to work?"

"Er, sure," I said, and Fry turned around and continued to mop.

This world—this world I had entered just kept getting more interesting. Magical learning devices. I would have said "what next," but I didn't want to jinx it. For all I know if I predicted something crazily stupid it would happen, and if that was the case, I would never forgive myself.

Stupid trains of thought aside, I examined the machinery and equipment that filled the kitchen, basking in the knowledge that I had somehow acquired through less-than-normal means. That was the missile tube controller. There was the walk pattern intelligence dock, where the strider watched the bot's path to make sure it stayed balanced. Everything had a purpose, everything had a meaning, everything was for the control of the machine so that the pilot, October, could do her job without getting mired in the small details.

I accessed some of the knowledge that I had learned without realizing it.

60% of a team member's job is outside the restaurant, as boots on the ground.

Boots on the ground. So that was where Fry got his scar—I wondered if any of the other team members had scars like he did. Perhaps not. Fry had been lucky.

The employee door opened, and October stepped through, wearing her bulletproof apron, carrying another one on her arm.

"Put this on," she said, handing it to me. "It's sized for you, as close as you can get with the way they size them."

"It's not tailored specifically for me?"

October looked surprised. "What, do you think they'd waste equipment like that on a grunt like you?" Then, she grinned. "Don't worry. You don't need to have it custom-fitted. It'll go on like a glove, or whatever, as long as you fasten it right."

I took the apron from her. It was heavy, not as heavy as I was expecting, but heavier than it should have been if it were just an ordinary apron. Which was obviously the case, as it wasn't just an ordinary apron. It looked more like a bullet-proof vest, to be honest, and it had several straps that hooked around, as well as back plates, which I'm sure no ordinary apron would have.

"Do I get a helmet?" I asked.

"You get a hat," she said, handing me a ball cap.

I grabbed it—and my hand immediately sank downwards under the weight. It wasn't an ordinary team member cap. That much was clear. I pulled it over my head, and immediately a heads-up display appeared as if I was in a video game.

"Whoa," I said, a little buzzed from the fact that it was so cool. There was a vitality meter, an infrared overlay, informational tabs, and other stuff that I knew the function of but couldn't put it in words. All in all, it felt like I was Master Chief or Iron Man or something. I held my fist out. "Let's go, Cortana," I said.

October tilted her head. "My name's October."

Fry leaned over the counter, looking at me with a sympathetic expression. "I thought about making that same joke the first time I put on my team member ball cap." He looked at October. "You really don't know your video games, do you?"

"What does that have to do with Cortana?" asked October. She seemed genuinely confused.

I sighed. "October, Cortana is the AI that Master Chief has in his suit."

October looked even more confused. "Master... Chief?"

"You know what, never mind," I said. "We'll play Halo together sometime when we get back from deployment."

October brightened. "That reminds me. We have to be ready for portal entry at eighteen-hundred."

Fry checked the clock on the wall of the dining area. "That gives us twenty minutes. We better start now if we want to get the checklists done in time."

Checklists. I knew what those were all about. I even remembered every single item on them, and how they were related to each other, despite never having learned it. It was really starting to amaze me. How cool my new life was, that is. Would I be seeing more technology like this? I sure hoped so.

George, Kyle, and Andrew left the break room as a group, chatting to each other, each team member holding a tablet that shone with bright, futuristic techno-colors and had a sweet holographic display. Kyle had two. He made eye contact with me, and then tossed one over.

I caught it. I knew what my job was—weapons manager. I was the one who kept everything needed for top-side out-of-vehicle operations safe and maintained. That meant that I was just dead weight during battles where we stayed inside the bot, but for when we left, it was vital that everything be maintained and in proper working order. My position wasn't a necessity—before I came everyone shared the duties—but there was definitely enough work for a whole person, at least during the checklist period.

We finished the checklist at 5:51, which was 17:51 military time. Nine minutes to spare. October gave me a thumbs up just before she got into her captain's seat.

The restaurant shuddered, as October managed the controls, as the other team members worked their stations. The walls collapsed in on themselves, revealing long, thin bones made of metal and plastic and red and yellow colors. The light fixtures turned into gears. The tables folded down into the floor to become armor. The dining area disappeared, replaced by a large screen that showed the outside world, a three-sixty display area with a full view of the metropolis that was Benton, California. I could see the Walmart, and the Burger King across town.

"I'm getting a message from Burger King 10345," said George. "Patching him in."

"Hello, October," said the voice of King. It was still as bad-guy sounding as ever. "We won't be fighting each other during deployment, but know that I won't like working with you, whatsoever. We have a mission to complete, and a world to protect. Afterwards, if you want, we can have another showdown to decide who gets to control this town."

October's face changed, and she assumed the full captain personality that I had seen her take on the other day. "You're on, King. In fact, if you aren't too chicken, let's have a contest to see who can bring down the most bad guys."

King laughed. "You'll lose, for sure. This Burger King is a well-oiled machine."

"We just got a powerful new team member," said October. "Potentials through the roof. You won't believe his stats. We'll take you on, and we'll win by a mile."

King continued to laugh. "Put your money where your mouth is and we'll see who wins this one."

The contact ended. The Burger King across the town formed into its bot mode, and started walking down the middle of an avenue. Cars swerved around its feet.

"It's eighteen-hundred," said Kyle. "Portal is opening south-southwest, grade A stable. Making headway."

"Begin walking sequence," said October, gripping the controls.

The McDonalds bot began its walk towards the blue, fiery mess of energy that mysteriously appeared right at the intersection of First and Main. A portal. The men in black suits from before could be seen in various spots around the town, watching.

The Burger King bot made it to the portal at the same time we did. Just as we were about to enter, King's robot jammed its arm out, knocking us aside.

"Damn," said October, as we tilted precariously. "That guy!" She took a deep breath. "I really, really don't want to work with him."

"I think saving the world takes precedence over petty rivalry," said Fry, as he nudged some controls.

"Who knows if it's saving the world," said Andrew. "It could just be another brushfire war."

"We wouldn't be called out on such short notice if we were just going to be playing police state," said October. "This is serious. Especially since we're going to Xen. That place has been the nexus of some serious alien invasions in the past."

"What's Xen like?" I asked. That kind of knowledge hadn't been passed to me through the magical paper-pushing teaching machine, for some reason I couldn't fathom. It would have been so easy. But no, I had to learn it the slow way and look like a total idiot in the process.

Not that I ever cared about looking like an idiot.

"Xen is a dry place, I've heard," said Fry. "The place is just a pocket dimension compared to even other small dimensions. Just one piece of land that's as unstable spatially as any black hole up here. That's probably why it's where most alien invasions come from—it's real easy to make a beachhead there into this area of the multiverse."

"You keep mentioning alien invasions. What do you mean by that?"

"I mean what I say. Alien invasions. The Earth is some prime real estate, and there are forces that really wouldn't go well with humans."

"And what does McDonalds have to do with all this?"

"That, I can't tell you," said Fry. "Just go with it. You'll get used to it eventually."

"Right," I said, still feeling unsettled to my stomach. Things were happening way too fast for someone as normal as me to truly comprehend. I had the feeling that it would all hit me eventually, probably in a big wave, but for the moment everything had a slight tinge of unreality that I knew protected me from the problems that would come with me accepting the fact that I was now part of a team of soldiers who fought inside of a giant robot made out of a

McDonalds restaurant who were about to save the world from an alien invasion coming from another dimension.

October piloted us into the nexus of the portal that had opened in the middle of the street, just as the last bit of the Burger King robot disappeared. In the distance, I could see what must have been a Wendy's restaurant marching towards us, and in the even further distance there was what could have been an Arby's or maybe a KFC. It looked as if everyone was gathered for deployment—for a second I idly wondered where the people of the city were going to get their cheap, tasty food with all the fast food restaurants off to protect them from an alien invasion. I figured maybe obesity would decrease by a measurable amount while we were gone—that would be an interesting thing to study.

My mind snapped back to the present when we passed through the portal, a tearing feeling ripping my body to shreds without actually harming it or even really touching it. I felt like I was the Millennium Falcon in Star Wars going into hyperspace with all the stars going wonko-bonkers around me, becoming trails that disappeared into blurs of light before the camera cut away and showed my body jumping into the nonexistent horizon.

We came to in the middle of a desert, in the outskirts of a compound that looked a lot smaller than it really was—and I could tell it was big in actuality because of the distance readouts on a screen nearby, because I had been taught how to read it by a magical teaching machine and all that. It was several kilometers away, the main building.

Other giant robots began appearing around us, at first a few, and then dozens, and then hundreds, until at least a thousand robots were in my field of vision, with more coming in every second. For a moment I reveled in the fact that the aliens were going to get what was coming to them, until I realized that the army was this big for a reason.

Some serious stuff was about to go down, and I was going to be in the center of it all.

King's Burger King bot was just a couple of meters to our right, standing in a resting position. October watched it for a moment, her face showing a conflicted mix of frustration and what might have been remorse, before she turned away and gripped the controls tightly.

"Forward, set legs long stride," she said, and the crew got to work calibrating, tuning, and controlling the various aspects of the bot.

The only job I had was to sit in a corner and watch the outside through the view screens. I was sure that eventually I would be given a task to do, but for the moment, my job was finished.

As we traveled I thought about what was to come. A sniper—that's what they were turning me into. What did it mean? Why did I get involved with this? Where was my life taking me?

Was this all a dream?

I decided that it wasn't, because even a dream wouldn't be as crazy as the world I was living in now. And besides, everything felt too unreal—everything had that sort of shaky tinge that could only come with disbelief, that feeling that you get when you can't believe something is real and yet it really is. If everything felt perfectly real, I would have been convinced that it was an elaborate dream.

But this was reality. And I was about to go to war.

The compound in the distance came close remarkably fast. All around us dust was being trampled into a large cloud by the thousands of bots that walked in tandem with us. It looked as if every single fast food restaurant in America was with us—which was probably true. I saw the regular assortment of McDonalds, Burger King, Wendy's, and KFCs. I saw In-N-Out, with a yellow arrow design that looked both ridiculously cool and ridiculously stupid. I saw a Popeye's, a Taco Bell, a Whataburger.

It was too much. My brain was overloading with the stupidity of it all. I looked away from the view screens and found my eyes drawn to October.

She looked serious. Womanly, in a powerful way. Almost Amazonian. It was in direct contrast to how she looked in school, which was to say, very polite, well-mannered, with a kind of girl-next-door feeling to her movements. Here she looked the part of a pilot and a captain. Especially with her uniform, which complimented her form surprisingly well.

She caught my gaze and smiled. There it was, a sign that she wasn't an untouchable badass, that she was just a normal girl on the inside. If I didn't know any better I would have said that her expression was almost embarrassed. Then she looked away and the moment was gone.

Fry maneuvered his way through the equipment up to me and put his hand on my shoulder. "Are you okay?" he said.

"Yeah," I said, not meeting his gaze. "I'm fine. Just feeling a little out of it."

Fry laughed, his voice full of reminiscence. "The first time I saw the Franchises and its allies arrayed in full form like this I felt exactly like you did."

"When was that?" I asked.

"About two years ago," said Fry. "I'm halfway through my four-year term of enlistment. Just like you, I went into action right after I got hired. It was a real dimensional war, against the Covenant."

I paused, unsure if I had heard that right. "You mean, the Covenant from Halo?"

"Yeah, it was real bad, too. Somehow a pocket universe where Master Chief died around the second level got mixed with a white hole quasar and achieved a reality status equal to that of our universe."

"I... See," I said. "And who are we fighting this time?"

"Oh, no one you know," said Fry. "Most of the universes out there are governed by small-scale ideas that germinate out of a small group of people. My first war was an exception to the rule."

"So how did it go?"

"How did what go?"

"Your war with the Covenant from Halo?"

"We fought off their incursion and locked them into their own universe. That's usually what happens."

"Ah," I said. "So I have nothing to worry about this time. We're just going to go kick some alien ass, and lock those sorry excuses for movie tropes back into their own universe."

"Not quite," said October, bearing in on our conversation while still piloting the restaurant. "This time we're dealing with a magical enemy." She paused. "It's about time I let slip what I've been hiding. Don't get mad at me for not saying this before, but it's a secret that can't be circulated too close to a dimensional rift. Otherwise, we'll have some serious problems on our hands. This time what we're up against is none other than Sauron himself, brought out of a universe from The Lord of the Rings spinoff video game Battle for Middle Earth and blasted into the space age through accidental contact with a universe where Russia won the space race."

I didn't know how to take it. "That sounds..."

"Bad?" said Fry. He laughed, darkly. "Communist space orcs sounds like a good band name."

I laughed with Fry, unable to do more than marvel at how amazing my life had become. "That sounds good," I said. "That sounds real good."

And so my life got even crazier.

4

***

Charlie

Communist space orcs. That was what we were up against:
Russia and Sauron, buddies in war against all of humanity, or at
least, all of America's fast food restaurants who were a bastion
against them. We were sandwiched in between two dimensions that
were starting to sound a lot like a rock and a hard place.

Not that I found the place to be too hard. The knowledge that
our enemies were something as ridiculous as communist space orcs
calmed the feeling of nervousness that was beginning to take over. I
sat on top of a counter near the back of our bot, watching the march
towards what I assumed was the Franchise compound, probably a
forward operating base from what I knew of military tactics. Not that
any of those would apply to an army made up of fast food Gundam
lookalikes in a war against communist space orcs.

We reached a massive, spread-out tarmac where several
hundred strange-looking airplanes were arrayed in rows, at least a
dozen deep. They had a flat top and were covered in green and
orange protrusions. All of them looked exactly the same, which
shouldn't have been a surprise, but was anyways because of the
crazy assortment the Franchise bots were.

"Pemex," said October, her voice betraying a sort of disgust that
I hadn't heard before.

"Who are they?" I asked. "Some sort of restaurant that you can
only find in Virginia?"

"No, they're Mexico's only gas company. All gas stations there
are state-run operations—it's a government affair."

"And why are they here?" I asked.

October shook her head. "I don't know. All I can say is that the
enemy is stronger than we could have imagined, if the Franchises
are desperate enough to call upon help from socialists."

"And that's a bad thing?" I asked.

"It's a bad thing," said October. "Almost as bad as working with King."

"So it's not that bad."

"You don't understand how much I hate King," said October, running her hand through her hair in what was most likely an absent-minded show of frustration.

"I see," I said.

"You say that a lot."

"I know. It's because I don't have anything else to say in the face of how strange my life has gotten."

"You'll get used to it," said Fry, as he stared at a computer readout.

The march of restaurant bots stopped as the thousands of massive machines reached the tarmac and began to array themselves in ragged lines that were obviously of such little importance that they didn't need to be straight. It was distinctly un-military, which the Pemex planes made very clear, contrasting the Franchise restaurants with their uniform, solid lineup.

A voice came over the communications system, one I didn't recognize, but which sounded deep and heroic enough that its purpose was clear.

"We have gathered here under the united North American trade committee's banner to fight against an ancient and yet powerful enemy that is knocking at the gates of our own dimension, our own world, the world that we love and the world that we live in. The enemy is powerful, and we need to be resolute in the facing of this threat, standing strong against the hordes of blackness that have come out of the very pits of hell itself."

The speech continued on for a long time, stupidly elegant, probably written by a kid just out of college who was listening to too much movie music. It sounded like a speech straight out of a video game. The world was about to end, we were the only ones who could stop it, someone was the hero to save the world blah blah blah.

October could sense my disinterest and gave me a consolatory look. I met her gaze and managed the best smile I could.

"Communist space orcs," I said. "Right? Can't be that bad."

"Magic is a dangerous enemy," said Kyle, sitting down next to me. His hands were shaking.

"Aren't you needed somewhere?" I asked.

Kyle took a deep breath, in, then out. "Yeah, but my hands are shaking too much." He paused. "My job is run by an AI mostly, anyways. But magic, magic sucks. A spell caster can kill an entire battalion of men in a single thought, and ever since Eragon popularized the idea, it's become much more common."

"Don't we have spell casters on our side?" I asked. "Any mages? Sorcerers? Clerics?"

Kyle shook his head. "Our dimension and magic don't mix very well. From what I've heard, we've been negotiating with magic users for some time, but there's just too much in the way. Though, things have gotten better since my first campaign."

"I assume that's where you learned to fear magic."

"Yeah, before the advent of Eragon fever and its brand of magic, magic and technology were equally matched. Magic wasn't well understood, and the people who used it weren't usually of the truly military type. Sure, there were your universes based off of Dungeons and Dragons, but large-scale magical combat doesn't really fit well with that magical ruleset, and every other ruleset was either too arcane or not well-known enough to become a real problem." Kyle paused. "And then Eragon came out—or rather, its sequel, Eldest— and everything changed. My campaign was just a little while after Eragon and its sequels. Our analysts hadn't anticipated the power of that kind of magic. I remember a quote from the book—it's burned into my head. 'You can kill with as much effort as it takes to lift a pen,' I think was the general idea. I was lucky. I was wounded in a battle with a dragon and wasn't with my team when the mages appeared." He paused. "There were over a thousand restaurants, at least five thousand people. There were maybe ten mages. All of our army was wiped out, like that."

"So, how did Earth not end up conquered?" I asked.

"The Franchises deployed a Dr. Device."

"A what? From Ender's Game?"

"That's what we call it," said Kyle, "But it isn't the same as the book. That's just where it got its name. It basically collapses space-time in a radius of several astronomical units. Needless to say, it's really, really dangerous. The Franchises had a tough time cleaning up after that one."

"How long ago was this?" I asked.

"About ten years," said Kyle. "Give or take."

"You don't look that old," I said.

Kyle laughed. "No, how old do I look?"

I examined Kyle. His body was youthful, lithe, looking not more than twenty-five years old. "Thirty," I said, guessing high because of the information I'd been given. That would have made him twenty at the time of the war, which was plenty old, considering that October was seventeen and already the bot's pilot and captain.

"Thirty-two," said Kyle.

"And you still have acne."

"Just a little bit."

"I don't believe you."

"He really is thirty-two," said October, from her spot in the center of the kitchen. "He just looks younger. It makes it hard for him to get drinks at bars."

"And how do you know that?" I asked.

October laughed. "Just know that I know."

The speech had ended some time ago. Now, the massive number of machines assembled around the compound were splitting into groups, and some of the Pemex planes were taking off from the runway. It felt like a real military operation, like D-day was going to happen again, except with giant walking fast food restaurants instead of those sorry-looking grunts you always see wading through the water under fire on the History Channel before it became the Ancient Aliens channel, back when it was all about Hitler's reign instead of Hitler's escape from death.

October piloted our restaurant towards a group near the center of the tarmac, right next to where the Pemex planes were taking off. A couple of restaurant bots stopped next to us, including King's Burger King. King's voice came over the comm.

"Working with you in squad 112 again, eh, October Autumn?" said King.

"The count is still on," said October. "I'm going to win it."

"This reminds me of a certain movie."

"Oh, shut up. You know as well as I do that this is serious business."

'Then how about this," said King. "If I win, you give me control of everything past fourth street. If you win, I'll give back all the territory I've ever taken from you."

"You're on," said October. "You'll regret making this bet, and I'll make sure that the Franchise auditors enforce its consequences."

"The same goes to you."

Another voice came over the radio. "Stop it, you two," it said. It was female, older-sounding, more mature in its tonality. "We're going to be working together for the next couple of months, and if you don't stop arguing I'll knock you both upside the head when you aren't looking."

King laughed. "Such a thing to say over the open comm, Layla."

"If I don't do it I'm sure the Franchise auditors will do it for me. I bet they're as tired of your antics as I am."

King continued to laugh. "Did you hear that, October? She called our argument 'antics.'"

"I don't see what's so special about that," said October.

There was silence on the comm for a while. Then, Layla spoke. "As acting regional manager, I'll take the lead in resolving team disputes from here on out. Your bet has been recorded, and I'll make sure it gets the backing it deserves."

"You're being awfully accommodating," said October. "What's the catch?"

"That you behave," said Layla. "And don't sabotage each other like you did last campaign."

"I promise," said King.

"So do I," said October.

"Good," said Layla. "We have our assignments. There's a contingent of orcish warships landing on this dimension's equivalent of a hothouse planet. It's completely flat, as gravity doesn't work the same here as it does back home—so outboard missions aren't going to be that easy. Also, the atmosphere isn't breathable anywhere, so you had better keep up with your suit maintenance."

"Roger that," said October.

"I understand," said King.

"Then we're off," said Layla.

We followed Layla's robot—it was a Wendy's—towards a distant point on the horizon where a row of portals was set up in what looked like a hasty fashion. The thousands of restaurants that had appeared at the forward operating base were now filtering through them, off to fight the war that was very obviously not at all conventional in its territorial strategy—it was obvious because teleportation was a thing, and there is no frontline if that is true, or any concept of territory for that matter. Battles can happen anywhere and everywhere. That meant that they would happen around strategic targets, around the defense and conquest of those targets.

We made it to the portals and stepped through, the five bots that were part of our squad. We were all from the same region—in our division there were several dozen bots total. The Franchise system of leadership was operated in the same way as their business, that is to say, general orders were given that were then interpreted by the franchisee, or in the case of war, the captain—otherwise known as the manager. This was one of the things taught to me by the magical device.

So we were free to accomplish our goal through whatever means we deemed appropriate. I didn't know what kind of plan October, Layla, King, and the other managers had, but I was sure there was something, as October had a determined look on her face. It was obvious that we weren't going in blind. She had mentioned a brief before, and I suspected that there were a whole bunch of things that she was keeping to herself, probably because it was on a need-to-know basis, or maybe because she couldn't risk a dimensional rift or whatever other mumbo-jumbo was reality here in the dimension of Xen.

We stepped through the portal. Again, I felt like I was going through the Star Wars Millennium Falcon hyperspace jump on crack mixed with a serious dose of Benadryl when taken intravenously. In other words, I felt like my brain was going to crack open my skull and bleed out of my eyes.

Obviously, that didn't really happen. I came to my senses in a world of green, green everywhere outside, the call of strange birds and animals loud in the background of the jungle that I knew was where our mission was going to be. It looked like a scene imported straight out of the movie Avatar—for all I knew, it really was Pandora—with humungous trees that dwarfed our restaurant, and gigantic creatures flying in the sky that looked like a cross between a whale and an elephant with delta-wings like a jet-fighter. Whatever they were called, I was sure their bones would make an interesting exhibit at the aquarium, hanging by those long, thin cables that I was always afraid would snap and bury me underneath a pile of dead whale.

"Our mission calls for outboard operations," said October, looking at me. "Is our equipment ready for battle?"

"Yeah," I said. "I checked it all three times over. We aren't going to suffer any convenient equipment failures, unless whoever's writing this story wants to add some much-needed tension to our battles."

"Did you really need to break the fourth wall like that?" said October.

"I wasn't aware there was one," I said.

October laughed. "That was a joke. Obviously this is reality, not a story someone is writing. Now, let's get our boots on the ground."

October maneuvered the restaurant into a crevice underneath a large, hanging rock with vines adorning much of its surface. She knelt it down, and a ramp extended to the ground, separated from the kitchen by an airlock that used to be the men's restroom.

Kyle, George, Andrew, and Fry passed by me, each one grabbing their issued equipment from the lockers behind me. Rifle, sidearm, SAW for Fry, LAW for Kyle, machetes for everyone, gas masks, oxygen tanks, other paraphernalia that would be needed during an incursion into enemy territory.

"Why aren't we using our bots?" I asked, oblivious to the grand strategy.

"Because we've been ordered not too," said October. She paused. "I understand your curiosity, but I can only say that there is a reason why we're dismounting, and it's a very good one. That, and maneuvering in a forest this dense with a machine like this would put us at more of a disadvantage than it would benefit us."

"I see," I said. "And we're not going to fight giant blue people in mini-walker robots? With gigantic combat knives?"

"We do have a dismountable walker," said October, a strange expression crossing her face. "Though I would prefer not to use it."

"Why?" I asked.

She looked away. "You'll see, if they order us to use it."

I was curious to see what would put off October when even communist space orcs wouldn't. Was there something even crazier that I didn't know about just around the corner?

October motioned with her arm. "Grab your equipment, Max," she said. My locker was last in the row of equipment storage units. In it there was a sidearm, environmental equipment, and a sniper rifle that was almost as tall as I was. Even though I had never touched it before today, I was trained in its use and knew every little detail about its function, its tactical doctrine, even some useless history bits like how it evolved and how militaries have used it in the past.

The gun itself was yellow and red, in alternating patterns around decals in several places that proudly displayed the McDonald's logo. It was a jarring sight, to say the least, one that I hadn't yet gotten used to—everything in the Franchise military was branded, like the logo was for some sort of sportswear company. It gave everything a NASCAR-esque feel.

I picked up the sniper rifle for the first time, feeling its surprisingly familiar weight in my hands. Almost immediately I could feel fatigue in my limbs, as the thing probably weighed more than forty pounds. I remembered what Fry had said about my muscles not being suited for the task. I hadn't expected it to be so clear, so immediate. How was I going to do my job when I could barely point the thing straight?

I instinctively kept my finger off the trigger and the safety on as I loaded a single round into the chamber. The rifle was bolt-action, a function that had a long history and yet strangely modern in execution.

As part of my job during pre-deployment, I had taken apart the gun and cleaned it, and so I knew that it was okay and ready to go. Even so, I checked it one last time for dirt or cracks or anything that would adversely affect its performance and perhaps endanger me. I had the fleeting idea that it was kind of scary how much had been taught to me during those two hours in the office, while I had been filling out paper forms, unaware of what was happening.

I slung the rifle over my back and put on my environmental gear, my face-mask and my oxygen tank and the knee-high boots that were colored a bright McDonalds red. The Golden Arches emblazoned everything.

I looked like a clown. Maybe that was what was intended, given that the company's mascot was a clown. I wondered how we would camouflage ourselves. Did we even need to? Or was there some sort of technology or tactic that made camouflage outdated? I really hoped that was the case, as I didn't want to be painted up like a bulls-eye in the middle of a jungle while there were communist space orcs around.

We stepped into the airlock. October keyed a few commands into a panel hidden underneath the bathroom mirror. I could feel the atmosphere change, my skin tingling as the toxic air of the planet outside seeped in through the now-opening door. There was a sudden change in pressure, my ears popped, and that was that. Humidity immediately clung to my arm hairs. The world felt distant, seen through the glass face-mask I was wearing. I felt constricted. Like I was about to suffer a claustrophobia attack.

October spoke and her voice came through an earpiece that was attached to my mask. "Our mission is one of infiltration," she said, as she walked down the ramp into the outside world. "The main army is battling it out on the plains of Xen, which is the namesake disk of this dimension. We're here to disrupt the chain of command. Take heed, because enemies could appear at any moment."

"Yeah, and they'd see us before we saw them," I said. "With the crazy color scheme we're sporting. What is this, a circus or something?"

"The enemy has detection magic that can register a human from miles away. A little bit of extra color won't change that fact."

"So basically we're walking into a trap."

October shrugged. "It's a war of counters. They sense us, we counter them with technology, they counter with something else, we counter with something else. The chain goes on above our heads. It's not our job to fight the electronic war or the magical war."

"Right," I said. "I still feel uncomfortable standing out like a clown in a jungle. In fact, I am a clown in a jungle."

We reached a clearing where the rest of our squad was gathered, including the team members from King's bot. I noticed King looking at me—I recognized his face from the face-to-face chat from the first day—and I avoided his gaze. He seemed to think it was funny and said something to one of his team members.

I looked around at the three dozen or so people who were gathered around the clearing. All of them wore garish colors, in different schemes, and all of them carried weapons that were as gaudy as they were deadly. Over near the edge was the Wendy's team. The Burger King team was close to us. There was another McDonalds team, the guys from across the freeway relative to where our store was located. There was a Del Taco and a Taco Bell, which was kind of ironic. That made up the entirety of our strike team.

Layla fired up a hologram and the managers, including October, walked up to the center of the clearing to talk about strategy. After about fifteen minutes they broke and walked back to their respective teams. October came back to us with a pensive expression.

"We pulled the unlucky straw," she said, her voice low. "We're going to be the vanguard. Our mission is to seize control of an electronic warfare station that's one of several strategic targets command has decided need to go. Our arrival was probably detected right away, and so they'll be waiting for us." She turned around and marched towards the edge of the clearing. "Let's go."

The three dozen team members in the clearing began to spread out and head towards the setting sun. As I walked I could feel something different about the planet's gravity—it was supposed to be different, and I hadn't known what that had meant until I felt it. I felt as if I was leaning at an angle, constantly about to fall to my right. I suppose that direction was the center of the planet—no, the disk— that I was on. Supposedly the whole thing was flat like a pancake.

We hacked our way through thick greenery with accents of color from orchids and mushrooms and brightly-decorated butterflies that lifted up in swarms when we approached them. I found myself getting nervous. My hands were sweating. How would I react when we got into combat? Would I panic? Would I manage to shoot? I didn't feel bad about killing these enemies—they were communist space orcs, and it really didn't feel real yet—but at the same time I imagined what would happen when I came face to face with one of them. What would they look like? Would they be wearing Stormtrooper armor? Would they be half-naked, like traditional orcs, or would they look a lot like us?

I took a look at George, in front of me, and did a double-take. The colors of his suit and his clothing blended in with the background seamlessly, even though the colors were bright and stood out. It was as if they belonged in the jungle even though they were unusual. I took a look at my own clothing and saw the same effect. It was as if the colors belonged. They blended in like I didn't think reds and yellows could. Maybe it was a trick of technology. Maybe it was magic. Whatever it was, it was pretty cool, and it eased some of my tension to know that I wasn't a painted bulls-eye just waiting to be shot. With what, I didn't know—did the communist space orcs use lasers? Bows and arrows? AK-47s? October did mention magic, and so there probably would be some interesting stuff happening later on—all of it dangerous, possibly meaning my death.

My death. The idea that I was in a life-or-death situation finally hit me. This wasn't a game. I really was going into combat where the enemy would be trying their hardest to kill me, even if they were communist space orcs. Death by communist space orcs was definitely up there in terms of utter ridiculousness.

October raised her arm. We stopped.

"I'm getting something," she said. "Possible contact. North-Northwest, bearing at a slow speed. Could be Charlie."

"What is this, Vietnam?" said Fry, his radioed voice loud in the silence.

No one spoke for a while. Then, George nervously laughed. Everything was silent. No one moved.

Layla's voice came over the comm. "October. Why have you stopped?"

"I'm getting a contact," said October. "Moving to engage." She gave the hand signal for "caution" and crept forwards.

We moved silently through the brush. My sniper rifle was starting to get really heavy, and I shifted its weight on my back. The planetary disk's atmosphere did strange things to my open skin, numbing it in places, making it tingle in others. It made me wish for a full space suit, even though I knew that would make me unresponsive and unable to fight well in combat, where quick movements were a necessity. I understood this, and yet I didn't like it.

October rounded a large jungle tree and stopped again, holding her hand up.

"More contacts," she said.

There was silence. The tension in the air was palpable. I wanted to reach up and tear it away, but I couldn't—I was as tense as everyone else, perhaps even more tense, because this was my first time on a campaign. This was my first time in combat.

A laser bolt whipped past my face and singed a massive hole in a tree trunk not a foot to my right. Everyone around me dropped to the ground almost instantly. I stood there, stupefied.

"Down!" yelled October, loud enough that I heard her real voice through her mask and mine. It overlapped with her radio voice.

I stupidly contemplated that fact while my body responded, hitting the ground before I knew what it was doing. More laser bolts flashed past. October, George, and Kyle started laying down suppressive fire. The noise was tremendous. I had never heard a gunshot before, and I wasn't prepared for how loud it would be. I thought my magical training would have prepared me for this, but I realized that it couldn't. This was just something I would have to get used to. My facemask had little squishy bits on its side that lowered into my ears, dampening the sound of bullets and lasers.

My heads-up display flared, outlining friendlies in green, enemies in red—there were several up ahead, hidden in the brush, probably centered around a machinegun nest, judging by the density of laser blasts that were flying overhead.

What was I supposed to do? I lay there, trembling, unable to move my body. It wouldn't listen to me. I tried to return fire, pulled the trigger of my sidearm, but it wouldn't move—I started panicking. Then I remembered the safety was still on. Too scared to be mad at myself, I pointed the handgun into the forest and fired, fired, fired again until the clip was empty.

Proper procedure flooded into my head unbidden. I felt the calmness of knowledge enter my brain, sedating my fear. I took several deep breaths.

My sniper rifle. In this situation, I was a tactical asset. I should have kept myself aware of the terrain, searching for possible sniper nests—that was the doctrine in this situation. My job wasn't meant to be a frontline combatant. My job was to support from behind the front lines.

And so I got up and rushed away from the firing, away from the shooting and the flying laser bullets.

"Watch out!" said October, her voice cutting through my head. "They're flanking us!"

Lasers flew past me, almost hitting me several times. I ran, hunched over, towards the middle of the group. I should have been there in the first place. Why was I on the front lines? Why was I in the vanguard?

There was no time to think. I found a nest in the middle of some tall trees that were gnarled together, and I climbed up using vines as handholds. When I reached a nook in the branches, guarded by several thick trunks, I unslung my rifle and leaned in on an orchid-covered piece of wood. The weigh was tough for my arms to bear. My hands were shaking. Would I hit anything like this?

A stray laser bolt blasted away some of the flowers to my left. Even in my position, I wasn't completely safe. I searched the surrounding trees through my scope, watching for the red outlines that would mean enemies.

I saw one. There it was: my first contact with a communist space orc. I wasn't laughing. It wasn't a joke now. Everything had just gotten very, very real.

5
*** * * *

Potential Fulfilled

The sound of my rifle was like the world tearing apart, the fabric of reality being ripped asunder. I was in no way prepared for how much kick my gun had. For a moment I thought about the stupidity of having an untrained rookie like me in this role, before my magical training took effect, forcing me to observe, confirm, and search for my next target.

Of course I missed. But that was beside the point. I was working for a dual purpose, learning how to shoot while at the same time providing support. This wasn't so bad. It wasn't like being on the front lines, where I would get shot at directly. Here, the only thing I had to fear was another sniper. Or a magician. Or a stray laser bolt.

I considered the fact that nowhere was safe on a battlefield, before sighting my next target and firing.

I hit it. On my second try, I hit my target in the right shoulder, spinning it around, into the open where I could get a good look at it.

The humanoid was like a classic orc, with a twisted face, massive teeth, and green skin. However, it was wearing some combat armor that vaguely reminded me of Mass Effect while still retaining a Russian-spacey look, reminiscent of the silver shininess of Sputnik. It was quite the ridiculous fashion, made serious by the seriousness of being shot at by real lasers.

I wondered where their mages were. Were we fighting them right now? Was there a battle going on above our heads that I couldn't see?

I sighted another target. This one was behind a row of vines, and I only caught him because of the red outline my team member ball cap heads-up display put around it. I lined up my scope. Fired, and missed. The target dived to the ground, putting a rise of dirt between him and me. I sighted the target, and fired, the bullet pinging into the brown earth. I wasn't going to hit him anytime soon, and so I searched for another target.

My blood was rushing. I felt alive. Exhilarated, powerful, like I was on the world's tallest roller-coaster and was in the center of its deepest fall. Again and again, I lined up, fired, confirmed. Each time, after I had spent my round, I pulled back my rifle's bolt action and loaded another bullet in. The empty shell was humungous, as thick as a baseball bat, or at least it seemed that way as it pinged through the branches back down to the ground.

Even through my earplugs the sound of my gun was loud. Each time it fired, there was a jolt of epic proportions centered in my shoulder that slammed me into the back of the tree. It was a wonder that I was able to hit anything with the recoil that my gun had—as it was, I hit only once in every ten shots, an accuracy rating that was an eighth of what it was supposed to be. Of course, I was doing pretty well for my first time fighting. I didn't even have any training.

After a while the forest grew quiet. There were no more lasers, no more suppressing fire.

October's voice came through the comm. "Charlie's gone. Let's get a move on."

I dropped down out of my tree—and immediately I collapsed to the ground, shaking all over. My gun dropped out of my hands and caught in a vine. I was terrified. My life flashed before my eyes.

October rushed up to me. "Max?" She looked into my eyes, lifting my head up. "Max! Are you okay? Speak to me!" She wrapped her arms around me.

After a moment I disengaged, stood up, and retrieved my gun. I was still shaking slightly, but the moment had passed. "I'm fine," I said. "Don't worry about me. Worry about yourself."

October shook her head. Was she crying? "I don't want to lose you," she said. She was crying. What had done this to her?

I put my arms around her. "It's going to be fine." Then I stepped away. "You have a job to do, right?"

October took a deep breath and smiled. "Yep. My job is being your boss." She paused, obviously troubled. "Forget that ever happened. Don't tell anyone about it."

I looked around. There was no one in the immediate vicinity—though it was hard to tell, considering how surprisingly well our uniforms blended into the forest. I tried spotting bright colors but my mind just glazed over the background and I only spotted one soldier, a Burger King worker wearing blue and red. It wasn't King.

October and I walked through the forest back to where the frontlines were. On the way I stepped over the body of an orc. It wasn't the one I had killed, but I examined it anyways, marveling at the reality of my situation. They were real. They were actually, totally not fake or a product of my imagination. And, they wanted to kill me, unless I killed them first.

I prodded the body with my foot, surprised by how soft the armor was—it was silver in color, and when I looked closer, I could tell that it was made with traditional orcish style, sort of like how I imagined orc armor looked like when I played Dungeons and Dragons. It was a strange combination. Both low-tech and high-tech, fantasy melded with science in the same way that branding was melded with military in the Franchises. Perhaps we weren't so different after all.

"What are you staring at?" said October. "It's dead."

That got my attention. I looked at her. "Did we lose anyone?"

"Yeah, a few guys from the other teams bit the dust, a few more wounded. We've sacrificed a couple team members to bring them back to our landing zone. That means we're down to about two dozen soldiers."

"Aren't we going to get help?" I asked.

October shook her head. "Nope. This is a small-scale operation, not really crucial to the war effort, more of a completion thing."

"I kind of thought I would be at the center of it all when I was briefed."

"You wanted to play the hero?"

We continued walking through the thick jungle, towards where the rest of the group was heading. October walked side by side with me when she could, taking a position in front of me when the way was too narrow.

"I guess," I said. "I just had a fantasy that because I was put into this weird situation that I'd be important or something. I felt like I would matter."

"Well, you don't," said October. "And you had better get used to it. You're disposable like the packaging that a Big Mac comes in. So are we. We're all disposable."

"Then why are you fighting?" I asked. "If you're disposable, what gives you the will to fight?"

"I want to protect the Earth," said October. She paused. "But that's a little to naive to be a real goal. I guess... I guess I just got roped into it like you did." She paused again, this time for a long period of time. Finally she spoke. "I fight for my friends. I fight because I don't like King and want to one-up him." She was silent. We caught sight of Andrew, who waved us over, and he joined us, saying nothing. About that time I figured that me and October had been speaking over a private connection; Andrew made no sign that he knew what we were talking about.

"I remember reading that silly things like that are what keep soldiers alive in war," I said. "You're not any different from the warriors of the past. You're fighting for perfectly noble goals. Our mission is a good one, at least to us, and we're lucky to be fighting against an enemy that really is an enemy. I've read about how horrible Vietnam was, what with the enemy being so vague and shadowy. When you're not sure who the enemy really is, when you're not sure who is in the right, that's when bad things really start to twist you."

October smiled at me, slowing down her pace so that she could get closer to me. She gave my hand a squeeze and then pulled away. "You can be surprisingly wise when you want to."

"What," I said, taking on a joking tone, "You thought I wasn't wise before?"

"I had you pegged as the nerd type."

"And I assume that's the type you like, since you're into me."

October laughed. "I guess you can be a nerd and be wise as well." She stared off into the distance. "I just wasn't expecting to be consoled about my war trauma by a guy who just got started with this yesterday. Was it yesterday? That seems like so long ago."

I laughed, more to let off steam than because I found her statement funny. "I know, right?" I said. "I feel like I've been a soldier forever."

There was a long silence in which no one spoke.

"I had a pet cat that died," said Andrew, surprising me and from the looks of it October, as well.

There was a short pause. Andrew stepped over a tree trunk and almost stumbled, October catching him just in time. Andrew brushed himself off. "He died because I wasn't there to watch him. I was off fighting a war. The restaurant offered to replace him but I don't think any other cat could replace Fluffles."

"You named your cat Fluffles?" said October.

"What?" said Andrew. "He was fluffly."

October laughed, this time a pure sound that wasn't obstructed by stress or any other negative emotion. "Thanks," she said. "That cheered me up."

Andrew looked confused. "What's so cheerful about my pet cat dying?"

October calmed down and put her hand on Andrew's shoulder. "Remind me not to let you name my pets."

"I wasn't going to do that anyways," said Andrew, looking even more confused.

I pulled October away from him. "Stop harassing the younger kids," I said, my tone not that serious, more light than funny. I didn't want to stop the comradery; it was just that Andrew's face made me feel embarrassed for some strange reason.

Andrew looked at me for what I felt was the first time. He seemed to finally notice that I was here, finally get it into his head that I was fighting alongside him. Then, his eyes darted away, showing a number of complicated emotions. Andrew wasn't a simple kid, I could tell. My first impression of him had been of the quiet type, the type that kept everything to himself, all bottled up.

Was I reading too deep into him? Probably. But at the same time I felt an empathy for his position, wondering how a sixteen-year old—I was pretty sure he was sixteen—was in this position, and how he felt about it. I knew that the real Earth military, at least America's military, didn't take recruits under the age of eighteen. I wondered what made the Franchises different. Was there some sort of advantage that hiring high school students gave the warriors? Was it because we had the most open minds, because we could accept the fact that things were in no way what they seemed?

Yeah, I was definitely reading too much into it. I told myself to take things in stride and tried to stop thinking.

"Do you have any pets?" I asked October, glancing at her by my side.

She stepped over a tangle of vines, and then helped me over. Andrew climbed over on his own, trailing further behind us.

"No," said October. "Not now. I used to have a lot of pets, some rabbits, a Guinea pig, a dog, a parakeet. Now my house is pretty quiet. Ever since my mom left we haven't gotten any new pets."

"Your mom left?" I said.

October's expression told me I shouldn't have asked. Backpedaling, I thought of what to say to salvage the situation. Before I could, I noticed October's expression change from one of irritation to one of sorrow. Still, she said nothing. She was probably beating herself up for getting angry at my question.

But I knew not to step on that landmine again.

"So," I said. "Why don't you play video games when so much of what you fight derives from them? I mean, you said it yourself. Our enemies are an offshoot from a video game universe."

October looked happy for the change of subject. "I don't know," she said. "Video games just never appealed to me. Why would I want to play at war when I've seen the real thing?"

That was a good point. I said nothing, and the two of us pushed our way through the underbrush until, up ahead, there was a change of scenery.

A space station-like compound was embedded in the side of a rocky hill. It was grey, had lots of antenna, and flew a flag that was a mix of the USSR's hammer and sickle and the Eye of Sauron. A chill ran through my spine as I examined the flag through my rifle scope.

"What do you see?" asked October, crouching down low. Andrew and Kyle were close by us. My heads-up display showed that the rest of our squad wasn't too far away.

I checked out the rest of the compound through my scope. There wasn't much else to say. There were a few guards, holding laser rifles, and the doors to the compound were barred shut with energy beams. I was wondering how we'd get through, before they opened of their own accord, and a caravan of vehicles rolled through. They were surprisingly old-fashioned looking, the old-timey USSR feel really hammered home by the muted coloring, the sloped angles, the red hammer and sickle and the eye of Sauron. I was surprised to see that the vehicles were driven by humans. When about four jeep-looking vehicles had passed through, the doors closed, but the energy beams guarding them did not reappear.

"There's a road past the outpost," said October, beginning to creep forwards.

I followed her, and so did the rest of our squad.

"We should be safe," continued October. "That was probably a command squadron, or perhaps an equipment delivery. One or the other."

We made our way to the edge of the compound. The trees around it were kept back several meters, the space having been cleared by an excavator of some sort. It was open ground. It would be hard to traverse, at least without being seen.

October held up her hand. The signal to stop and observe. She alone continued to move forwards.

King's voice came over the comm. "What are you doing, October?" he said, his irritation obvious. "Don't go there. You'll reveal our position."

"They already know we're here," said October. "They're probably waiting for us to make our move. I say we storm the compound."

"I agree," said Layla. "This isn't such an important strategic asset that they would sacrifice more than a handful of troops from the frontlines."

"It could be a trap," said King.

"It's always a possibility," said Layla, "But our briefing was clear. Storming the compound is an option. Let's move into position."

I found a nook between two rocks that allowed me room to maneuver and rest my rifle without obstructing my vision of the compound. It was hidden enough that I didn't think I would need to try hiding myself.

"This is Max, I'm in position," I said. "Over-watch is secured."

Several more squad snipers relayed in their confirmations. I didn't recognize any of the voices—I probably wouldn't have even recognized their faces if I saw them.

October crept forwards, and I had the sudden, inexplicable feeling that something terrible was about to happen. I shook the feeling off. This wasn't supposed to be a dangerous mission. It was of little strategic importance, just one small piece of the big puzzle happening all throughout the entire dimension, however big it was. We were just pawns.

But that wasn't what made me afraid. The lack of conflict, the ease with which we got this close. Something was wrong. Alarm bells were ringing in my head.

Before I could say anything, October burst out of the bushes and sprinted towards the compound. At the same time, Fry laid down suppressing fire with his squad machine gun, the chatter of the other squads joining in with his. Tracers burned lines through the air. About twenty people rushed towards the main building, underneath a spray of bullets. There were very few lasers fired in return, and those that were shot went astray. We had succeeded in surprising them, even if they knew we were here.

A sneaking suspicion broke into my consciousness. They had let us get here. It was a trap. I couldn't explain why, but I was certain of it.

And then it hit. The white blindness that came out of the sky and obscured everything from my vision.

"October!" I cried, without thinking, jumping out of my hiding place. I rushed onto the field, only to run into an orc with a laser gun pointed right at my head.

I dove to the ground. The orc fired once, twice, in short bursts, the blasts flying over my head and singing the ground. I rolled over instinctively and used my rifle like a club, batting the orc's legs out from underneath him. He hit the ground with a thump, his uniform reflecting the bright light from above into my face. Without thinking about other options I rammed the butt of my rifle into the orc's face, once, twice, three times, unable to do more than bloody his fat nose. I remembered that orc skulls were supposed to be very, very hard. Cursing myself for not thinking about it earlier, I drew my sidearm and fired several shots into the orc's chest. He shuddered, spitting blood, and then he fell still.

The sounds of battle were all around me. I was lost, alone in a sea of blinding light, unable to see my way through anything. I heard the sound of engines in the distance. Was it those same vehicles that had left, earlier? Why were they returning?

A blue light appeared in front of me, and then time froze. Everything was still. A figure in a deep purple robe stepped out of a door into the very fabric of space-time. He had a dignified face, though it was too bright for me to make out the details. His beard was long, well-kept, and shining silver in the harsh lighting from above. His eyes sparkled. He stepped towards me with slow, measured paces.

"Hello, Max," he said, his voice very familiar and yet alien to my ears. It was smooth. Soft, and I wanted to hear more of it, though it was too strange to be real at the same time. It gave me tingles down the back of my spine.

"I'm here to bring you a message," said the man. "My name does not exist, and yet my essence is at the core of every wizened wizard and hero's mentor in the universe. I am the being who guides. The Obi-Wan Kanobi, the Brom, the Gandalf, the Hitchhiker's Guide to the Galaxy." His voice was long, slow, and gave serious credibility to his claim.

"The dimensional planes have aligned," said the man in the cloak. "You have been chosen as the hero who will save the world. To that end, we will give you one power, one ability that you may take with you to aid you in your quest. It may take any form."

I thought. My mind was whirling. Even if this was a joke, even if this was a trap, I was stuck in it, and so I figured that I would just go along with it.

Anything I wanted. For no reason at all. At a moment when everything I knew was about to end. I needed something that would allow me to save her. October. At that moment I realized something. I loved her. I didn't want her to die. And, in this situation, she surely would.

"Can I ask to end this war?" I asked.

The man shook his head, though his eyes were kind. "I cannot affect anything other than your person. If you wish to end the war, I can give you tools that will allow you to do so, but you will have to carry out the plan yourself. And, I cannot advise you in your choice. You will have to decide for yourself what your path will be."

I thought, for a long time, the world doing nothing around me, the brightness never fading, never wavering. The brightness was obviously the trap that we had run into—it was some sort of magic that created a light that was blinding enough to disorient us. That was the trap. October had warned us about magic. Now I saw how dangerous it could be.

Magic. There was something there, something that was missing, something that I could take advantage of that would turn the tides. How much power could I wish for? Could I make myself like a god?

But that wouldn't do any good for the people that were fighting around me. They would be dead before I could help them. I needed something that would get everyone out, and fast.

"Be quick about it, boy," said the man in the cloak. "There is great evil about, more so than you can imagine. The Russians and Sauron are the least of your worries."

Russians. Sauron. The McDonalds restaurant. Everything being so strange, it was hard to believe. It was like—it was like everything was inside my own head.

"Give me the ability to make my thoughts reality," I said. "Give me the ability to create real things using my imagination."

The wizened old man bowed. "You have chosen rightly, as was destined. I will instruct you on the rules, which must be imposed, as with not rules there is no power. Firstly: as you have requested, you will be able to form objects into being with only your imagination. However, you will not be able to create life. And, you will only be able to create an object that you have seen for yourself. As well as this, you will not be able to manipulate a reality that already exists, no matter what, so be careful with what you create. As with all powers, there is responsibility involved. I will not lecture you on it, but do know that you are being watched, both by forces of good and by those who wish to attain what we have given you."

Then, the man in the robe disappeared, leaving time stopped. I knew instinctively that it was going to start again in a couple of seconds, and so I quickly tested out my new power.

It worked. I imagined our McDonalds robot into existence, and it appeared, as if out nothing—or rather, literally out of nothing, if what the man in the robe had said was true. The robot was a welcome sight. And then, time started again. The bright light flickered to life, became more potent, though some of its brightness was blocked by the robot. That gave me an idea. I ran through my head a list of possible objects that I had seen in my life, and quickly selected a large hot air balloon, which appeared out of nothing, surrounding the light in cloth. The light was muted by the fabric, leaving only an afterimage. I saw the field, the open ground. October was still alive, looking startled as she stared at the McDonalds robot that was parked right in front of her.

"Max!" She shouted, darting towards me through a storm of laser fire. "What happened? Why is our bot here?"

I ran to meet October underneath the bot's legs. "I was given a power!" I said. "A power to save the world!"

"What do you mean?" said October, her voice a little too loud through the comm system, which was designed to facilitate conversation in the loud environment of a battlefield.

"Let's get in," I said, pointing to the bot.

October looked at me in confusion, then seemed to make a decision. "Will do," she said. She called for the rest of the squad, who seemed to be equally perplexed. On the way we maneuvered around the pile of fabric that had been the hot air balloon. Once we were inside our bot's kitchen, October grabbed hold of the controls, firing the bot's engines up. Andrew, Kyle, Fry, and George all piled in, running to their various stations. Fry grabbed a mounted machinegun that was in a ball turret that I hadn't noticed before. The sound of its chatter was especially loud in the close quarters.

"Load Big Mac round!" said October, her captain's attitude coming back to her. She maneuvered us around the other squads, who were still running about in confusion while suppressed by several dozen laser-toting orcs who were hidden in various places in the building. October lifted the bot's arm up and fired. The bolt smashed into the compound's wall, vaporizing it. Half of the roof came crashing down.

"Well, I guess we did what we came to do," said Fry. He sounded confused, as I was sure everyone else was.

The firing died down. On the ground, I could see the surviving members of our squad gathering around our bot.

I had created the robot out of nothing. Me, an ordinary kid, had brought a billion-dollar fast food machine out of nothing. What were we going to do with the original?

And then the man in the robe's words hit me. *Be careful.* I created the bot on the spur of the moment, but the implications of its appearance were far, far too large to be comfortable. It was an obvious sign that something was up with me. I decided, then and there, to only reveal as much as was needed. The man's warnings continued to reverberate through my head.

October faced me, her face full of conflicting emotions. "What happened?" she asked. "How did our restaurant end up here?"

She was obviously looking for answers, and wouldn't stop until she got them. And, I was willing to tell her.

"Let's talk in the airlock," I said.

October shook her head. "We can trust the people in this kitchen. Tell us here and now. What did you do?"

"How do you know it was me?" I asked.

"Now I do know it was you."

"Ah," I said. Then I let out a deep breath. "A random guy in a purple robe froze time and gave me a superpower that allows me to create objects out of nothing."

October's eyes narrowed. "The Watcher."

"You know of him?"

"I did not think him still active in the affairs of mortals," said October, "Pardon the cliché phrase."

"Cliché phrase excused," I said.

October cracked a half-smile. Then her face became serious again. "The watcher visited you." She sounded like she knew it would happen. "When I saw your potentials on the aura reader, I thought it was broken. Now I know it wasn't."

"What's this about potentials again?" I said.

"Potential is the innate ability of a being to be, well, heroic. Powerful. A person with a lot of potential in an area will attract big events to him like flies to honey. And your potentials are so high that they broke the scales. They must be far, far higher than I could have imagined if The Watcher came out of his centuries-long hiatus to grant you a heroic ability. And, a powerful one at that."

"He said I could choose what ability I wanted."

October scoffed, though obviously it wasn't at me. "The Watcher always asks that of someone. The true test is to see if the person picks the ability that he was destined to pick. If he doesn't, it means that the person isn't meant to have any ability." She paused. "Though, I have never heard of an ability that can manifest an entire restaurant out of thin air."

"How can you tell it's not teleported?"

"I'm not blind," said October. Then she paused. "Though a normal person wouldn't notice, this restaurant handles significantly differently on a fundamental level than the one I'm used to driving. I can tell it's a different beast." She paused, her face contemplative. "Though, I do think I enjoy the change. I feel more in control, and the motions feel more fluid. How, exactly, did you create it?"

"I imagined it," I said. "And it became real."

October tilted her head. "Really."

The rest of the crew was also watching me, which made me uncomfortable. Only October seemed to be completely comfortable with me. Everyone else looked, to put it simply, a little shocked and suspicious. I would be to, were I in their situation. Here they were, inside a machine that I had conjured out of thin air. I wonder who they thought I was?

October noticed my gaze. "Are you thinking that they hate you now?" she said.

"No, that's not it," I said. "Why would I think that?"

"Because maybe they're jealous. Because maybe they're suspicious of you."

I waited a few moments, composing my response. "I have a little bit more faith in humanity than that."

"In humanity? Not in your comrades-in-arms?" asked October, leaning towards me. "I would reword that."

Fry leaned back against a wall with half a smile on his face. "You just became a very important person, Max," he said. "I'll get to brag that I knew you before you were famous, even for a couple of days."

"Wait a minute," I said. "Who says I'm going to be famous?"

October raised both of her eyebrows. "You mean you don't know? You can't figure out what happens to pretty much everyone who gets contacted by The Watcher?"

"No," I said. "I just got his job two days ago."

October sighed. "I would have expected you to guess anyways."

"It's not that I can't guess," I said. "Just that I don't really believe anything anymore. The world is too crazy for me to make any conclusions. For all I know, the power I manifested could be a common thing. In a world with communist space orcs and McDonalds restaurant Gundam robots, that isn't too far of a stretch. Maybe there's an X-men universe somewhere, or a Heroes universe, or any other comic-book based system. I mean, look at pretty much any magic system in any story. There are plenty of people who have powers that I couldn't even begin to imagine even now."

October said nothing for a while.

Before she could speak, Layla's voice came over the comm. "What happened, October?" she said. "Report. Tell me what's going on. Why is your restaurant here? How did you get it through the jungle? Did you teleport it?"

"No," said October. "One of my team members manifested an ability given by The Watcher."

"This isn't the time for humor," said Layla, her voice obviously irritated. She didn't believe it, which probably meant that she was a rational human being even amidst the craziness of the world I now inhabited. "But you can brief me later, when you're feeling more serious. For now, we have to make sure that the outpost is actually neutralized. As well as this, we have to see what's really going on here. We have to answer the question of how we managed to walk into a trap like the one we encountered."

"You guys can take care of that," said October. "We'll stay in our restaurant and make sure that no enemies approach from the perimeter.

There was silence for a long while. Layla was obviously debating her response. Then she spoke. "Agreed, October. I'll take the rest of the squads to do a full sweep of the interior. We'll relay what's happening, and if we need your support, we'll call."

The comm went dead. October looked at me, her head at a slight angle, interest clear in her expression.

"Show me what you can do," she said.

"What do you want me to make?" I asked. It was more for my sake than for hers, because I suddenly pulled a blank regarding items that I could possibly create in the cramped space of the kitchen.

"A cup," she said.

I imagined a cup like the ones I had in my house, and one appeared in the middle of the kitchen, falling almost immediately and shattering on the ground.

October looked more interested than annoyed.

"I'll clean it up," said Andrew, grabbing a broom and dustpan.

As Andrew cleaned, October watched me. "Can you make it not appear floating in the air?"

"I'll try," I said, holding out my hand.

Sure enough, I could materialize the object in my grasp. It wasn't hot and it wasn't cold, surprisingly so. I had expected it to feel a little bit more magical and less solid than it did. I almost dropped it in surprise when it had suddenly appeared, and it took me a few seconds to recover.

"How about something more complicated?" asked October. "Obviously you can recreate the artificial intelligence that controls most of this ship's functions with even more precision than the original builders could. I want to see what you can do. Can you make me an Iphone?"

"Sure," I said. I materialized an Iphone in my hand. It was my own—I knew it the instant it appeared.

October held out her hand. I handed it to her. She tried to type in the password.

"It's mine," I said. "It will only take my password."

October handed it back to me. "Are there any limitations? Any rules you have to follow? Or are you really a cold fusion-type with total disregard for the laws of thermodynamics?"

"I thought this was a world with magic in it," I said.

"Even magic has to obey the laws of thermodynamics, even if it does interpret them rather loosely. What you're doing is totally ignoring them. The objects have to come from somewhere. Where are they coming from?"

I knew the answer. It was so simple, I had no idea why no one could think of it. "My imagination," I said. "Inside my head. They are created in there from my memories and then they appear in the real world."

October leaned back in her chair. "So we've discovered a new type of magic. A magic of which the limit is imagination. In essence, limitless."

"I can't create life."

This gave October pause. "Can you create organic compounds?"

"Like, food?" I said.

"Try," said October.

I materialized a steak on the grill. October looked at it. Fry walked up to it, poked it, and took a bite.

Kyle, George, and Andrew stared at him as if he was crazy.

"What?" said Fry. "If he can't create life, it should be sterile, right?"

The three crew members looked surprised, and glanced among themselves. Andrew raised his hand. "Can I have some ice cream?"

"Sure," I said. "What kind?"

"Mint chocolate chip," said Andrew.

I materialized him a mint-chocolate chip ice cream cone, pulled directly from a memory I had as a child, walking along the pier of Balboa Beach with my family, stopping at the rather expensive ice cream cart, the cone melting in my hands underneath the summer sun that was still cool due to the fresh sea breeze. The sound of a carnival floated overhead. There were seagulls in the air.

I snapped back to reality, inside the kitchen. Everyone was looking at me, watching me, judging me. I felt naked.

"It's all going to be okay, right?" I said. "Nobody's going to dissect me, no one is going to try to kill me?"

"Not if I can help it," said October. Her eyes met mine. They were ferocious, and would have been frightening if I had not known that behind them was a will to protect me. As it was I was happy that she cared so much for me, and at the same time confused as to why she would. What had I done for her that made her think of me so highly?

I remembered my realization from before, when I had been kneeling in front of The Watcher. I remembered the feel of my rifle in my hands. I had decided then that I loved October—or at least, I wanted to love her, felt something for her though I did not yet know what it was. And so I was happy to be in the situation I was in.

Fry walked up to me and put his hand on my shoulder. "I'm with you," he said. "And not just because getting on your bad side would probably get me killed." He smiled, wolfishly. "That was a joke. I don't think you're that kind of guy."

George and Andrew nodded with him.

Only Kyle looked troubled. He turned away when I tried to meet his gaze, and crossed his arms in as if he was offended. Something was obviously bothering him.

October glanced over at him. "Hey, are you in on this, or what?"

"I don't like it," said Kyle. "It smells rotten. Like something bad is going to happen. It's too much of a good thing to be true—there has to be a serious catch."

The kitchen was silent for a long while. Everyone was watching me, probably waiting to see my reaction. I gave them one: I tried my best to appear as innocent and friendly as possible. Eventually it looked like Kyle's suspicion had relented, or at least been assuaged for the moment. He stamped his feet on the ground. "I still think something serious is going to happen. Whenever The Watcher appears, bad things occur. There are no exceptions to that rule."

"Well, he's a hero for a reason, right?" said October.

"I don't know that I'm a hero, per se," I said. "I'm not sure what I am. I feel like a freeloader. Like I don't deserve this. I'm still trying to take everything in."

"You'll earn your ability, I'm sure," said October. She smiled, though it was more consolatory than happy. "We'll make sure that you do."

I wasn't satisfied, but I stayed silent because there wasn't anything else to say. Several minutes passed.

Layla's voice came over the comm system. "Hey, October?" she said. "You had better get back." There was a burst of static. "They're everywhere. Nuclear missiles. Giant spiders. Zombies." There was more static. "Get out of here." She was obviously trying very hard to regulate her voice. It sounded about to crack apart. "Get out of here! Warn the Franchises! They're not just who we thought they were! They're everywhere!"

I could hear gunshots coming from inside the compound, through the rubble that we had created. What was inside there, that would shake someone like Layla? Nukes? Giant spiders? Zombies?

October gripped the bot's controls, her knuckles going white. "We're not leaving," she said. "We're staying here until all of you get out."

King's voice came over the comm. "Oh, October, always wanting to play the hero when you really aren't." His voice was as strained as Layla's, perhaps more so. "I really regret this, I truly do, but it looks as if I'll be killing more enemies than you this campaign." He paused. "Pity I won't be alive to see the gains my restaurant made."

"Don't you die on me!" said October. "If you're dead, who are we going to fight? We'll trash your restaurant! Do you want that to happen?"

There were more gunshots, and some other loud, unidentifiable noises.

"It's a missile silo," said Layla. "And they're about to go off. Please, get out of here while you can."

"I don't understand," said October. "What's happening down there? It doesn't make any sense!"

There was a blast of static. "Hello, people inside the restaurant that trashed my lovely compound here."

It was a deep voice. Calm, steady, and very appealing in its low notes. It was shame that the comm system distorted it.

"You won't get out of here alive. Thanks to you, I've had to start my plan two days too early. That means that things won't go as smoothly as I had hoped."

"Who are you?" asked October. "And how are you on this channel?"

"I'm the bad guy," said the voice. It laughed, a laugh that actually didn't sound that bad-guy-ish at all, not like King's voice had. It was a strange feeling. Everything was starting to make sense now. I was fighting someone. Someone with power. Someone that I had just stumbled into contact with.

And he didn't sound at all like he would go easy on us.

6

* * *

Evil Incarnate

I was afraid. I couldn't feel a reason, couldn't see why I should feel the way I did, but I was shaking in my boots, a figure of speech I didn't understand until now. It was how everything had come together. How the man's voice sounded to my ear. I knew, deep down inside, that something very, very bad was about to happen.

"Let's take Layla's advice and get out of here," said October. She looked at me. "I don't suppose you have a way to get his bot through the thick jungle?"

"I..." I couldn't answer. "I can only make objects appear that I've physically seen in person."

"Have you ever seen an industrial logger? How about a helicopter? Anything to get us through the jungle?"

"Can't we just hack through?" I asked.

October shook her head. "If we could, we would have come in our bots. We hoofed it because we had to, not because—"

The rubble of the compound shifted, falling in waves off the side of a massive, black, scaly, terrifying figure that was slowly rising out of the scree that surrounded it.

I was clouded with horror. My eyes focused in on a tiny spot in the center of my vision. Unspeakable things ran through my mind, my spirit unable to process them, unable to wrest control of my body as it convulsed in utter fear. There was the enemy. There was the bad guy.

No. It wasn't even the real bad guy. Just a projection of his aura, a little piece of him that was stored away in this tiny facility deep in the jungle. And yet I was so afraid.

"Get... It... Together!" said October, through gritted teeth. The McDonalds robot moved. Slowly. But, it moved. I clawed my way back into control, my body not responding as it should, my eyes focused entirely on the misty-black figure about as large as our restaurant that was approaching us at a slow ambling walk, almost as if it didn't care if we escaped.

I thought, desperately trying to figure out anything that would get us out of the situation. I had an idea—I summoned an oil tanker, one of the trucks I had seen pumping gas into gas stations back home. It appeared in the sky above the monster's head, smashing into it cab first, spilling its contents all over.

"Yes!" cried October, moving the bot so that its main hand cannon pointed straight at our enemy. "That's the way to do it!" She pulled the controls with obvious difficulty. "Load Big Mac round!" she cried.

"I'll do it," I said, materializing a round in the chamber. I felt freed. My power was working. I was fighting against a monster that put even what I had to shame, but it was working. I was doing something. Even if it was as haphazard as what I was doing in the moment.

"Fire!" said October, and Kyle pushed himself onto a counter, pressing a few buttons awkwardly.

The round roared out of the chamber, lighting the monster on fire, blasting all of us out of our terrified stupor. October turned our machine on its tail and sprinted towards the jungle. We crashed through the trees, our legs tangling in the undergrowth, October pushing the machine to its limits to get us out. We barely made it a hundred feet before we were too mired to get anywhere. The jungle was thick. There was a reason why we hadn't brought our machines.

"Everyone out!" cried October, and we all piled into the airlock, hastily donning our masks and our environmental suits. In the background, flaming red walls of fire lit up the kitchen with an eerie glow. I could smell gasoline in the air—it must have been strong if it penetrated the restaurant's life support systems. We stepped out of the airlock more in a pile than anything else, stumbling along blindly through the burning, smoky jungle. The fear that had encapsulated me was still there, burning away with the flames of gasoline and death, but we were able to run. And so we ran. We ran until we reached the deep jungle, where October turned to us and looked us each in the eye.

"We're getting out of here," she said. She turned, looking satisfied with what she had said. She continued to push through the underbrush.

We made it to the clearing where our original bot was stored in about half an hour. All of us were exhausted. I couldn't run anymore, not even if my life depended on it. It took all my effort to climb up the boarding ramp and enter the machine.

The airlock hissed as we entered. The ramp pulled back, and October sat down at the controls. She flipped a few switches and looked around through the view screens at the abandoned restaurant robots around us. She saluted.

"You will be missed." Then, she manipulated a few controls that connected to a portable portal machine—I hadn't thought to materialize one of those, though now I wish I had—and fidgeted for the ten minutes that it took to open up. When the portal had finally been connected, she stepped through.

And immediately we stepped into the center of hell itself. Smoke filled the air, the sound of gunshots and the clash of metal on metal, loud enough and crunchy enough to let us know that there were robots battling it out with their fists in close combat.

"Command!" said October. "Give us a status report!"

There was static. Then a voice. "Are you all that's left of squad 112?" it asked. "Where are the others? Gone?"

"What's happening here?" asked October.

"We're under attack by an unknown enemy of supreme power," said the voice. "We need all the help we can get. Get to the front line, do as much damage as we can, we're almost overrun here."

"Roger that," said October, piloting the restaurant through a field strewn with broken machines and the bodies of a dozen different creatures of the dark, orcs and zombies and giant spiders among them. There was something serious going on. Among the bodies I could pick out dead team members, standing out because of their bright clothing and branded decals. There were far too many dead for my comfort.

The area of the battle we stepped into looked to be mostly over. And, looking around us, it was clear who had won. They had. There were at least a dozen giant elephants, several Cthulhu-like monsters, and a dragon, though none were as fearful as the monster we had seen in the jungle.

And then the missile fell. A single rocket, bearing down almost vertically, landing in the center of the compound. There was a flash—my eyes went spotty, and for a moment I couldn't see. And then there was a roar, so massive that it shook the very foundations of my bones. I fell to the floor, paralyzed in fear. The compound. Humanity. Our war effort. All of it flashed through my mind.

No! This couldn't happen! I needed to save them, I needed to keep the enemies away from Earth! That was my job, that was what The Watcher had assigned me to do!

A mushroom cloud appeared over what was left of the compound. In the distance the remnants of the Franchise battle bots fought a last desperate stand against the forces of evil, the Godzillas and orcs and who knows what else that were everywhere on the plains.

We were fighting a losing battle. That much was obvious.

"The portal," said October. "We have to close it."

"How are we going to get there?" asked Fry. "It's several kilometers away."

October gripped the controls. "It's time to get creative." She looked at me, her eyes determined, filled with expectation that I was both afraid of and grateful for. It snapped me back to reality. I was needed. "You have thirty seconds," she said. "Find a way to destroy that portal."

Ten seconds passed before a thought even passed through my mind. I spent ten more seconds cycling through every vehicle I had ever seen. This was a lot harder than it looked. For a moment I considered using something I had seen in a movie, but I knew that wouldn't work. I had to have seen it with my own eyes. My own eyes—that was a strange rule.

How far away could I materialize objects? That idea popped into my head. And then, I knew what to do.

It was a boring idea, but it just might work; no, it had to work. I imagined the nuclear missile that had just a minute ago destroyed the compound. The mushroom cloud was still growing in size. It flashed through my memory first, and then I saw the missile with my mind's eye.

A nuclear missile appeared over the portals, over three kilometers away. I willed it to explode. It didn't. Instead, it simply buried itself in the ground.

And that was it. The monsters reached the portal, hundreds of them, passing through in waves, soon entering in the thousands, Kaiju and Decepticons and Sith lords and who knew what else from every fictional universe and then some.

"Well," said October. "That's that. Looks like we aren't going to have a home to go back to."

"Can't we do anything about that?" I said, watching as everything I knew swirled away into nothingness. "Aren't the franchises powerful enough to stop this?"

October looked at me, her eyes unfocusing, focusing, unfocusing again. She looked to be concentrating very hard. Then she nodded. "You may be powerful enough to stop this," she said. "We need to get you some training." She looked at the rest of the crew. "It looks like the burden of saving the world has finally fallen on our shoulders. And, it looks like we'll be taking a journey through the multiverse." She looked at me. "You remember what the portal machine looked like, right," she said.

In the distance, the assorted fictional monsters and bad guys in the distance were closing in. Very few Franchise bots were left to stand against the enemy. A couple of them were heading towards us—they might not make it, I knew, and there were just a couple, but I was cheering for them all the same. We needed all the help we could get.

"I remember the gate," I said. I thought for a moment, concentrating, and a portal gate appeared in front of our bot. It was that easy. However, it wasn't activated—and I knew from experience that the ten minutes it took to activate was a very long time when we were pressed against a wall. October furiously pressed buttons on a retractable keyboard in her chair. Every other crew member in the kitchen bustled around without looking at me. October glanced in my direction.

"Give the environmental suits a once-over," she said. "We're going to need them. Make sure they weren't damaged during our run."

It was a mundane task for such a tense time. The bad guys—I didn't know how to classify their diversity, the only thing they had in similar was that they were all classically bad guys—continued to march closer. There were several restaurants coming at the fore, ahead of the forces of evil.

The forces of evil. How strange that we would be fighting such clichéd enemies in a world like the one I lived in. Something seemed off about it all, though I couldn't piece together in my mind what it was.

As I checked Fry's environmental gear, the image of the trucks with human drivers leaving the compound flashed through my mind again. What were they doing? They were the only normal humans I had seen so far. Every other enemy I had encountered was either an orc, an alien, or a monster. Something was definitely going on. But I had no idea what it could be. I considered possibility after possibility as I checked through the last of the gear, running through the checklist that had been imprinted in my mind by the magical teaching machine.

Magic. Something magical was going on. That much was obvious, but...

"We're live," said October. She pressed a button on her keyboard in a strangely frenetic fashion and the comm system cut through. She put on her headset and spoke into the microphone embedded in it.

"This is a message to all surviving Franchise restaurants. We are rallying at the location of this sender, preparing to evacuate to a safe zone. Any and all facilities that make it in the next six minutes will be brought along. All others will be left behind. That is all."

The bots in the not-so-distance sped up, tossing sand beneath their legs. The plane we had entered, the plane on which the compound was built, was completely flat, covered in a thin layer of sand that was now whirling around in the wind of the nuclear explosion. Even through the storm, everything was still visible, thanks to our bot's detection software.

A few tense minutes passed. First one, then two, then five and then six bots rallied at our side. When we reached eleven, the gate opened.

"Advance!" said October, leaping into the portal. The kitchen shook with the force of the desperate move. I felt it again, the feeling that my brain was being kicked across hyperspace like a football of the gods. And then, we came through, into a clear and simple meadow that looked about as far from conflict as could be desired. A dozen other restaurants materialized at our side. And then, there was silence. Nothing more happened for a long while. Several crews dismounted, looking obviously frazzled.

October leaned back in her chair, rubbing at her temples. She took a deep breath, in, then out, then in and out again. She closed her eyes.

"We can't save Earth," she said, her voice low. "But we can hope to take it back." There was silence for a long moment. Then she opened her eyes and looked at me. "I believe in you, or rather, The Watcher. I think you have the power to save the world in this time of crisis. At the very least, we'll have an infinite amount of material if we want to mount a campaign to retake the Earth."

"You're already talking like Earth is conquered."

"It's as good as done," said October. She frowned. "I don't like one thing. Where were the Pemex planes during the battle?"

I started. I hadn't noticed that; the Pemex planes, the trucks—they were connected somehow. I could feel it in my stomach.

Pemex was a state-run company, and so there was a clear motive for them to join forces with the Russians—maybe they were behind it.

No, it couldn't be. Not with the amount of evil that I had seen on that plane. I don't think even the Russian government at the height of its power could control Godzilla and Darth Vader and who knows what else; it was too ridiculous to think that the Russians were even truly evil like that. They were human too.

"Is the atmosphere on this planet breathable?" asked Fry, as he leaned against a wall.

"It is," said Andrew, checking a readout. "The composition is the same as that of Earth. Probably because this planet has been terraformed."

"What dimension are we in?" asked George. He looked more shaken than anyone else in this ship, probably because he was the oldest and understood the implications of what had happened the most. He had grown up during the cold war and had long feared nuclear-powered destruction—that much was certain. Seeing humanity, or at least our version of it, brought low by a nuclear missile was probably horrifying to him.

October didn't answer George's question immediately, instead looking each crew member in the eye. "We're in D'Yarth," she said. "Not a dimension anyone would know. This one isn't based on a fictional universe. It's, as far as I can tell, natural."

"And what's our plan?" asked Fry. "We obviously can't take on an entire army of enemies with just twelve restaurants. Not when several thousand failed."

October slammed her fist against the armrest of her chair in an uncharacteristically violent move. "We could have done something. If we had done enough research, if we had had enough intelligence... We could have averted this. What were the people in charge thinking? What happened that they allowed the enemy to get the better of them?"

"I know it's frustrating," said Kyle, "But it's what happened. We can't blame command when we don't know the details. All we know is that we have someone who has a superpower of epic proportions here, and we need to harness that power for the good of humanity." He sounded reluctant when he spoke, as if he was fighting against something inside himself that was averse to relying on me. Had I done something to offend him?

But he was talking about the good of humanity, and personal troubles were the least of our worries. We had to find a way to do something about the army. I had power. I had been given a key. Now, all I had to do was figure out how to use it.

It seemed that October had an idea. Her face was determined, not confused, composed and powerful. In all honesty she looked beautiful, but it wasn't the time or the place to be admiring that. I was just glad that she was still alive.

"What's on your mind?" I asked.

October looked like she was thinking. Then she spoke. "We may have a solution to getting you trained in the use of your new superpower."

"I wouldn't call it a superpower..."

"Even though there hasn't really been a hero who has had your power, exactly, I'm sure that it could be considered a superpower under normal rules of classification." October's expression was slightly amused. "We're going to find a manifestation of The Watcher and persuade him to teach you a method of using your power that could get the Earth back."

"Will it be that easy?"

October fingered the keyboard that projected out of the front of her chair. It was an idle motion, but it was all that filled the silence that reigned in the kitchen.

Finally, October spoke. "I don't know. I obviously have no idea about what's going to happen next. I'm not"— her face was troubled. "I'm not strong enough to handle this. Everything is on me now, I'm"— she took a deep breath, her face rippling with emotion and then dying down as calmness overtook her expression. She breathed in, breathed out. "Sorry about that. I'm going to meet with the other managers outside." She got out of her seat, issuing a query through the comm system.

A reply came back. "This is Robert Green. It looks like you outrank all of us. I'm just an assistant manager."

"Are you one squad?" said October.

"Two," said another voice.

October nodded, an absent-minded gesture, and stepped through the airlock.

We waited for several hours as the managers conversed. Eventually, October came back into the kitchen, covered in a sheen of sweat. It must have been hot outside.

"We've decided to make headway towards a city in the East. This planet should be under the control of a space-faring civilization known as the Tek. They're human, but barely, and none of them speak our language. We've contacted them before but only for small things like passage through minor hyperspace routes. We have to be careful. There's no knowing what could happen when they see our restaurants."

We ate a meal of ration packs that were surprisingly healthy-looking, not at all like I would have expected given the fact that we were in the middle of a fast food restaurant. It still retained that classic McDonalds feel, that low-quality cheapness that permeated every corner of every restaurant, but it was a little different, just enough to be noticeable.

When we were finished October got back in her seat, preparing to launch. We waited for the rest of the squad to form up around us.

The procession of twelve fast food bots through the plains and low shrubbery was both exhilarating and saddening. I had seen bots walking before, but never in such close proximity. It gave me a sense of power that I hadn't felt before. I felt safe, even though I knew there was danger about. The enemy was near.

I materialized an ice cream cone in my hand and stared at it, not wanting it anymore, even though just a second ago I had felt the craving. It began to melt. Forcing myself to eat it, I thought on the events that had transpired during the last few days: the battles, the reveals, the strange occurrences, the nuclear blast and the army of monsters. The specter of the nameless horror in the forest haunted everything, refusing to go away. And with that, I slipped into a state of semi-sleep.

7

* * *

RVs are Cool

When I awoke there was a city on the horizon. It was beautiful, sweeping buildings designed with aesthetics in mind that reflected the sunlight striking their sides in a million different directions. The clouds floated across their surface, mirrored perfectly. As I got closer I could see that the buildings were in fact very, very tall, much taller than the tallest skyscraper on Earth. It was very much the city of a space-faring civilization, made all the more apparent by the loads of spacecraft coming in from orbit, as well as the tall space elevator that was too thin to notice at first but eventually became very visible, stretching upwards and upwards until it disappeared into outer space.

If anyone could help us win the war against evil, it would have to be these guys. Unless they were evil themselves.

A number of flying craft surrounded us as we came closer, flying alongside us. They were sleek, designed in a curvaceous style that was a little disappointing in its sci-fi mundanity, sporting four blue-spitting ion engines each as well as an assortment of mini-guns and rocket pods.

"Et allus kupelia," said a voice through our radio.

George was frantically maneuvering through a screen cluttered with information. Then, his eyes lit up. "Found it! The language has been identified, it's on our records."

"Fire up the translator," said October. "This just means we're where I meant to go."

There were a few beeping noises that sounded distinctively like the noises I heard from normal McDonald's kitchens. Then a screen dropped down in front of October. She typed in a few words. There was a moment of silence. Then the radio crackled again.

"Wual usis namur?"

October typed in some more words. The translator machine beeped in a manner that sounded frustratingly like talk-back, as if the machine had a mind of its own. Perhaps it did, and I just didn't know about it—from what I knew about translation between languages, I could tell that this machine was very advanced. Though, it didn't surprise me that we had one on board. Nothing surprised me anymore.

The conversation continued on for a few minutes, and then the flying machines floated away, their engines firing at full burst, leaving blue streaks in the air. I filed away the machine in my head in case I ever needed a flying machine—one I couldn't pilot; however, I was happy enough to get at least half the deal. That was the problem with my ability. I could create machines, I could create weapons, but I couldn't create people with the ability to use them. Maybe what The Watcher had given me wasn't so powerful after all. At least I knew how to drive.

October continued to march our restaurant towards the city, the rest of the squad following her, until they reached the city outskirts.

"The officials say we can stay here under refugee status for one week," she said. "We have until then to find the right person who can teach Max how to use his power."

"Do you have any ideas?" I asked.

October shook her head. "No. But if what I've heard is correct, this city is an informational hub where you can find out anything about everything, in every dimension. While we're here we might also find out a little bit more about who defeated the Franchises, and how."

"I feel like an adventurer," I said. "Someone who has a power to save the world, who's going to do something amazing."

October smiled at me, half amused, half admiring, though I didn't know why she would be admiring me.

"I was just spouting the first thing that came to mind," I said.

October said nothing, only took my hand lightly and brought it up. "Be careful. Can you promise me that?" she finally said.

Kyle snorted in an annoyed manner. "We'll all be careful," he said. "You don't need to tell us that. We're on the run from an enemy that is much, much more powerful than us, and we have to find a way to fight it. That's a dangerous undertaking."

October frowned. "Nobody asked you, Kyle."

Kyle turned away, displeasure written on his face.

I looked at October. "Was that a smart thing to say?" I asked.

I could see Kyle's anger bubbling just beneath the surface. What it was for, I didn't know, and all I could tell was that I probably shouldn't be pushing the man's buttons.

October ignored Kyle's unease, and my comment. She walked to the airlock and turned around to face us. "So, are we going to get out of here, or what?"

The rest of us followed, entering the bathroom airlock while machines disguised as bathroom fixtures regulated air pressure and volume. The door to the kitchen closed, and the boarding ramp extended. We walked off the machine and into a district of the city that was full of low-ceiling warehouses and rough, unkempt streets, though they were still obviously high-tech, the center divider shining with an inner light. The sidewalks were empty except for the rest of the survivors who had come through the gate with us. We met up in a large group and started heading towards the center of the city.

Most of us were carrying weapons. Though I wondered about it at first, I stopped wondering when I saw the other people on the roads. Everyone was carrying weapons in open view. Was this place some sort of wild-west town? Was there a reason why the populace was armed as such? Everything felt distinctively fictional, put together, as if I was watching someone else play a video game. October had said that this world hadn't come out of a work of fiction, but I was starting to doubt her. I had questions.

My rifle weighed heavily in my arms. The air was sweltering, the skyscrapers around us reflecting the heat and radiating it outwards in a classic example of the concrete island effect, the effect that made New York city much hotter in the summer than it should have been. I would have thought that a civilization this advanced would have come up with a fix for that, but it seemed that they hadn't. My skin prickled with sweat beneath the oppressive humidity. The temperature only went up as we walked towards the center of the city, over tunnels filled with rushing vehicles, past elevators lined in glass, and through crowds of people who looked just a little bit off, just a little bit like they weren't really the kind of humans we knew.

Their language was everywhere, in billboards, on signs, riding floating holographs in the air. It was a very precise script, one that did not look at all like it was from an alien planet, and looked more like it was from some Middle-Eastern country, or perhaps a South Asian country.

Everyone wore light clothing that was made out of what looked like tinfoil. To me, it seemed cliché in its appearance, but after thinking about it I realized that there was probably a good reason for that.

"Do you know where we're going?" I asked, unsure of how to proceed.

"No," said October. "I'm just looking for a place where we might be able to stay."

"Can you read the signs?" I asked.

October held up her smartphone, pointed it at a sign, and pressed a button. The script in the sign changed immediately to English; it read: Barlich's Bar and Grill. I nodded my head in appreciation of what could only be technology pilfered from another dimension.

"We need to find out everything we can about this place," said October. "I have reason to believe that the forces of evil may want to take this place over as well." She paused, looking at me. "You— you've seen a hotel before, right?"

"Yeah," I said, unsure of where she was going.

"Then, could you manufacture one?"

"I–" I said, and then I stopped. "I guess, I guess I can."

October clapped her hands together. "Good! That's where we'll be staying tonight." She paused. "Or, rather, never mind. That would bring too much attention. Pull into existence a couple of RVs instead. You can do that, right?"

I was relieved, though I couldn't tell why. "I will," I said. "Where?"

We walked until we found a dark alleyway where there were no people. It was underneath an overpass, several of them piled up on top of each other, and the shadows were long despite the time of day. I doubted that anyone would see what we were doing, and if they could, they probably wouldn't care. I guessed that I could fit three RVs in the space underneath the bridge. Would that be enough to hold the forty or so people in our group? Several of them were still filtering in; we had split up along the way to avoid calling too much suspicion to ourselves.

Once we were all there, I concentrated, and pulled into being three RVs, exact copies of the one I had ridden long ago when I was a kid on my trip to the Grand Canyon. That RV had been large enough to fit ten people with a bit of squeezing, and so I figured forty people could fit into three with a lot of squeezing.

We waited for the night to come while October talked over plans with the other team managers. It was still sweltering hot, though eventually I entered the RV and turned its air conditioning on—to power the vehicle, I called into being enough gasoline to fill the tank. I was starting to get used to my ability, strange though it was. Maybe I really could do something with it. Maybe I really could bring the universe to salvation by fighting against the evil powers that threatened to take it over.

I smiled. The thought was so ridiculous that I dismissed it and instead thought about what I wanted to eat. I was hungry. In the end I decided on pancakes and shared them with the five other people who were in the RV with me, including Andrew and George. Kyle was sitting along on a ledge outside, and Fry was talking with October and the other managers, as he held the mostly honorary title of assistant manager for our restaurant.

The day came to night, and we all bedded down in the RVs.

I was woken in the middle of the night by a siren. Everyone was scrambling. The RV's engine churned, once, twice, three times and it started. October was in the driver's seat.

"Everyone get down!" she yelled, turning around to look at me, checking that I was there and turning back around. We blasted out of the underpass and rolled along the side of an aqueduct that was filled with green algae and little water. Behind us one of the other RVs followed, and behind it was a ball of fire that I feared was the third RV. A dozen of the flying machines from before were on our tail. Some of them were shooting. A voice burst through the radio, cutting the sound of sirens.

"Elgas! Hotnat kinfi!"

"Do you understand it?" I asked October.

October shook her head. "We don't have our translator on board. But I can tell that he's angry!"

An explosion ripped apart the concrete to our left, tilting our RV at a dangerous angle. Everyone in the back toppled into a pile, drowning me in a sea of limbs. I clawed my way into the front where I took a seat next to October, free from the stuffiness of the back.

October brought her communication device to her lips. "Andrew! Are you there?"

"I'm here," said Andrew, through the radio. He had stayed the night in the other RV, the one behind us.

"Tell the driver of your RV to follow me. I think this aqueduct leads out of the city."

"Got it," said Andrew.

Another explosion rocked our vehicle. The night sky lit up bright with orange and red color. Several rocks pelted the walls. October twisted the wheel violently and swerved us around a corner, just barely missing the walls of the river itself. A few more inches and we would have been taking on water. The RV righted itself just as Andrew's vehicle rounded the corner. An explosion separated us. Andrew's RV pushed through the smoke as if being born anew out of fire. I looked back ahead of us, only to see three flying machines coming straight at us.

"A cannon!" said October. "Find us a cannon!"

I clapped my hands together and prayed for a vision of something, anything to shoot them with. I got an idea—an LAW. I had seen one in the outboard gear.

"Roll down the window!" I shouted at October, materializing a rocket launcher in my hands.

October held down a button, and the glass moved downwards, painfully slow. I leaned out as soon as I could fit and aimed the launcher. There was a small iron sight, but everything was moving so fast that I couldn't line anything up. I fired. The streak of smoke from the rocket swished past the closest flying machine.

A miss. I tossed the launcher out the window and materialized another one in my arms. This time, I took my time to aim. The flying machines were keeping pace with us now.

Just before I fired, a machine gun opened up on us, forcing me to duck my head back in. Several bullets hit the window, cracking it.

"I can't see!" shouted October.

It was dark, and the cracks in the windshield just made everything harder to see. The lights of the tall buildings around us reflected off the river made the edges hard to pick out.

I looked at the launcher in my hands. This wasn't going to work. I tossed it into the back and racked my brains for an alternative.

I came up with an idea. Make as much ruckus as possible. Basically, flood the world with objects that would screw up their tracking and allow us to escape. I decided I would push my power to its limits.

I imagined a hundred RVs, all of them moving at the same speed we were, and then I materialized them. All of them came into being at the exact same time. Most of them appeared in mid-air, most over the river, all of them crashing to the ground or splashing into the water. Some of them continued to rush forwards around us, confusing the flying machines. Their bullets sprayed somewhere else, at one of the decoy RVs. I continued to materialize them as the ones that I had before either slowed down, got mired in the river, or exploded.

"What the hell was that?" said a voice from the back.

"Shut it!" said October, her face reading intense concentration.

An empty RV crossed the road right in front of us, and we almost rammed right into it. Just in time I materialized a sedan underneath it that vaulted it upwards in a summersault that sent it packing into the river with a splash. We barreled past, and I materialized a dozen more RVs. The pursuit had to be confused now. There was no way they weren't.

Why were they after us? What had we done to warrant such an attack?

There was no time to wonder about it. All I knew was that there were dozens more flying machines heading our way, from all directions.

And then a strange thing happened: time stopped, again. I looked around, surprised, but more than that, aggravated.

"You again?" I said. I was instantly sorry—The Watcher had given me a power, after all, completely free of charge.

The Watcher appeared, through the portal, wearing his purple robe like before. He smiled at me. "Having fun with your new power?" he asked.

"Yeah," I said. "Well, not so much fun as... well... I don't know. I'm still learning."

The Watcher bowed his head. "You have much to learn, young one." He smiled, and his smile was a kind one, full of warmth and grace. I liked it. It made me feel comfortable. "I will give you a hint," said The Watcher. "You must stay in this city. Do not leave, learn more about it, and you will find yourself rewarded. Though, you will have to take more precautions than you have been. I will say that running a gasoline-based engine inside of this city is an offense that will get you killed. This city is full of strange customs. And, it needs help. Help them, and they will help you. That is the way of the world, and of the multiverse." The Watcher bowed. "I must take my leave. Do continue to use your power as you do; I find it very entertaining." With a soft chuckle, The Watcher was gone.

And then time sped back up. An explosion just inches from our side shook me to my core. We swerved, almost running into the river, before October regained control.

"I just had another visit from The Watcher!" I yelled, over the din of crashing RVs.

"What did he say?" yelled October.

"Now's not the time," I yelled back. "Though he told me to stay in this city!"

"I was planning on that!" yelled October, though she hadn't been a second ago. "Now shut up and let me drive!"

We swerved around another corner only to find almost a hundred flying machines waiting for us, and a barrier along the aqueduct. We couldn't pass. I tried to materialize enough RVs to break through, but they were all shot down by vehicles that appeared to be tanks but had much, much bigger guns. We slowed to a stop. Seven tanks lowered their guns at me.

Well, I thought, resignation taking me over. *At least I have another cool toy to materialize.* I decided to not materialize one, mostly because it wouldn't do us any good. We were surrounded.

Andrew's RV pulled up next to us. A group of uniformed men ran out from the barrier, all of them carrying weapons, and surrounded us. An amplified voice echoed through the aqueduct.

"Amfish. Clasyum holist."

"I think he wants us to get out," said October. She looked at me. "You promise to get us out of trouble if things get too bad?"

I nodded. "I promise." I was afraid. Not as afraid as I was back in the jungle, when looking at the nameless horror, but still afraid. I was afraid in a different way. I was scared not of being killed, but of the fact that I didn't know what was going to happen next.

We stepped out of the RV, one by one. At least a hundred guns were pointed at us.

"Do you think you can materialize some translation software?" October whispered to me.

"I can try," I said, thinking of the part of the McDonalds robot that did all the translation. This was the first time I was calling back a part of something instead of a whole something, but it worked. A tiny microchip about the size of my thumb appeared in my palm.

"That's it?" asked October. She shrugged. "Well, as long as it has an output."

I materialized the screen that went with it. It was heavy, but it worked. I gave it a power supply and hooked it all up. Everything was as I remembered it, taken from the innards of the McDonalds bot. Apparently, even if I had never directly looked at the hardware, I could materialize it because I had seen it in effect. Otherwise I would never have been able to make working machinery. The men with guns watched the procedure with intense interest. One of the men, who looked to be in charge, held up his arm. He spoke a sentence in his language.

"You don't need to provide translation," said a mechanical voice. "We have our own software. You are from the planet Earth, are you not?"

October nodded her head, dumbfounded. The translation hardware that I had just materialized was neglected.

"I am sorry to hear about what happened," he said. "We give our deepest condolences to you, refugees caused by that accursed darkness." The man paused, though the translation machine took a few extra seconds to finish talking. "However," said the man, and the machine. "Running a gasoline engine in this city was a stupid move on your part. We cannot ignore such offenses, even if they were made in ignorance." He looked less angry and more righteous, less mad at us and more concerned with following the rules. "However," he said, "We see that you have... Special circumstances. Show us the one with the power to materialize objects at will."

Without hesitation, I stepped forwards. I needed to do this. If I could save the remaining squad members, it would be worth anything. "I am he," I said, chiding myself for being needlessly formal.

The translation machine spoke softly into the commander's ear. The commander nodded his head, and then he motioned with his arm. "You will come with me, then," he said, his emotion readable even though I couldn't understand his language—the machine's voice was metallic, emotionless.

I followed the man into one of the flying machines that had landed behind the row of men with guns. October held out her hand.

"Wait!" she said.

The commanding officer looked back. "What is it?" he asked.

October let her hand fall. "What are you going to do with us?"

"You will stay in prison until we see fit to release you," said the commanding officer. "It is only on account of this boy's special ability that you have not been shot where you stand."

I shivered. The words were terrifying in their reference to an ultimatum that was given without hesitation. We would have been killed in any other circumstance. October might even be killed anyways—I decided then and there not to work with anyone until I had set forth conditions that allowed them to go free.

I was lifted up into the air by the flying machine, and I watched the figure of October getting smaller and smaller below me. I heard her voice, buffeted by the loud ion engines around me.

"What?" I yelled, cupping my hands over my mouth.

October followed my example. "Be careful!" She shouted. "I—" and then her voice was too faint to be heard.

I what? I thought. Then the thought faded away as I was taken across the city.

8

* * *

Breaking All the Rules

The room was large, an aircraft hangar for all I could tell, filled with nothing but bright white light and the lines of tiles that looked as if they had come straight from the game Portal. I was too stunned to speak for a moment. Then, the commanding officer who had taken me away from October and the rest of the team nodded to me, speaking a line in his language.

"Show us," said the translation machine.

I looked out over the room. We were on a catwalk halfway up the wall, which mean that the ground was thirty meters away and the ceiling was the same. The room must have been as large as a football stadium in terms of length and width, maybe more.

I looked for a moment out over the emptiness, and then I held in my imagination one of the flying machines, an exact copy of the one that had taken me to this room.

The machine appeared about a meter off the ground—I had meant to have it appear resting on the ground, but I missed—and it settled to the floor with a loud crash. The commanding officer folded his arms, his face pensive. Then he spoke.

"You—you have met The Watcher, have you not?"

"I have," I said. Nervousness of what was about to come flooded through my body.

The commanding officer extended his hand. "Your cultural database tells me that this is the way to extend a cordial greeting. Is that correct?"

I shook his hand, bewildered and not that unhappy. The man smiled, and thought it wasn't a happy expression, nor was it for my sake, I felt myself comforted. The man wanted me to be on his side.

That much was apparent. I had some bargaining space, some ability to get October and the rest of the team out of whatever prison they were staying in. I decided to take the plunge.

"If I work with you," I said, "You'll have to release my friends."

The commanding officer nodded his head. "Is that it?"

I nodded. "There's nothing more you can give me."

"My name is Khal," said the officer. "Khal is written with the letter for Green and Blood, the ichor that comes from the hisfret my linage hunted in the far past."

It was a typically foreign introduction, made surreal because it sounded so similar to what I had encountered in fiction. Of course they would have a foreign way of greeting. Of course he would have a strange name. It all made sense, didn't it?

And yet it didn't.

I looked around the room. "What else do you want me to do?"

"A man," said Khal. "Summon a man."

"I can't do that," I said.

Khal nodded. "Then, can you summon a tank?"

I nodded, and imagined one of the tanks that had stopped our flight from the city. It appeared in the room, this time right on the floor so that it made no noise when it materialized. I was more proud of the accomplishment than I should have been.

"You are valuable," said Khal, motioning to me. "You will meet my superior."

I nodded, following Khal through the building until we came to an elevator, which we rode up for several minutes, the walls turning to glass halfway up so that I could see the entirety of the city in its glittering nightly brilliance. From up here it didn't look too different than a city back home. That got me wondering. How much could I really materialize? Could I call an entire city into being just by thinking? Could I create a continent? A planet? There had to be a limit to my power.

I had a feeling that I would encounter it soon. The people who were in control would undoubtedly make me show my true potential.

For a moment the city reminded me of home. Earth. My parents. I wanted to see them—I had gotten roped into this adventure and I was stuck here, but I wanted to be where I could protect the people that I loved. They were probably suffering right now. Earth's military must have been fighting a losing battle. Were my parents already dead?

The elevator doors opened with a ding, and Khal stepped out. We walked through a corridor that was full of people in uniform, not a few who stopped to watch as I passed, interest on their faces, or sometimes surprise. There must not have been very many interdimensional travelers spotted up here.

We came to a conference room. Khal opened the door, bowed, and led me through, withdrawing as soon as I had passed the threshold.

"Welcome," said a distinctly human voice.

"Er, hello," I said, to the figure at the head of the table. The table was long, oval, surrounded by distinguished-looking men in uniform whose eyes were all trained on me. I felt uncomfortable. Like I was being dissected.

"Do sit," said the man at the head of the table.

There was an empty chair right in front of me; I sat.

"We have watched a demonstration of you power," said the man at the head of the table. "And we have decided to deem you a strategic asset. Cooperate with us, and your friends will go free. If you don't, they will be executed in accordance with the law."

"I'll cooperate," I said. "Tell me what I need to do."

The man pressed his fingers together. "We need ten thousand main battle tanks. Five thousand hovercraft. Twenty thousand rifles, and twenty thousand armored uniforms. That is the price of your friend's release. As well as this, we need your continued cooperation in the creation of more weapons, such as starships and orbital weapons."

"I'll create them," I said. "What of our restaurants?"

"They have been seized for research and development purposes, as they are very peculiar machines. It seems that they double as places where one would go to receive a cheap meal; is this correct?"

"It is," I said.

The man did not look like he cared one way or another. The only thing I could read on his face was a slight amount of amusement. I realized that I could kill him right now by simply materializing something, and then I realized that would be a very bad idea. My friends were riding on this deal.

"I'll do it," I said. "Give me a space to create the machines, and I'll do it."

"So be it," said the man. "I have verified your existence. First Operator Khal will now lead you out of this building and to where you will fulfill your pledge."

I was suddenly struck by the realization that these people were not safe; they were building up their army for a reason. At least their military was normal, but I had the feeling that some surprises were in store for me.

On the roof of the building there was a landing pad, where a hovercraft picked us up and took us to the outskirts of the city. We made it to a massive, flat parade ground in the center of a military compound that was guarded by hundreds of tanks and had a spaceport in its center where starships lifted off and landed by the dozens. All traffic stopped as soon as we flew over the grounds.

I looked at the large, empty space. Ten thousand main battle tanks. Could I do that many at once? I estimated the amount of room that would take, and them imagined ten thousand tanks all lined up next to each other. And then, like that, they were real. Ten thousand tanks just like the ones that I had seen earlier that night.

It was awe-inspiring. Khal looked as surprised as I was; I hadn't expected it to be that easy. I really was powerful. There was something inside of me that had immense value. I materialized five thousand hovercraft, and once Khal showed me the kind of rifle they used, I materialized ten thousand of those. Then, I materialized the uniforms. They appeared, neatly placed in rows along the parade ground. Already hundreds of people were running towards the massive amount of new material, looking like ants from the door of the hovercraft.

"A starship," said Khal. "Like the one you see there," he pointed.

I made one, then two for good measure. They were huge, filling up a quarter of the field, which was already pretty full.

This was starting to get fun. I wondered why I had been given such an immense amount of power, without any apparent drawback.

"Do you wonder?" I heard, and time stopped. The Watcher stepped out of his portal, wearing his characteristic purple robe. "With great power comes great responsibility, as one comic book character once put it. You simply have a power that eclipses pretty much every other superpower in the books. All this means is that your enemy is that much more powerful. You will need every ounce of power I have given you to complete your task, and then more."

The Watcher made as if to leave.

"I have a question," I said. "Why me? Why am I the one who was chosen?"

"Ask Peter Parker," said The Watcher. "Or Bruce Wayne. Ask any hero and you will hear the same answer, which I'm sure you already know." He tipped his wizard's hat. "And with that, I will go, to haunt you again when the time is convenient."

He disappeared, and time flowed again.

I looked at the things I had created, the massive army I had given rise to. If I were to acquire something of immense power it would be game-breaking. And with that realization came the realization that my enemy would be ready for that.

I braved asking the question that was on my mind. "Why do you need all this equipment?" I asked. "Couldn't you just manufacture it yourself?"

"A great evil is coming to this galaxy," said Khal. "This is but a drop in the bucket of our arsenal, and yet we will need many times that to fight the battle we need to fight."

"Let me guess," I said, knowing the answer to the question already. "The forces of evil are coming from another dimension, aren't they?"

"They are," said Khal, a look of surprise on his face, before he must have realized that we were refugees for a reason. He looked at me with a slightly different eye than before. "You're running from such evil, aren't you?" he said.

"I am," I said. "And quite possibly everyone I know will be killed by them." Saying it out loud made it sound a lot more true than I thought it would. I felt insecure. Afraid. Everyone was in trouble. For a moment it was too much, and I only stared out of the door of the hovercraft, at the thousands of machines that I had just created.

I knew my mission. I knew what I had to do.

"If I create weapons for you, will you be able to fight the forces of evil?" I asked. Though, the phrase "forces of evil" sounded empty and hollow in my ears, after I had seen what they really were. A collection from the darkest depths of the psyche that had materialized into being from alternate dimensions and were now about to take over the multiverse, for no other reason than that they wanted to spread chaos. That was a kind of enemy that anyone could unite against.

But still, I was stuck with the nagging suspicion that something wasn't right, that the ancient evil that was awakened wasn't like I had imagined. The encounter in the forest came back to me in a flash, and I felt a chill. The monster—it was too evil to even be called that—had sent fear through my entire body that hadn't been there even when the nuke had fallen.

I looked at Khal. He was now an ally. Someone to be trusted. "Take me to my friends," I said.

As soon as Khal's translation machine made my request understood, Khal gave an order to the hovercraft's pilot. We tilted away from the large parade ground filled with military equipment and headed towards another portion of the city, this part with more low-lying buildings than skyscrapers, looking like a poor part of town. So even high-tech wonder cities had slums.

We landed in the center of a high-walled compound with watchtowers placed along the length of the walls. Searchlights passed back and forth across the open ground. We dismounted and Khal led me through a series of increasingly secure gates until we reached a section of the prison that was separated from the rest. There I found October, and the rest of the squad, four of them to a cell for a total of six cells. October stood up when she saw me and walked up to the bars.

"Max," she said. "You've come."

I placed my hand on the bars, wrapping my fingers around hers. "I'm getting you out of here."

Khal gave an order to the prison warden, and the keys were passed over. The doors slid open with a mechanical click and October walked out. The first thing she did was wrap her arms around me.

"I thought you would never come. I thought I would never get to see you again."

Khal watched with a slight interest in his eyes that I found unwelcome. I embraced October for what seemed like an appropriate period and then disengaged, looking her in the eye. "We may have found allies in our fight," I said.

October looked at Khal. "How so?"

"Let's let out the rest of the team first."

When we were all free, Khal led us out of the prison to the roof where there were several waiting hovercraft. We loaded up onto them and flew over the city, back to the military base where I had created the equipment. From air I could see our restaurants being disassembled in front of a compound of low, brightly-lit buildings. It didn't worry me that much as I could always summon replacements—but October looked incensed.

"The bastards are taking apart my restaurant," she said, annoyance obvious in her voice. "Do they realize what a valuable piece of equipment they're destroying?"

I put my hand on October's shoulder. It was tense; unnaturally so. "It's okay," I said.

October took a deep breath. "Sorry. I don't do to well in tight spaces, especially prisons."

"Well now you know, so we can avoid that predicament in the future."

"Yeah, I sure hope we do," said October. "But our mission has just started. Undoubtedly we'll be in some situations that will be far more serious than a few cramped spaces." She paused. "I need to get ahold of myself. It wasn't that bad. It wasn't"— She looked down, at the ground several hundred meters away. "I'm sorry." She wasn't looking at me, and I wasn't even sure if I was meant to hear that. "I'm sorry for bringing you into this. I'm sorry that you had to go through all this simply because I—simply because I had a romantic interest in you."

I took October's hand in mine. She turned towards me. I looked her in the eyes; they were flashing with the lights of the city. The hovercraft's engines droned in the background. George was leaning against the wall on the other side of the craft next to Andrew and some other team members I didn't recognize. We were as alone as we would probably get for quite some time.

"You don't have to be sorry," I said. "I'm the one who made the first move. And, if I had known that all this would happen, I still would have done it."

October's expression showed that she had recovered herself. She grinned mischievously. "What are you doing, saying something so romantic like that? It's almost like you want to seduce me." She tilted her head. "Is that what you want?"

I could see in her eyes a storm of conflicting emotions that I could only begin to understand. Hers was a depth of character that I couldn't fathom. She was inscrutable. Her personality changed constantly from quiet to romantic to brave and swashbuckling. She was a character of a woman, and I was coming to respect her more and more each hour I spent with her. I was glad to know her, and more than that, I felt something for her.

We landed in the center of the field where our restaurants were being taken apart. Khal pulled October aside and spoke to her, a conversation I couldn't hear thanks to the wind the hovercraft's engines whipped up around us. October nodded and stepped outside. Khal followed; the rest of us were off soon after. We walked among metal parts that were gaudy in color and emblazoned with the logos of Burger King, McDonald's, Wendy's, Popeye's, and a number of others. I ran my hand along a section of shoulder plating that had come from our bot. It was cold to the touch.

October talked to the person who seemed to be in charge, and then she began to direct the people who were running about taking things apart and packaging them up for study. She didn't seem as incensed about their disassembly as she had from the helicopter.

Her hair was outlined in harsh colors from the spotlights that lit the grounds. I watched her for a long moment, admiring her, and then I turned to Khal.

"Do you need me for anything else?" I asked.

Khal's response came after a delay as his translation machine spoke into his ear. The machine relayed his words. "Nothing for now. Soon you will be needed. There are many things at work in the Electoral surrounding the appearance of you and your friends. Even though we maintain connection with other dimensions, it is rare that we encounter them out here in the outer reaches of our domain."

If this was an unknown planet by D'Yarthian galactic standards or whatever, then why had October chosen this place to visit? I decided to ask her when I had the chance. Maybe she knew something that she wasn't sharing yet. Some piece of information that couldn't be spoken of for some strange reason or another.

Or maybe it was something as mundane as the fact that this civilization was known for being in contact with other dimensions and harboring refugees.

Khal watched me, his expression unreadable in the darkness, though I doubted that I would have been able to read it had it been light outside. As it was I got the feeling that he was observing me. Testing me, perhaps, in some way that was unique to his culture or even to him as a person. I wondered what he was thinking. Were the people of this dimension the same as us? Or were they radically different in some way?

Time would tell. For the moment, I busied myself explaining to Khal the various things that had happened to us that had brought us to where we were. He was apologetic about the deaths of those who had been in the third RV. Apparently they hadn't considered that we were the refugees from another dimension; the first responders had simply seen some illegal gasoline-driven vehicles and had operated according to procedure.

I hadn't known any of those who had been in the third RV. Even so, I felt sorrow at their loss, even though many, many more humans had been lost during the battle of Xen and during the conquest of Earth that was going on even as we spoke. There had been ten people in that RV.

We watched as our restaurant bots were disassembled in front of us. October eventually came to my side and stood next to me, silently, her hands on her hips.

"So," she said. "What next?"

"I thought you had it all figured out," I said, a little worry creeping into my voice, though it was mostly because I was just tired.

October shook her head without looking at me. "No, why did you think that? I don't think this situation can be figured out. We're in deep over our heads. We're drowning here."

I stood still as the implications of what she said settled down into my brain. We were in deep. We were drowning. There was nothing we could do. Then I remembered.

"I think the people of this dimension are preparing for war with the same guys that took over Earth."

"The forces of evil?" said October, her voice level.

"Yeah, but I don't like that name. Too cheesy."

"Why are you worried about the real deal 'forces of evil' being cheesy? They're real. Who cares what it sounds like." October's expression turned into a smile, and then she laughed. "I can trust you to lighten the mood. Too cheesy, hah!" She paused. "Then what do you want to call them?"

"How about Sauron-Voldemort-Darth-Vader?"

"How about 'The Evil Empire?'"

"Evil Tea Party?" I said.

October laughed. "That sounds like a speed metal band. How about 'This is how the dinosaurs went extinct?'"

"Was that really how they went?"

"Yeah, the dinosaurs were an intelligent space-faring civilization that was destroyed in an interdimensional war."

"I can't tell if you're joking or not," I said.

October grinned. "I'm joking. At least I think I am." She paused, her expression thoughtful. "How about this. We'll call them Darksiders."

"That's a cool name," I said. "Where did you come up with it?"

"Off the top of my head."

I watched her, examining her, testing her to see if she was serious.

She shrugged. "What? Are you entranced by my beauty or something?" She grinned, and put her hand on my cheek. It was cold.

"You look terrible," she said. "Get some sleep. Conjure up a bed or something. I'm sure these people won't mind, considering what you did for them."

I yawned. I really was tired. Seeing that I could imagine into existence an entire army of tanks without breaking a sweat, bringing a little house or something to sleep in wasn't that much of a stretch. The only problem would be where to put it, and if the Tekians would let me. Maybe if I just summoned up a mattress and laid it on the ground.

That would do. For kicks, I imagined my bed from home, a simple wooden frame with more notches and scratches than I could count. It appeared without much fanfare right in front of me. As a courtesy to the rest of the crew, I summoned twenty more copies of my bed, and then I fell onto one of them and was asleep in a few minutes.

9

* * *

Total War

I woke up to the sound of a bugle. It was still almost dark out; I felt as if I had only slept for a few minutes. My sleep had been dreamless. I wanted it to continue, but I soon realized that in the middle of the parade ground was not a place to be doing that. The twenty beds that I had materialized the night before were still there, almost all of them occupied. I figured that the Tekians had let us sleep here because they felt sorry for us, or maybe because they appreciated what I had done for them more than I could tell. A couple of men were already working on the continued disassembly of the restaurants. Our McDonalds was almost completely in pieces, the important and secret bits having been stripped away and taken to a facility where they could be tested. It surprised me that a place like Earth, which wasn't at all space-faring, could hold technology that a civilization like the Tekians would want. Maybe Earth was more advanced than I thought.

I remembered my first day on the job, the battle with King's Burger King. I remembered the Men-In-Black style memory erasure that had occurred, the hyper-fast repair of the damage that had been caused. That certainly hinted at something that was going on behind the scenes. Maybe my home dimension really was technologically advanced and we just didn't know it.

The sound of gunfire, in the distance, startled me out of my reverie.

"They're here," said October, who happened to be standing right next to my bed, looking at the horizon. "The Darksiders have found us, and them. I'd hate to abandon these people before we really got a chance to help them fight, but it looks like we'll have to abscond."

"How do you know it's them?" I asked, peering into the distance. I was fully awake now.

The sound of gunfire rose and fell in the distance. Hundreds of hovercraft lifted off from the military compound we were in and headed off towards the source of the noise.

I looked up at the sky and saw that it appeared to be boiling. Large flowers of red and yellow were visible even against the morning sunlight. Several flickering explosions left spots even as I watched.

"It looks like they have it difficult up there," I said. "Is it the communist space orcs that are fighting them? Or someone else?"

"Let's get out of here before we find out to our detriment," said October.

The rest of the team members were getting up, one by one. I materialized several restaurant bots—they appeared with a thump as they hit the ground—and I walked up to the copy of my restaurant. I put my hand against the side of its foot. The metal was cold, covered in a fine dew. I pulled my hand away.

"We're not going to help them fight?" I said.

"We have to leave," said October. "I had hoped to stay here and find who I was looking for, but it seems like they may not have been here anyways."

"How do you know?" I asked.

October looked into the distance again. "Let's just say I didn't sleep last night."

"Are you okay?" I asked.

October said nothing, only rolled her shoulders as if to massage them and climbed aboard our restaurant. Andrew, George, Kyle, and Fry passed me, each one giving me a nod of acknowledgement as they passed. Kyle still had a look of frustration or perhaps suspicion when he met my gaze.

The rest of the teams loaded up, fitting haphazardly as most of them were from different stores. In total we filled six bots. The Takian military around us didn't seem to mind that we were taking off; in fact, they gave us a wide berth and didn't bother us at all.

That was, until a row of tanks crashed through the barrier separating areas and pointed their guns at us.

"We cannot let you leave," said a robotic voice. "Your power is too vital to our cause. We cannot afford to lose you. Surrender now and you will be given the utmost care in your treatment. We do not wish to hurt you."

"What do we do?" I asked of October, who was staring into the view screen with a pensive expression on her face.

She looked at me. Her eyes were expectant. "It's up to you. Do you want to help them? Or do you want to escape while we still can?"

Many things went through my mind at that moment. The war with the Darksiders. The fact that I hadn't even come into real contact with them before—everything I knew about them I had learned from a distance. The fact that there were millions, billions, maybe even trillions of people who were in the dimension that needed my help. The people pointing guns at us were just scared, fighting for their universe, their way of life and the people that they loved.

I couldn't just abandon them. I made a decision. "We're staying. Tell them that if they can find the men to staff the machines, I'll create them."

October relayed my statement through our restaurant's PA system.

The robotic voice replied after a long pause for translation. "We are grateful. We would request that the one with the power step out and come with us. Those who are with him will be sent to somewhere safe."

"We'll be fighting in the battle too," said October.

The silence was strangling. Finally, the robot voice replied. "Very well. However, you must follow our orders. Your machines are unique enough and powerful enough that your aid would not be unappreciated."

October's grip on the controls tightened. "Let's go," she said. "Max, you disembark." Her face displayed resolution, her eyes strong, holding in them a well of emotion that was just below the surface, though it wasn't about to come out—she had control over herself.

I saluted, and then I entered the airlock. Before the door closed, I materialized two long-distance walkie-talkies like the ones my dad had bought me for my eleventh birthday and tossed one to October.

"Channel seven," I said, just as the doors closed.

I felt the change in air pressure as pops in my ear. The sweltering heat of this part of the planet Tek washed over me as the bay doors opened and the boarding ramp descended. I walked down the ramp and into a ring of officers, all of whom saluted to me. Khal stood in the fore with his hands behind his back.

"Your assistance is greatly appreciated," he said, through his translation device. "You will now come with me. We have much to do."

We walked along the parade ground strewn with scrap metal that used to be our original restaurants. October and the rest of the squad marched away towards the site of the battle after I had traveled some distance.

The sky lit up with explosions by the hundreds. Khal looked up every couple of seconds, his expression looking more desperate each time. We reached Khal's hovercraft and got on through the large, open door.

I got a good look at the machine for the first time in the light of day. It reminded me of those drones with four propellers, only much bigger and with rockets instead of blades. There were two open doors opposite each other, each one with a mounted machine gun hanging out of it. Both of them were manned on this craft. Exposed wiring and hydraulic systems covered most of the interior. The cockpit was below the riding compartment, and all I could see of the pilot was his helmet.

We took off, the military compound growing smaller beneath us until I could see it all in one glance. The vast field where I had materialized thousands of vehicles was now half-gone, empty, the machines having been taken to the front lines during the night, or so

I presumed. We headed over the tops of buildings to an area near the front lines that looked to be a staging site, where hundreds of vehicles idled in rows waiting to be repaired, or waiting for their crews to return. From here I could see the enemy. They were the same motley assortment of evils that had taken over the compound in the Xen dimension. I wondered what sort of defense this dimension, D'Yarth, had put up against such an army. Undoubtedly they had responded like Earth had, probably with some secret society of sorts, and the conflict with their real military involved was a last-ditch effort to stem the tides coming in from other dimensions. They looked to be losing.

It didn't matter how much equipment I produced; if they didn't have enough trained men to staff them, there was no use. We couldn't go any further than that.

I watched Khal's face for any indication of what was about to come. I got nothing. His face was unreadable, scarily so, reminding me that he wasn't exactly all the way human. We stopped, hovering, over the center of the staging area.

"This is where you will"— A missile arced through the air and exploded not two meters from the opposite end of the hovercraft. We spiraled out of control, heading towards the enemy lines, the shapes of monsters and kaiju and other evils becoming distinct against the backdrop of a burning city. I needed to do something, fast, but my mind wouldn't work. I was too stunned. My ears were ringing. We plummeted through the air, and right before we crash-landed, I managed to materialize a mountain of plush bedding, the kind of fluff that I had once found in my stuffed bear when a dog ripped him apart. The memory flashed through my mind as we crashed. My body was launched out the open door, and I landed with a puff in the mountain of white bedding. The rest of the people in the craft were not as lucky. The metal had caught fire, burning, and then the ammunition compartment exploded, lighting the early morning sky up with red and yellow.

Khal limped towards me, holding one arm dead at his side.

I keyed in my long-distance walkie-talkie. I had almost forgotten it at my side.

"October!" I said.

"Max! Are you all right? I saw your hovercraft get shot down!" It was October's voice, strangely calming amidst the chaos that was around me. "I'm fine," I said.

I looked again, and took back my words. The front lines had been pushed back, and we were now behind enemy lines. A group of orcs in silver battle armor were approaching from the direction of the city, and a kaiju the size of a skyscraper was not five hundred meters away towards the plains.

I needed to do something. I had checked the emergency flares in our restaurant's outboard equipment as part of my job, and I materialized one now. Even though it would be dangerous, I figured that I could get myself into a car and avoid the monsters as they closed in.

Once I had the car—my own Nissan, the one I drove to school every day—I stuck the flare in the door and lit it. Khal got in on the passenger side.

"Are you okay with this being a gasoline-driven vehicle?" I said, a tinge of dark humor coming over me.

Khal said nothing, only gritted his teeth. I shrugged, and fired up the engine. The kaiju was less than a hundred meters away. It obviously wanted to pick us up and eat us or something like that—I wasn't going to let it. I gunned the engine, dropping straight into second gear, and we roared off across the plain, the burning city sparkling in my rear-view mirror. I wondered what my own city looked like. How had the military fared? Undoubtedly they had been overrun, if even the D'Yarthian military couldn't handle the flood of Darksiders.

We veered through the Kaiju's legs, the scaly skin coming so close I could count the individual overlapping parts. They were a deep, dark green color.

The Kaiju reached down below, hand grasping, and just as it was about to wrap around my car, a red and yellow fist smashed the monster in the head. It was October. Her McDonald's restaurant was battered, scratched in many places, but it was still working. Around us the other restaurants in the squad fought the Darksiders to a standstill. They opened up a clear area, giving me enough time to fling open the door, jump out as soon as it felt safe enough, and sprint towards the lowering ramp coming out of the back of my restaurant.

I jumped on before it was all the way down and scrambled into the airlock. The door hissed shut behind me and then the kitchen opened up. I stumbled onto the linoleum.

"Are we picking up Khal?" said October.

It was too late. Khal made it halfway to the boarding ramp before a kaiju grabbed him by the torso and lifted him up to its mouth. October jackknifed the kaiju in the side, but it didn't dislodge Khal, the kaiju instead stumbling to the side. Khal's body was limp. He had been killed by the pressure of the hand around him.

I offered up a silent prayer to whatever gods watched over this dimension and turned to October.

"Get us out of here," I said.

Time froze. The Watcher came out of his portal, wearing his customary purple dress. Instead of talking to me, this time, The Watcher sat down on a chair that had appeared out of nowhere and looked at me, watching. He nodded his head once, twice, three times, and then hummed.

"What do you want?" I asked. "I know you told us to help them. But how are we supposed to fight against this kind of enemy?"

"Help can be rendered in more ways than one," said The Watcher. His voice sounded frustratingly mysterious. I wanted to yank on his beard and force him to tell me what I wanted to know.

"There is a map. Find it and you will be able to see where you must go next."

And then he disappeared, time flowing again just as if it had never stopped in the first place. And then, out of the corner of my eye, I caught sight of a caravan of trucks running through the chaos. They were the same trucks we had seen at the compound. They were driven by men, humans, who didn't look evil so much as they looked dangerous. I pointed to them.

"Follow those trucks!" I yelled.

October turned the restaurant around, and then she caught sight of the vehicles. Her hands clenched the controls. "Get us balanced," she commanded. "We're about to enter sprinting mode. This may get a little bumpy."

The restaurant's stride increased by double and the kitchen began to shake back and forth. I stumbled against the wall and gripped the edge of the deep fryer to keep myself steady. We were catching up to the trucks. On closer inspection they appeared to be in a style that was indicative of the late nineteen-seventies. Maybe in the world where they came from, style had never advanced past that point. It was certainly possible in a world where the USSR had won the Cold War. Style was a very American thing.

As were fast food restaurants. A mounted turret on the back of one of the trucks opened fire on our robot. The bullets pinged harmlessly off the metal armor, but they still made me nervous nonetheless, as some of them caused the view screen to short out. We gained ground slowly, passing through a landscape filled with battling figures, mobile front lines, missiles flying through the air from both sides. We narrowly dodged a laser beam that was colored green and reminded me of a popsicle with its neon brightness. Only, this popsicle was made out of vaporized plasma and would destroy our restaurant if it hit.

Thinking that I should do something to help, I kept the enemies at bay by materializing random large objects, obstructing their movement, blocking bullets, misguiding missiles. Several times I tried to plant road blocks in front of the line of trucks only to see them swerve around them with an inhumanly short reaction time. They were headed into the city. We had to intercept them before then, as we would never be able to chase them through the narrow streets that were surrounded by miles-high towers, some of which were in the process of collapsing. Images of nine-eleven flashed through my brain, and something went off in my mind. Could I do it? Could I create an entire city out of nothing?

I imagined buildings, hundreds of them, placed in a wall around the line of vehicles.

And, they appeared. There was a small gap for us to enter the trap zone. However, when we made it in, the line of vehicles was gone.

Several kaiju were trapped inside of the ring of buildings as well. We slammed right into the side of one of them, metal groaning, the monster's roar ripping through the air with the sound of a hundred elephants. October punched the monster in the face, its bones crunching, its jaw collapsing, our metal fist bending under the pressure. Orange and red paint was left on the monster's skin, scraped off by its scales. The imprint of the Golden Arches smoked beween its eyes.

A second kaiju swung its spiked tail at us. October blocked it with an arm and drop-kicked the kaiju in the stomach, sending it reeling.

"Load Big Mac round!" She commanded, sweeping her hand through the air to reach controls that were above her now. Her fingers played over the hundreds of buttons as if it was a concert grand piano. The other crew members all furiously worked away at their various stations, keeping the bot balanced, loaded, and ready to respond to any attacks. October pointed the main hand cannon at the kaiju, grabbed it by the neck, and fired, a blast of red and yellow spraying out from between the restaurant's fingers and the back of the kaiju's neck.

The last kaiju rammed into us from the side, and we went tumbling to the ground in a heap. October blasted us back into the standing position with some pre-loaded springs, and the kaiju stumbled backwards, covered in dust. October pointed both hand cannons at it and fired one round, two rounds, three rounds, commanding each one to be loaded after the next. The kaiju stood still for a moment, smoking, before it collapsed in a heap to the ground.

There were no more. The buildings around us were beginning to collapse. Ideas about what to do next flashed through my head. We needed that map. The Watcher had alluded to something that would tell us where to go next. We needed that map, and we needed it bad. Otherwise we would perish here, underneath a never-ending swarm of monsters and orcs and Sith lords. The Darksiders would have their conquest, and I would be dead. More importantly, October would be dead.

The map. The line of trucks. I knew it instantly—I had seen the trucks, I could materialize them, or any of their constituent parts. I imagined a map that would show us where to go, attached it to an image of the trucks, and concentrated. A little ball of metal appeared in my hand. It was easy. Almost too easy. There had to be a rule against this. I examined the object in my hand.

Instantly I knew that it was a key. It was also a map, sure, but more than that it was something that would unlock both physical treasure and imaginary mysteries. The map would guide us. It was meant to be hidden, but my power had awakened it, and now we were about to embark on a journey that would take us to the edges of the universe and back.

All in a Gundam robot made out of a McDonalds restaurant. *This,* I thought, *is going to be interesting.*

10

*** * * ***

The Rules of Magic

The portal opened after ten minutes of nervous waiting. Even though we had a map, we had no way of using it—it was encrypted, and there was no connection port in our machine quite like the terminal sticking out of the bottom of the metal sphere. Just to be sure, I tried every option, feeling like an old man with a USB drive in a tech café. Sure enough, nothing worked. We wouldn't be able to use the map.

And so October came up with a plan B. We would return to Earth. What was left of it, at least. We would hope that the person October had in mind was still alive, and we would find him.

The gate opened. Just before we stepped through, a red lightsaber came flinging through the air and sliced the portal in half. I looked to where it had come from. There, standing in a space between two buildings, was a Sith lord from Star Wars complete with skeleton-like mask and black cape. He held out his hand and our entire restaurant began to quiver on its foundations. We were lifted into the air like so much playdough and summarily tossed against the side of a building. We crashed through rows of offices, shattering glass, tearing up drywall and bending steel.

October's hands flew over the controls. Alarms were going off everywhere. The rest of the crew worked intently at their stations, the danger of our situation showing on their faces. George especially looked as if just barely holding on, just barely keeping himself together so that he could perform his duty.

I realized that I needed to do something. I had power, I had something that I could use to protect us. But nothing came to mind. I couldn't think of a single object that I had seen in real life that would protect me against the advances of a Sith lord.

Our restaurant shuddered. Through the view screens, through the wreckage of the building we had crashed into, I could see the Sith lord approaching.

I realized that I had something other than my power. I had a rifle. I had a weapon that, if aimed correctly, could get past the defenses of a Sith. I hoped.

I threw open the outboard equipment compartment and grabbed my rifle, my hands wrapping around the M decals, the red and yellow paint job, my arms holding the now-familiar weight.

"Do we have a top hatch?" I yelled at October, knowing the answer right away anyways.

We did.

"We do," said October, her concentration elsewhere. Then a look of realization crossed her face. "You're not really planning to—"

"I have to take this shot," I said, running for the part of the kitchen where there was a retractable ladder. I pulled it down and began to climb, rung over rung, my rifle slung across my back.

"You can't do it," yelled October. "He's just going to block it!"

"Distract him!" I said, over the noise of the restaurant and the collapsing building.

I popped open the emergency hatch and poked my head through the top. I braced my back against the edge of the door and kept my legs on the top rung of the ladder. The restaurant barged through the walls of the building we had fallen into, reinforced concrete crackling and falling all around me. The Sith stood in the center of the ring of buildings I had created, watching us.

I lined up the scope. Our restaurant's arm pointed at the Sith lord. At the same time, the restaurant and I fired. Both projectiles hit simultaneously. When the smoke cleared, there was nothing.

And then there was a bright blade of red pointed at my neck. I stumbled, falling back through the trapdoor, my hand catching on the closing mechanism by pure chance, shutting it quickly enough that my foot was almost caught.

I lay on the ground, breathing heavily.

October shook her head. "I told you it wouldn't work."

The sound of a lightsaber against metal resounded through the kitchen.

October cracked her knuckles. "We're going to go playing in some concrete," she said, sending our restaurant into a sprint towards a building. We crashed into it, barreling through rooms, busting through steel beams and drywall, tearing up desks full of paper. We came out the other side. The noises had stopped. Behind us, the building was collapsing, grey dirt flowing out from its underside as bright flames lit up the sky.

"Portal!" said October. "Now!"

I materialized a portal. It was already connected. I figured I could do it, because I had seen it in that state, and it turned out I could.

We jumped through.

Hyperspace kicked me in the head with a steel-toed boot, and the whole world went blank for a few scary seconds. And then, we were back home. Well, sort of. The place we had come out in was a green forest, a clearing in the center of it, filled with poppies and white flowers that looked like roses.

But all was not calm. In the distance, smoke rose from a thousand individual fires and formed together to create a massive cloud of grey that obscured the horizon. October watched it, her facial expression unreadable.

"Where is this person we need to meet?" I asked.

"In a cabin in the woods," said October. She got out of her seat. "He wouldn't react well to us barging in on him with an entire restaurant, so we'll have to go on foot."

The entire crew lined up at the outboard equipment lockers, and soon we were ready for an adventure. We entered the bathroom airlock and left by way of the boarding ramp. It was great, being in the atmosphere of my home world. I hadn't noticed it before, but it was rich, thick with sweet oxygen, easy on my lungs even though there was a distinct note of acrid smoke. It was a lot better than breathing canned air.

I took a deep breath and looked at October. "We'll follow your lead."

She nodded. "Hopefully the GPS satellites are still in orbit." She took out her smartphone, and pulled up the map function. When she saw the display, she sighed in relief. "We're good. The Darksiders haven't taken down our network yet." She began to walk, looking at her phone for direction.

"So you do know where we're going?" I said, following in her footsteps, carrying my rifle over my shoulder.

George, Andrew, Kyle, and Fry walked in a spread-out formation around us, like professional soldiers. I felt like I was part of a real military expedition, just like in the jungle. Our red-on-yellow outboard clothing blended in with the temperate forest surprisingly well even though those colors didn't occur naturally at all, like they did in the jungle. At least there, there had been vines and orchids and flowers that were brightly colored.

We traveled through the forest for a long time, climbing up a gentle slope that was scattered with occasional boulders and covered with a deep layer of pine needles and fallen leaves. Our feet left impressions as they crunched through the debris, and I couldn't help but feel that we weren't being very careful about not being seen. I trusted October's judgement but at the same time I felt a little uneasy.

A flight of jet planes soared overhead. The V formation split, leaving behind a long contrail, and several missiles were launched. I noted the composition of the jet—what it looked like—for future reference, so that I could call one up if I needed to. Though, I wasn't sure how to find someone that could pilot one.

We came upon a thin game trail that looked as if it wasn't just a trail used by animals. There were signs of human habitation: shoe marks here, an empty beer can there, further up along the road a gum wrapper shining brightly against the ruddy forest backdrop. We moved in a single-file line. October took the lead; she seemed much more nervous than before, which in turn made me nervous and I assumed the same for the rest of the squad.

When we reached the edge of a small cliff, she held her hand up. Stairs were carved into the cliff's edge, made by some rough tool, shaped haphazardly and blended into the rock by years of aging. October moved on her own up the steps, slowly, one foot at a time. When her head poked over the top she stopped. Then, she dropped her arm.

"We're good," she said.

Once we were all up the cliff, October led us to the edge of a fence with a sign that read "violators will be shot," splashed with white paint against an old piece of plywood. October put her gun on the ground and cupped her hands over her mouth.

"Ben! Hey, Ben! I know you're there!"

There was silence for a moment. Soon after the trees rustled and an old man carrying a shotgun that looked as old as himself stepped out of the brush. He was wearing camouflage print pants, size large, and a solid green shirt. His eyes were intelligent, though it was more of the wild kind than the educated intelligence that I had come to expect from people. He wore a long beard and a ball cap with a logo too faded to be read. Even though he had an unkempt air about him, he did not seem unclean.

He frowned when he saw October. "I told you not to come back until you had left the Franchises," she said.

"The Franchises are gone," said October. "We're not part of them anymore. We're just using their equipment."

The old man—I presumed he was Ben—smirked. "Oh, and next I'll hear that you're the ones who can save the world from this craziness that's come out of nowhere."

"Actually, yes," said October. "Let us in and we'll explain."

Ben muttered to himself. I caught something about "all the Franchise's fault," though the rest was too low to hear. Ben opened the gate onto his property, leading us along the game trail we had found, until we came to a small cabin in the woods with a Chevy pickup truck on cinder blocks in front of its door. The car's metal was rusted, the paint was chipping, and large cracks ran along the windshield. Leaves covered the top and filled the back.

Ben walked around it to his door and opened it with a key. He led us inside, and immediately I knew it was going to be a tight fit. Most of the room was occupied by junk, trash, spare parts and tires that were stacked up to the ceiling in some places, almost toppling over in others. Somehow, I wasn't surprised. The interior of the house resembled the man who lived in it.

Ben sat down in the only open chair and crossed his arms over his ample belly. "So what brings you here?" he asked.

October presented the map. "We need you to analyze this," she said.

Ben scowled. "I quit messing with technology years ago. You know this as much as anyone else."

"We need your help," said October. "You're the only one who has experience with technology from other dimensions."

"I'm sure you can find others," said Ben. "Or you can run to the Franchises like the dog you are. I'm sure they'll throw you a bone."

"The Franchises are gone," said October. "They were wiped out by the army of darkness."

"And good riddance," said Ben. "If it wasn't for them messing with dimensional portals none of this would have happened. I'll say that it's because—"

October cut him off with a wave. "Let's not get into the politics. Look, Ben. All we need is for you to analyze this map. That's it. Just figure out how to get this thing to tell us where to go."

"And why do you need to go?" asked Ben. "Why can't you fight the forces of evil in your abomination of a restaurant?"

"We've tried that," said October. "It doesn't work. This map holds the key." She tossed it to Ben.

Ben caught it, and then examined it with a look of reluctant interest. "Ah, it's a fine specimen," he said, "Though I can't tell you immediately which dimension this is from. It's not mass-manufactured, like so much of the stuff from D'Yarth. It's not hand-made, either, unlike most of the tech from Farland. And it's probably not a magic-tech hybrid, as I don't sense any cosmic perturbations, though that may just be because this dimension isn't hooked up with many of the mana channels that flow through places like Zand or Telroth. And it's definitely not an aetheric vessel. No spark chambers, no sign of metalmancy. I'd have to say that this isn't a data storage unit. Most likely it's an artificial intelligence. Depending on where it really came from, it could be anywhere from the so-called AI on your smartphone to a real, all-out HAL-type artificial super-mind. I wouldn't risk activating it without knowing first."

"Can you find out?" said October.

Ben sighed deeply. "Sorry," he said. "I destroyed all my analytical equipment when I quit. I can't do anything for you without it."

"Then, can you use the equipment in our restaurant?"

Ben crossed his arms. "I'm not getting aboard that abomination."

"But you helped develop it," said October. "Why do you hate it so much?"

"Look here," said Ben. "I know you're going to try to convince me. I know that you probably won't give up until I relent or we're all dead by way of giant monster or maybe little green-eyed aliens with laser beams. However, I'm not going to make it easy on you, because an old man has his pride to maintain." He paused. "Do you understand?"

October nodded. "I understand." She looked him in the eye. "Max? Show him what you can do."

I nodded, and held my hand out in front of me, in full view of Ben. In my head I pulled up an image of an apple, the best-looking one I could remember. Without any ceremony the apple that I had imagined took on form and appeared in my hand.

Ben raised an eyebrow. "What kind of trick did you just pull there, boy? I wasn't aware of any manna channels activating just then. Is that an aetheric power?" His eyes narrowed. "Though," he muttered, "Aether leaves a slight burning smell..." He took a deep breath through his nose. "And I don't smell anything." He leaned back in his chair and frowned. "Show me that again. And this time, do it slower."

I materialized another apple. Now I had two. I tossed one to Ben, and he looked at it, his expression suspicious.

"Are you going to eat it?" said October.

Ben scrunched up his nose. "And risk being poisoned by whatever unholy non-magic created this thing? Not likely." He paused. "Your ability," he said, to me. "Where did you get it?"

"The Watcher," I said.

Ben huffed. "I should have guessed. The Watcher, The Watcher, The Watcher. Always meddling in the affairs of the multiverse. Always the one to appear when things are getting troublesome. It's been so long since his last appearance that I had all but thought him gone."

"You know about him?" I asked.

Ben scoffed. "Of course I know about him. No self-respecting denizen of the multiverse wouldn't. The only reason why most people on Earth don't know about him is because he's disguised, because the Franchises and other organizations like it have been oppressing human progress and knowledge for centuries. I mean, just look at how they operated before everything went wrong. Do you call smashing up entire towns and then forcing everyone in them to forget it ever happened a good thing? Because I certainly don't. That's why I live here, in the mountains. I'm safe from the Franchises here."

"I take it you don't like fast food, then," I said.

Ben looked at me with a strange expression. "It's never been about the food. What made you think that was what it was all about?"

"What do you mean?"

"You figure it out on your own. We've been talking too long already." Ben tossed the map back to October, and she caught it. "My answer is no. No matter how much you beg, I won't do it."

"Not even to save the world?" said October, as she handled the orb.

Ben laughed. "Are you so certain that this will do it? A whole lot of people who were stronger, more valiant, and better equipped than you have failed at that task, my young lady. What makes you think you're so special? Is it because The Watcher has contacted that boy? Don't get so full of yourselves. There's nothing that you can do to stop the invasion of the forces of evil. The best you can do is accept your new overlords and hope to god they don't decide to purge this planet's population, which, by the way, the most certainly will." Ben rocked back and forth in his chair. "There's nothing you can do. There's nothing I can do, or that we can do together. It's all over."

October slammed her fist down on a table that was laden with books. The pages rustled, and several of the leather-bound volumes slipped and fell to the ground. A look of resignation crossed Ben's face.

October gritted her teeth. "There is a way. We know that it's a long shot, but how are we going to excuse ourselves if we didn't try? How are we going to know for certain that it won't work? I know it's a long shot, but you have to trust us. It won't take you that long, will it?"

Ben sighed. "I'll do it."

"Wait, you will?" said October.

Ben nodded as he got up out of his chair. "You'll just keep bothering me until I acquiesce or the bad guys come bursting in with their guns blazing. I think I'll take the path of least resistance here."

October grabbed Ben by the arm and shook his hand. "Thank you. Thank you."

Ben looked away, conflict showing on his features. A storm of emotions boiled beneath the mask that formed the surface of his expression. He walked to the door and turned around to look at me. "I'm not doing this because I think you're the hero of this story or whatever the hell we're experiencing right now. I'm doing this because if I don't, October's never going to let me live a peaceful life."

I got the feeling that there was a lot more to why he was going to help October. Though nothing was said, I could feel the history that the two had. They looked comfortable around each other. They seemed to know each other's tendencies, like they were friends that had just not seen each other for a while.

We walked out of the house in a group, though once we entered the forest proper the rest of the team spread out in a squad formation. October and Ben walked in the center. In the distance the sound of war grew louder. Kaiju towered over the buildings and the trees, cutting swathes of destruction, breathing fire, spitting acid, swatting jet planes out of the sky like bees.

I tore my gaze away and did my best to follow the group. There was nothing that I could do. Even with a power like mine, I wouldn't be able to help. That much had been made clear on the planet Tek. I wondered how they were faring; probably not much better than Earth.

Once inside the restaurant, October handed the map to Ben, who then eyed me with a strange expression on his face.

"You can materialize anything, right?" he asked.

"Only what I've seen in person," I said.

Ben looked thoughtful. "That should be enough. Make me a laptop, a soldering iron, some solder, and a pair of pliers. Also, some copper wire. Oh, and two USB ports."

I created everything he asked for. Thankfully, I had toyed around with computers and electronics not too long ago, and so I had encountered a soldering iron and everything that went with it.

Ben began to work. Every few minutes, he requested something from me. A screwdriver set. A blowtorch. A sheet of galvanized steel. Several large neodymium magnets—I was lucky enough to have played with one as a toy while working in a machine shop.

After about half an hour Ben stretched his arms above his head and leaned back against the wall. "Done," he said. "I analyzed the map's software, and since this restaurant is my baby I was able to twist its internal code into emulating whatever god-awfully complex architecture the map uses."

"Er," said Andrew. "I only got half of that."

"He means he did some sweet hax," said Kyle.

"Ah," said Andrew. He looked distressed. "It's not because I'm black, okay? I'm just not too good with computers."

"I wasn't thinking that," said Kyle, his expression both concerned and slightly amused.

Andrew blinked several times and then turned back to the work site. "So does it work?" he asked.

Ben held out his hand. "Map."

October handed the device to him. Ben placed it inside of a shoddily-constructed holster, and there was an audible click. The laptop began to hum. The cables connecting it to the restaurant's AI crackled with sparks. Several wires became red-hot. Ben typed furiously away at the laptop's keyboard, and soon, the map began to hum.

And then, as quickly as it had begun, everything stopped. There was no crescendo. Just a few clicks. The sphere that we thought was a map opened, and inside was a note, on a simple white piece of paper, written in Russian.

October lifted it out with shaking hands. "Can you read this?" she asked Ben.

Ben shook his head. "What, do I look like a communist to you?"

George cleared his throat. "I, ah, I took Russian in high school. I may be able to decipher it."

"That's right," said October. "You were in high school during the height of the Cold War. I thought learning Russian wasn't very popular then, though."

"My school taught it. It's been many years, but I think I still remember enough that I can get by. Give me the note."

October handed it to George. George peered at it, squinting his eyes, and then he moved his lips soundlessly. "It looks like... It looks like a message."

"Well, I mean, that much is obvious," said Kyle, folding his arms. "Tell us what it says."

"'Wrong way,'" said George, slowly. "'You can't get us that easily.' And that's it."

October sighed. "Yeah, I expected as much. They're toying with us."

"Who?" said Ben.

"The guys in the trucks," I said, to nobody in particular. "They might not be who we think they are. Maybe they're magical or something."

October rubbed her eyes. "We came all the way and opened this device. There has to be something else there."

"Well, I can say one thing about this device," said Ben. "I've thought about it, and the Russian in the note gave me an idea. The technology that this sphere is made of is too distinctly human to be made in a time stream that much different than our own. I thought it felt strange to me. This is Russian tech. Though it's a lot more advanced than I ever could have imagined, it has a distinctly Russian feel to it. I can't explain it more than that, but I feel like that's the thing that was bothering me about it."

"You're spot-on," said October. "The main enemy that started this all was a universe where Russia won the cold war and entered a space age."

"Well that explains everything," said Ben, half mockingly. "Just blame it all on the Russians. You know, the giant monsters, the guys with red lightsabers, the orcs in silver suits. Blame it all on those communist vodka-drinking bears and we'll all be all right."

"I think I know how to save this world," said October. "This map. It's leading us on."

"So where to?" I asked. "How are we going to do this?"

"We're going to go back in time," said October. "Or rather, to a specific point in the multiverse where everything collides. In order to do that, we have to find out more." She paused, looking at Ben.

Ben sighed. "Let me guess. I'm going to help you." He shook his head slowly. "I'm telling you, it can't be done. There's no going back in time, not without a significant amount of magic, aetheric energy, or both. None of those work in this universe."

"And so we'll go to another universe," said October.

Ben crossed his arms. "No. I swore that I would never get involved in the affairs of the multiverse again. Not after what happened last time."

There was a long silence. October stared at Ben, not blinking. Ben sighed again, deeper this time. "You're not going to let it go, are you?"

October nodded.

Ben turned his head away. "You're going to keep pushing until I relent, aren't you?"

October nodded.

Ben stood up, turning his palms over. "Fine then. I'll help you with your project. Just know that I don't think it will work. There's nothing a bunch of kids in one McDonalds restaurant can do to save the world from an evil so big it's trying to take over the multiverse. Not even if it involves time travel shenanigans."

"But you'll help us," said October.

Ben dusted his hands off on his pants. "Yeah, I will. Get this stuff out of here."

I sat back against the wall, watching the rest of the team disassemble what I had materialized and Ben had put together, thinking about the meaning of the message that had been given to us. *Wrong way. You can't get us that easily.* Had they known? Had they deliberately planned to lead us down this path so that we would be somewhere where they wanted us? Or was it from someone else entirely? Even then, it had given October an idea that probably wouldn't have come in any other situation, and so in that respect the note was exactly what we needed and exactly what they wouldn't have wanted us to get. If everything worked out all right. Which there was no saying that it would.

Everything was all messed up. There were no heroes to save the world in real life, or story, if this was a story. I was stupid to think that, even with my power, we would be able to take down an entire army of super-powered bad guys.

October packed up the last of the parts and came to sit down next to me.

"So," she said, letting her voice drop away. There was a long silence. "How are you? Are you getting used to your new power?"

"It's not that new anymore," I said.

October chuckled. "It hasn't been four days since you joined the Franchises."

"Ah, that's right," I said, losing myself for a moment. "Then, ah, it's only been four days since I said I liked you."

"And?" said October, raising one eyebrow.

"So what do you think of me now?"

October kissed me on the cheek. "I think you're a fine person," She got up and walked towards her pilot's seat. "You didn't need to ask, but I'm glad that you did. Don't worry. I'll make sure we both get through this alive, us and everyone on this team, and as many other people as possible." She turned back into her commanding captain mode. "Get this thing ready to portal jump. We're heading to Telroth."

We made the preparations in about half an hour. Since I hadn't seen a portal connected to this world before, it took fifteen minutes to start up after I materialized it. As well as this, the plane of Telroth was hard to connect to from Earth, or so October said as she furiously typed in commands on her keyboard. Ben watched over her and occasionally gave her direction.

We stepped through the portal and the universe hit me in the brain with a sledgehammer covered in nails. This time, purple beams of light spat out from a star in the center of my vision, and I could see the framework of the universe stretching, changing, becoming more elastic and not at all like I was used to. *That must be the magic,* I thought, as I watched it with a detached, calm feeling.

We appeared in the middle of a valley surrounded by low hills covered in grass and yellow flowers. I got the feeling that this place wasn't frequented by humans. Or if it was, they left no trace.

"We're probably going to have to do this on foot," said Ben, as he picked up the bag he had brought with him on board.

October knelt our restaurant down, powering it off, and then she stood up out of her pilot's chair. "I agree. We don't know what kind of people we'll be encountering. It's best we make a good impression."

"It's going to be hard with the kind of equipment we have," I said. "If this place is a pre-industrial revolution world, or maybe even a pre-enlightenment world, we'll make a huge impact with our high-tech equipment. If they've never seen a gun before we'll have a hard time dealing with that."

October nodded. "What Max says is correct. We'll have to tread lightly here, or else we'll risk our operation. Though it may be in a different fashion than what you expect. Telroth has a history of space-faring civilizations, and they've left their mark on the societies that live post-collapse. Here, the line between magic and technology is blurred. We don't know how they'll greet us." She paused. "We also don't know what language they speak, and we don't know if it's on file. This entire operation rests on our ability to communicate with the magic users that we find, so we'll just have to hope that the Franchise database collectors were kind enough to catalogue Telroth languages."

"A lot is riding on chance," said Kyle. "Not the kind of operation I'd like to be the only way to save the world."

"We don't have time to complain," said October, as she put on her suit. The door to the bathroom airlock opened, and we all stepped in. Ben was wearing the same clothes that he had come in on and he looked out of place as the only person not wearing colorful clothing covered in McDonalds decals. He still carried the old shotgun that he had pointed at us when we had first met. Compared to our military-grade weaponry, it looked a little out-of-place.

We stepped into an atmosphere that didn't feel at all Earthlike, though I could breathe it easy enough. It felt foreign, different, as if I had expected to drink lemonade and instead had gotten a mouthful of orange juice. Both were palatable, but the shock was enough to jar me into being surprised. I took a few deep breaths and calmed myself. The smell of flowers here was strong, as well as the smell of cooking oil coming from the robot behind us. October linked her smartphone to the bot, holding it up in the air to catch the signal even though she probably didn't have to, squinting as she looked up into the sun. The phone beeped. October held it out in front of herself and moved it around.

"This planet's magnetic field is about twice as strong as that of Earth's," she said, as she started walking. "Or at least that's what the encyclopedia said. It's got a gravity close enough to 1 G that we shouldn't notice a difference."

I tested my feet just to be certain. It was true, I didn't notice anything, but that was probably because I had been in a couple other gravity wells of varying power during the last couple days and my senses were all screwed up.

October started trekking up one of the hills that surrounded the valley. We all turned to follow.

She spoke without turning back at us. "If the wizards we encounter request payment, we can have Max here materialize just enough gold to get them to cooperate with us. It would be best if we don't reveal how much power we truly have, as they're likely to be suspicious of us already and probably won't take well to someone who can create everything they've ever seen at will."

We crested the hill and came upon a cart path, a dirt road with a big rut down the middle that had been trodden down by horse's hooves. There were no travelers in the area. October continued to walk while holding her smartphone in front of her.

I assumed the restaurant had some sort of radar system that allowed her to see the surrounding area, or maybe there was a system that could mimic GPS. Or, perhaps she was just using it as a compass; I really couldn't know. Back on Earth she had used the GPS system to find Ben's cabin, but here we didn't have that luxury.

Lucky us that we had a high-tech, sophisticated piece of equipment with us.

"Materialize us a car," said October. "The nearest town is out of range of our restaurant's scanner, but there's an inn about five miles down the road. We can risk the shock of driving up in a car if it means we get there before it starts to get dark."

It was true, the sun was setting in the distance, casting a golden glow upon the sparse clouds that filled the still mostly-blue sky. I looked at the scene for a few seconds and admired its beauty. Then, I looked down and materialized a car. It was the one I usually drove, a Nissan, which I had materialized simply because it was the most familiar to me. It came with a full tank of gas.

Everyone piled in, me at the helm, and we drove off across the road. Since it was unpaved we could only make about twenty miles per hour, but that was something compared to if we had been walking. We made it to the inn in half an hour. When we pulled up, a couple of curious peasants came out to look at us and point with long, bony fingers. Emaciation defined their features, the grooves in their skin filled with dirt.

We got out. Upon seeing our bright clothing and weapons they chattered amongst themselves in a language that sounded a little bit like Spanish, a little bit like Russian, not at all like Chinese. It was a very fluid language with fast syllables that rolled off the tongue.

October manipulated the translation equipment I had materialized for her. It was a hybrid between the D'Yarthian hardware and the Franchise database that Ben had put together sometime during the journey.

"Ah!" said October, as the machine beeped several times. "It looks like the language is on file. Though the lexicon is incomplete, and there are very few examples of their written language."

"Can you communicate?" asked Ben.

October nodded. "I think so." She stepped up to the peasants beside the inn. "Do you know any wizards nearby?" she asked, gesturing with her arms. The translation machine spoke for a couple of seconds after she had stopped. The peasants looked scared at first, talking amongst themselves, and then they gestured wildly with their arms. Their voices blended together. Several more people watched from the doorway of the inn.

October read a speech to text translation on a small screen in front of her eye. Her expression changed to one of thoughtfulness.

"It seems that there is a wizard who lives not far from here," said October. "But it also seems that they think we're wizards as well."

The peasants continued talking over each other. Then, they all stopped talking, backing away from us and the car and returning to the safety of the inn. A small child looked at me from between the legs of an older man. Her eyes were big, blueish-green, a color that I had never seen before. They were filled with apprehension and fear.

"It seems like the wizard is known to be a hermit and a little bit odd in the head," said October.

Kyle scoffed. "It's probably because of mercury poisoning. That's the kind of technology that wizards in this kind of environment get excited about."

"I don't doubt you," said October, heading to the car. "Let's go."

Time froze. The Watcher came out of his portal wearing his customary purple robes. He sat down on a stool in front of the inn and started puffing at a pipe. A few minutes passed, or it felt like that, though I had no way of telling whether the time-within-time I was experiencing was actually real. The Watcher looked at me for a long time. His eyes searched me, closing every time he took a draw at his pipe, opening again when he exhaled.

Finally he spoke. "I see you have come to my favorite domain," he said.

"This place?" I asked. "Telroth is your favorite dimension?"

"This planet in particular," said The Watcher. "There isn't anything quite like a feudalistic society with a solid understanding of the intricacies of magic. I find it much more palatable than post-industrial technologically advanced societies. The people who live in those are always so... Independent. Savvy. They won't believe anything you say to them unless they see it with their own eyes. Places like Telroth are gold in a sea of mediocrity."

"Are you insulting us?" I asked, not really feeling like that was true.

The Watcher laughed. "Oh, no, I'm just having fun watching you struggle to fight against an enemy that you do not understand, one that doesn't even acknowledge your existence, let alone your ability to threaten them."

"Then they're going to get a rude surprise," I said. "We'll bring them down. We'll save the Earth. You gave me my power to do just that, didn't you?"

The Watcher raised one eyebrow. "Did I? Did I really give you the power you wanted so that you could save your dimension? Or did I give it to you for some other, nefarious purpose? Which is it?"

I shook my head. This was going nowhere; I didn't believe that my power came to me for any other reason than that my world needed saving. Otherwise, it would be stupid. There would be no point. What was the meaning of having a superpower like mine if I wasn't going to use it against an enemy that was large enough to pose a threat?

The Watcher kept his gaze on me long enough that I become uncomfortable. The silence stretched on, and on, and on, never ending. What was he thinking about? What kind of advice was he going to give me this time?

"You had best get along well with your friends," said The Watcher, after taking a long puff from his pipe. "They may not be with you for that much longer."

A chill ran down my spine. What was he talking about? Was he foretelling that someone would die? I pondered his statement for a long time. The Watcher simply observed me.

"I'm going to save the world," I said. "Even though I know it's a long shot. Even though I know there are a lot of things that can go wrong. I think that I can do something for everyone. I think that I can do this with the help of my friends; I really think October's idea is going to work."

"Even though you don't know much about it? Even though you don't know how magic works?"

I thought about it. "Yes. I'm going to put my trust in someone like October, because she knows what she is doing. Even though she's young she still helped me out a lot. If I hadn't come with her on this adventure I would have been stuck back at home when the Darksiders came."

"The Darksiders, eh?" said The Watcher. "Nice name you have for the forces of evil."

"Who are they, really?" I asked. "Who is in control of them? Who is telling them what to do, and why are they attacking Earth?"

The Watcher took a long toke from his pipe. His eyes were closed when he spoke, smoke coming out from between his lips. "That, my boy, I do not know," he said. "The forces of evil are unfathomable. Probably they want power. Probably they want the power that I have given to you. Most likely they are after me—in fact, you can be certain that I am one of the reasons why this war is happening." He chuckled darkly. "I meddle in many affairs. I do not know why I am telling you this, but you can be certain that my hands are not as clean as you may think they are, or as you may have thought they were. I am no cleaner than any other wizard who has such power that he can spare a power like yours at the drop of a metaphorical hat." He laughed, this time infused with a brighter mood, meeting my gaze when he was finished. He toked from his pipe. "But I'm sure you have heard enough of an old man's ramblings. I'll take my leave now, though I will be watching you to see if your plan to travel back in time really does work as you plan for it to work." He winked at me. "Tallyho."

And then, he was gone. For a couple of seconds time stayed still. Then the world opened up and everything started moving again. I stood beside the car's driver side door, staring into space.

"Are you okay?" asked October, from inside the car, on the passenger side.

"Yeah," I said. "I just got a call from The Watcher."

October raised an eyebrow. "Ah, you did? What did he say?"

"He just rambled," I said. I got into the car and started up the engine.

Ben, sitting in the seat behind me, huffed. "The Watcher, eh? I'm sure he's up to no good again. This power of yours scares me. It's too powerful. Too convenient, and yet at the same time it isn't the right power for our needs. It's not like super strength, or the ability to fly, as both those powers make for a superhero who can save the day by brute force. But you, you're stuck with the ability to become a second-hand hero, someone who has to support from behind. You're special in many ways but the ability to fight the enemy head-on isn't one of your abilities." Ben leaned back in his seat and sighed. "The Watcher can be a real pain sometimes."

We drove down the now-darkening road, my headlights on, casting a beam into the blackness, uncovering only brown and dull shades of green. The world was very dark. I had heard about how dark the pre-industrial countryside was, but now I really felt it. Outside the beam was pure blackness that dissolved into a starry sky that wasn't at all like the sky of earth—a green nebula stretched up over the horizon, and the moon was a dull red color, much larger than the moon of Earth. As we bumped along the dirt path I stared at that sky, wondering. I felt estranged. Different, as if I wasn't myself anymore.

October reached across the cup holders in the center of the front seat and took my right hand in hers. I felt a small jolt of adrenaline through my body. Her hand was warm, not as soft as I thought it would be, but not rough either. We had been driving for several hours at about ten miles per hour when we finally came upon an old watchtower. It came out of the blackness at a frightening pace. The headlights reflected off of the damp and cracked stone.

We opened the doors and got out. October walked up to the tower's wooden door and held up her hand.

"Wait," I said. "They're probably sleeping. I know it probably isn't that late by our clock, but people went to bed at sundown before there was electricity."

October pulled her hand back. "I hadn't thought about that. Sorry, I just assumed that they would be awake."

"So what do we do?" said Andrew.

Kyle kicked at the dirt, illuminated by my car's headlights. "Bring a light with us. I don't know."

George sat down on the hood of the car and crossed his hands. Ben paced back and forth across the door.

"Make us an RV," said October. "We'll sleep in that tonight. Hopefully they won't try to kill us like the last people did."

"We should do it outside the visual range of the tower," I said.

Kyle nodded. "Max has a good idea. Let's get out of here so that we can come to them in the morning as if nothing happened."

October nodded, and we all piled back into the car. I drove it over the next hill and parked it in a depression where it couldn't be seen from the tower. Then, I materialized an RV in a nearby cove formed by several boulders. We all got in, the six of us, and sat around the table and the couch in the vehicle's center.

"So who gets which bed?" asked Kyle.

"There's an overhead, two bunks, the couch, and the back bed," said October. "Who wants the bunks?"

"I'll take one because I'm small," said Andrew. He got up and walked back to the area where the bunks were recessed into the wall. "Can you make me a toothbrush?" he said, turning to me.

I materialized a toothbrush and some toothpaste and tossed it over to him.

George got up from the couch. "I'll take the bottom bunk. I can sleep fine in a small bed."

"Who wants the overhead?" asked October.

"I'll take it," said Kyle, grabbing the ladder and pulling down the cushions.

I was starting to relax. All this was so normal, as if we were just taking a camping trip in the local woods without a care in the world, as if this was just a vacation. But it wasn't. Earth was a burning hulk, millions of people were dead. We were the only ones who could do anything about it. As well as this, we were in a foreign world, a foreign planet, a foreign universe. The green nebula in the sky only made that idea clear; I could see it through the small ceiling view-port.

"Me and Max will take the back bed," said October, in a tone that was both soft and purposeful.

I felt a little tremor go down my spine. I had slept in the bunk during the first night in the RV, and on my own the second night. What was October thinking? Obviously nothing was going to happen—we were in close quarters, after all—but all the same it made me feel nervous.

Ben smirked as he pulled up the couch, converting it into a bed. "Can I have some more blankets?" he asked, holding up the one that had come with the RV.

I materialized a thick cover and tossed it to him. He grabbed it and spread it out on the bed.

October got up and stood near the bathroom door until it opened and Andrew came out. I tossed her a toothbrush before she could ask for one, and she went in and closed the door behind her. I stepped outside the RV for a moment and relieved myself. It was dark, but at the same time the sky seemed brighter than it ever had, the moon burning like a red hot coal not an inch from the horizon. It had just risen, like a monolith coming out of hiding for the first time in a century. It looked almost alive, as if there really was a face in it—it was strange, looking at its pattern of craters, as they were completely different from the moon I was used to.

I wondered what kind of moon Middle-Earth had. Was it ever explicitly stated anywhere in Tolkein's writings? What kind of planet was Middle Earth? What was its gravitational force? What did its magnetic fields look like? Were there aliens in that universe? Because, obviously, it existed in real life somewhere out there in the multiverse. Otherwise there would be no problem.

It was cold outside. I shivered as I stepped back into the RV, just as October came out of the bathroom. I met her gaze and felt a little tingle in the back of my neck. She motioned to the back and I followed her to the bed. She looked at me with an apologetic expression.

"Sorry I made you uncomfortable. You can sleep in a different bed if you want."

"No, I'm fine," I said, getting underneath the covers. She did too, on the left side of the bed. It was big enough for the both of us with plenty of room to spare. I took two pillows and piled them up— I can't sleep unless my neck is at a certain angle—and soon I was almost asleep.

"Max?" said October, her voice low, the only sound in the night.

"Yeah?" I said.

"Thanks."

"For what?"

There was a long silence. I thought October had gone to sleep, until she spoke again. "For being there for me. For coming with me. I know this has been a surprise for you. I put your life on the line for my own selfish purposes."

"I don't think you were selfish," I said. Our voices were low so as to not disturb the other people sleeping in the RV. "You did what you thought was best. You brought me into something that could have been fun, could have been just another adventure. You didn't know that that day was the day the Darksiders would try to take over the world, and succeed."

October sighed. "We don't know anything about them. That's what scares me. We don't know where they really came from, other than the single lead that I have."

"Sauron meeting the Russians?" I asked.

"Yeah," said October. "That's what we're here to prevent. That's what I'm going to try to do. Go back in time and somehow, with your power, prevent Sauron from teaming up with space-age Russia."

"That's going to be a large undertaking."

"I know, you tell me. At least now we have a clearly-defined goal. Before this we were just on the run, just trying to survive."

There was more silence.

"Are you still awake?" I asked.

"Yeah," said October. "What do you need?"

"Why did we go to the plane of D'Yarth? You had a reason for taking us there."

"Because I thought there would be someone who knew what they were doing," said October. "I was hoping that the government there could help us. They've been our allies in previous campaigns, in the ones that have been interdimensional affairs, at least. I was hoping that we could get them to send an army. It was a long shot, and our hopes were shot the minute the Darksiders appeared on that plane."

"Will the Darksiders appear on this plane?" I asked.

"Probably," said October. "They may even already be here, somewhere on this planet. We can't know."

All I could hear was October's breathing, which soon slowed down and became steady. I lay awake for some time longer, looking out the window at the sky tinged with strange bright stars and a cloud of green.

11

* * *

Fetch me a Taco

We woke up to the sound of birds chirping. I looked outside; the sun had just risen and the sky was cast with an almost-dark blue color that looked as if it had been teased out of the blackness and was just now coming into its own. The red moon was low in the sky, almost at the horizon, having traveled around the world during the night. October rustled beside me. She sat up in bed, the covers falling off her body, still wearing the shirt she had been wearing last night which was now rumpled and creased with more wrinkles than before. Her hair was frayed at the edges and she had a tired, sleepy look on her face that wasn't unattractive.

She rubbed her eyes, and then looked at me for a couple of seconds before speaking. "I look horrible right now, don't I?"

I shook my head.

"Don't answer," said Ben, leaning into the back from the hallway. "It's a trick question." He had a toothbrush in one hand and a tube of toothpaste in the other.

Andrew dropped out of the top bunk and sat down on the edge of the back bed. He put his shoes on—he was still wearing his socks—and then he yawned widely. "'Morning."

"'Morning," I said, getting out of bed. I still had all my clothes on, the same clothes that I had been wearing for several days now. I just hadn't found a good time to clean them.

October leaned against my shoulder. "Can you materialize me some orange juice?"

"I want some cereal," said Andrew, walking to the table in the middle of the RV. "With milk. Two percent."

I got breakfast ready for everyone, materializing everything from bowls to spoons to cups and napkins and sausage and fried eggs.

Everything was already fully cooked and hot, as long as I imagined it right in my head.

Ben raised his fork, a piece of sausage on it. "A toast to Max, who has the most useful superpower I have ever seen."

"A toast," everyone said, together. They raised their various drinks up and clinked them together.

October looked at me and smiled. "It's times like these that I feel lucky."

Kyle leaned back against the padded bench. "I have to say, at first I wasn't really on board with this whole idea." His expression was pensive, thoughtful. "But I'm starting to see why everyone believes you'll save the world."

I looked down at my food. "Yeah..."

Kyle sighed, taking a bite of eggs and chewing thoughtfully. "I'm still not fully convinced, but it's not to the point that I want to leave anymore. You have my praise for being able to use your power for the good of mankind. If I was in your position, I would take it and run. But that's probably why I'm not in your position." He paused. "The Watcher has his own agenda, I'm sure, but I don't think it's a bad one. Not now. If it was an agenda for ill, he wouldn't have picked you." Kyle motioned with his spoon. "Not to insult you or anything, kid, but you're probably one of the naivest people I've ever met. Next to Andrew, of course."

"Ah, he's just in high school," said Ben, while he was still chewing on a sausage. "Don't get all harsh on him. The Franchise attracts naive people in droves. You have to be, to sign up for this kind of stuff. It takes a certain innocence to want to join up, or rather, to get tricked into joining."

"I wouldn't call it trickery," said October, getting up from her seat. "But now's not the time to talk about this. Let's get to the wizard's fort and finish what we came here to do."

I got out of my seat and made my way down to the RV's driver seat. I started the engine, pulled down the parking brake, and we started along the path towards the fortress.

Before we went five meters a fireball descended from heaven and splashed against the ground right in front of the windshield.

"Get off of my property, you damn Earthlings," said a voice, in perfect English. "I didn't come here to deal with your kind."

October grabbed the wheel and steered us around the fireball—I was too stunned to do anything about it. We veered off course and yet continued towards the castle.

"I said, get away!" said the voice.

"That sounds strangely familiar," said October, glancing over at Ben.

Ben shrugged. "What? I never went so far as to seclude myself in another dimension."

"Out!" said the voice. "Get out with your miserable cars! I don't want anything to do with your damned technology!"

"Keep going," said October, still holding onto the wheel. "We have to convince him. We're lucky that he's an immigrant."

"That happens?" I said. "I wouldn't have expected..."

"It happens a lot more than you think. Plenty of people have emigrated to other dimensions from Earth, and vice versa. It's just how things work."

We crested the hill at a ridiculous speed, the RV jumping upwards and getting some air before landing hard on its tires. For a moment I thought we were going to crash into a boulder before October pushed the wheel, jerking the RV, missing the boulder by an inch. The rock scraped paint from the RV's side. We careened past several trees, and then we came upon the watch tower itself, a hulking structure that was a lot bigger in daylight than it had seemed at night. Part of it was a mansion that looked as if it had been left neglected for several decades. The other half was a solid stone round tower that looked as if it had been constructed a century before.

"Go away!" said the voice. Then it spoke in another language, and then another language, and then a third that I recognized as German.

"I think he thinks we don't speak English," said Ben.

"Why would he think we spoke English in the first place?" asked Andrew, looking pale in the face.

"Probably because the RV says Winnebago," said October, as she drove the RV just past the tower's edge, stopping it in a small recession beside the road.

"Materialize me a megaphone," said October. She held her hand out.

I imagined a megaphone like the one I had once seen used at a school sports festival. It appeared in October's hand; she hefted it up to her lips while at the same time rolling down the window.

"We come in peace," she said, her voice amplified by the device. "We don't mean any harm. All we need is some help with a bit of magic."

A bolt of lightning arced from the top of the tower and struck the ground next to the RV. Everyone in the vehicle flinched. My ears rang.

"Next time I'll hit you square on," said the voice. "Get out of here! I don't want your kind around here! I left Earth for a reason!"

"It's okay!" said October, through the megaphone. "We have something to give you." She paused. "What do you miss most about Earth?"

The voice laughed maniacally. "Tacos! Oh, I missed tacos so much!" Then it coughed. "But you have no tacos! I can sense them from a mile away! Get out of here, you taco-less fiends! I'll kill you if you don't leave, right now!"

The voice sounded more insane than sane. I nervously gripped the wheel. "I think we should find another wizard," I said. "There are probably plenty—"

October grabbed my arm. "Make us some tacos."

I sighed. "Fine." I imagined a taco like the ones I had eaten in Mexico, straight from the food stalls. The smell of carne asada and guacamole filled the cab. I held the taco out the window.

"I have a taco," I said.

October held up her megaphone. "We have tacos. We come bearing tacos. Please let us in."

"Where did you get that?" said the voice, obviously confused. "How did you manage to come up with a taco so suddenly? Are you a wizard too? But, you can't be! In all my years working with magic I have never once been able to materialize a real life taco!"

October gripped the megaphone tightly. "We have a way to bring you an infinite amount of tacos," she said. "If only you'll let us in."

"You lie," said the voice. "That taco is fake. I don't know how you made it, but I swear to god it's fake. You can't trick me with your fake tacos, oh no you can't."

October poked me. "Can you materialize a taco from a distance?"

"I think so," I said, a little confused.

"Move!" said October, just as a blast of fire bore down on us. She stepped over the divide and pressed her foot down on mine. The RV lurched forwards, not making it in time, and the back half was blasted open with a force strong enough to tear through the metal walls. We drove with smoke tailing out of our rear end. Another ball of fire landed close to our left.

"Materialize a taco in the upper right room of the mansion," said October. "That's where he is."

"How do you know?" I said, desperately turning the RV to avoid a bolt of electricity. We made it through with scratches, but no more damage. Another bolt of fire landed not a foot to the right of the passenger side, and for a terrifying moment I feared for October's life.

And then she leaned over me and grabbed the wheel, her foot still on mine which was over the gas pedal. She looked me in the eyes. "I'll drive. You concentrate on getting that man a taco."

I imagined a taco, fresh off the grill, with a soft corn shell, full of salsa and guacamole. Then, I projected that image into the second story second room of the mansion. I made five tacos, in different places around the room, just to be safe.

The blasts of fire stopped. Our RV pulled a sharp turn, lifted up on its side wheels, and came crashing back down onto the dirt. There was a long silence.

Then the voice spoke. "They're poisoned. I know they're poisoned."

"You can check with magic, can't you?" said October, still holding the megaphone, though she could no longer lean out of the window.

"I—I suppose I can," said the voice. "But if there is poison I swear I'll wipe you and your dirty car off the face of this planet."

There was another long silence. Then the voice spoke again. "How did you know I liked carne asada?"

October handed the megaphone to me. "Tell him."

I put the megaphone to my lips, carefully, leaning out the window. "Carne asada is my favorite too." My voice bounced off the walls of the dilapidated tower, echoing across the empty landscape.

"You can come in," said the voice. "But no weapons. No technology. I left that stuff alone a long time ago."

October opened up the RV's door and stepped outside, stretching her arms. "Well then," she said, turning to me. "Shall we get going?"

I stepped out of the RV and stood next to October, craning my neck to see the top of the round tower. The rest of the crew and Ben came out the side door and stood in a group. The air smelled of dirt and raw greenery, of old wood and of cow fertilizer. The surrounding countryside was barren, and in the light of day I could see that it once was farmed intensively, stone hedges tracing invisible roadways that had once been like the main road we had driven down. In the distance a tiny, collapsed shack graced the top of a hill.

October walked up to the mansion's door and knocked once, twice, three times. Nothing happened for a moment. Then, several locks clicked, and the door opened to reveal a grizzled old man with a mean-looking face who wore a long beard and a wizard's hat. For some reason he reminded me of The Watcher.

October curtsied. "Hello, we're here on a mission to save the Earth, and we need your help to travel through time and prevent a meeting between dimensions."

The wizard grumbled to himself in a strange fashion that hinted at notes of insanity. "Come, come," he said. "Bring more tacos. Many tacos, I haven't eaten them in years, many many years. If you want to travel back in time, yes, I will have to eat many, many tacos. Many tacos."

His manner of speech was raving, maddening, repetitive. Ben leaned close to October and whispered. I was close enough to hear.

"Are you sure that's the wizard we want?" asked Ben.

October nodded. "We struck gold. This guy is the guy we need."

"If you say so," said Ben, stepping away.

"This guy kind of reminds me of a certain someone," said Fry, nudging Ben in the side.

"At least I didn't go hide in another dimension," said Ben.

Fry laughed. Kyle and Andrew looked at each other and shrugged. George walked somewhat behind the main group, a little distant—but I wasn't worried because he had always been a little distant.

The wizard led us into a main chamber that had a high-vaulted ceiling and was lit by magical were-lights hanging from the rafters. A large, wooden table took up the center of the room, stacked high with books, crystals, lenses, wands, potions, and other magical paraphernalia. I ran my hand along the table's edge as we passed and my finger came up covered in dust.

The wizard turned around when he reached the head of the table. "My name is Red. You shall address me as such. I have agreed to help you for the price of as many tacos as I can eat." He puttered around the table, grabbing several scrolls, a robe, and a carved wooden staff. "I need many things to create a time-traveling portal, many things that may be quite hard to procure. You must gather these things for me." He cleared a spot on the table by pushing off a mountain of stuff which fell to the ground in a cloud of dust. He arranged several potions, tacked a piece of parchment to the open space with blades, and began to paint furiously with a quill pen.

"I need the blood of a dragon, not more than two days old. I need the tooth of a skyshark, the tentacle of a land squid, and five ounces of goblin bile."

October looked at each member of the team in turn. "We'll split up to find the ingredients."

Andrew raised his hand. "I want to find the skyshark tooth."

"I'll go with him," said George.

Kyle and Fry looked at each other. "We'll take the goblin bile. We can handle a couple of goblins."

"I don't want to handle a dragon," said Ben. "But yeah, yeah, I'll help. There's probably a shop somewhere where I can buy some land squid tentacles."

"I guess that leaves me and October with the dragon," I said.

October looked at me. "You can do this. All we need to do is bring some heavy equipment with us."

Red puttered up to me and inclined his head. "Before you leave make me some tacos."

I materialized several tacos on a paper plate and handed them to the wizard. Red grabbed them with his fist and shoved them into his mouth in a grotesque display of horrible eating habits. It took him less than a minute to finish them all. When he was done, he held out the plate. "More."

I materialized several plates on the table, and pointed to them. "There. Take them, and we'll be back as soon as possible with all the items you need."

Red moved his hand in a shooing motion. "Go. Get out of here, there are many things I need to take care of before we can start he ceremony."

October looked at me, and I looked at her, and the two of us started retracing our steps to the entrance. The rest of the team followed us.

We made it outside to the place where our half-destroyed RV was parked.

Ben walked up to the RV. "I'll take this baby here. Get me a few extra gas cans and I'll be off to find a shop that will sell me some squid tentacles."

Fry and Kyle sat against a boulder, chatting, talking about their plans to hunt down a goblin and retrieve its bile.

"I want a Humvee with an autocannon," said Andrew. "Have you ever seen one of those before?"

I had. Two seconds later, there it was, shining in the bright light of day. I materialized some more gas cans, some weapons, and enough ammunition for them to shoot. George got in the driver seat, Andrew on the turret, and they drove away.

Kyle approached me. "We'll take two motorcycles," he said. "We'll head back to the restaurant with you to grab our weapons. We'll probably be gone before you get there, so don't expect to see us."

I imagined two motorbikes. They appeared without fanfare, shimmering a little before becoming solid. Kyle looked impressed.

"You picked right," he said, getting on board one of them. He started up its engine—it was loud—and held it upright with one leg. Fry got on the second bike, and the two of them drove off towards the place where our restaurant was parked. Though I could have materialized some weapons for them, they hadn't asked—probably because they had formed an attachment to the things they already had, the weapons in storage in the restaurant's employee lockers.

October and I stood alone in front of the mansion. "So," she said, looking at me. "Shall we take the restaurant and go fight us a dragon?"

I nodded. "I think my car is still where we left it, not too far from here."

We started walking. The day was cool, not too hot, but not too cold either. Neither of us spoke for a long time.

"So how has this adventure treated you?" October asked.

"I'm afraid for my parents," I said. "I'm afraid that they'll be dead when I go home."

"That won't be a problem if our plan succeeds," said October, her eyes on the horizon.

"I don't know about that," I said. "I just... I just can't imagine us saving the world. It's too much of a big task."

October elbowed me with her arm. "Come on, lighten up. We're on a mission to save the world. What could be more exciting than that?"

I could see that she was trying hard to cheer me up. I smiled, deliberately, though it was inspired by a real want to cheer up and take everything in stride.

We crested the hill. My car was behind it. The tracks in the grass made by our RV were still there, leading to the cove created by the mass of large boulders.

I got in my car and turned the key in the ignition. It felt familiar, safe, and it helped me clear my head of everything that had been whirling around. I was going on a mission. I was going to save the world. It was a really big job, sure, but I finally felt as if I could do it, even if the chances of the plan actually succeeding were low.

You can't get us that easily. The words of the message we had found inside the metal sphere rebounded through my head. I had the sneaking suspicion that all was not well, before I pushed it out of my head and started the car along the road to where we had parked the restaurant. The sun was making its lazy rise up the sky, and the last of the red moon had disappeared beyond the horizon. When we were at the top of each hill, I could see for dozens of miles all around, the sky filling my view like a gigantic bowl upturned on the planet and painted with fluffy, white clouds. It was a majestic sight.

After several hours of driving slowly over the dirt road we made it to where our restaurant was parked. I slowed; there were a number of people surrounding it, standing in a crowd some distance away from its legs. They all turned to us when we drove up.

Several of the people spoke at us in their language, the rapid-fire syllables passing in one ear and out the other. I materialized a translation device—Ben had taken the one I already had—and hooked it up.

They were expressing their surprise at seeing my horseless carriage, or at least that's how it was translated. They looked like peasants, simple, uneducated folk who must have thought we were a new breed of wizard. I got out of the car, making sure to keep my grip on my gun—I wasn't sure what was going to happen, but in the event that something bad happened, I wanted to be ready to defend myself.

The peasants chattered amongst themselves, pointing at me. They seemed harmless enough. When October stepped out of the car several of them spoke excitedly to each other and then approached her.

"I think they're saying you're pretty," I said, reading off of the translator. The file on their language was incomplete, and as well as this they had a rough accent that the machine was having a difficult time with. Thus, I had to interpret the machine's output more than I would have liked.

Eventually I was able to get them to calm down. October nodded, and then she opened up the restaurant's boarding ramp. We stepped inside before any of the peasants could think about coming in after us.

"Can we pilot this thing without a crew?" I asked.

October shook her head, walking to a corner of the kitchen and pressing a number of buttons at a panel. "We're going to take the walker. It has enough room for two people if we squeeze."

"I thought you said you didn't want to use it."

October sighed. "This situation calls for it. We don't have anything else that might be able to stand up to a dragon. I know you can materialize a tank or something of that caliber, but we'd have no way to pilot it. That kind of stuff takes training. So, the best thing we can do is use what we have on hand."

October finished what she was doing, and a small door opened behind a frying range. She stepped inside, motioning to me.

I got in behind her. It really was cramped inside the machine, and my body pressed up against October's in a way that wasn't unpleasant but at the same time was a little uncomfortable, mostly because my legs were squished into a compartment that was barely big enough for them.

"You'll be operating the main cannon," said October, as she started the machine up.

We detached from the main body of the restaurant and landed on the ground with a thud. I looked around us, unsure of what to think—I was beneath a glass canopy that was large enough to fit both me and October underneath. I could see at all angles. October looked a little uncomfortable, however.

"What's wrong?" I asked.

The peasants pointed at us with amazement clear on their faces. I thought it was just because of the shock value of a mechanical walker, but soon I saw that it was something else. Were they awed by the red and yellow color scheme? The McDonalds logo?

I put the thought aside and stayed still while October moved across the landscape, first at a brisk walk, and then at a run that was faster than my car had made on the bumpy, unpaved road. We were moving at about thirty miles an hour. It was a rough ride, but it wasn't bad, and I couldn't understand why October was so reluctant to use the machine.

"We're going to ask around the town to see if there are any dragons nearby," said October, her face expressionless as she concentrated on piloting the walker.

The walker had an on-board radar system, and eventually we made it to a small village with a wooden palisade somewhere off the main road. We stopped, and the machine bent down in a pose that enabled us to get off. When I stepped onto the ground, I immediately understood why October had been reluctant to use the machine.

The first thing that came to mind was the tacky plastic ten-foot tall Colonel Sanders mascot at my city's local KFC, the one that had been, on several occasions, stolen as a prank by the local high school. Except, this machine was patterned like the purple McDonalds guy, the one with a rounded body and big eyes, that I hadn't seen used in advertising for maybe ten years. If I remembered correctly his name was Grimace.

I would have been able to handle it fine if it had been Ronald McDonald. That was okay, and I even would have expected it. But, the purple dude? Grimace? Why would they still have him in stock if they stopped using him for advertising before I left elementary school?

I looked at October, and it was clear from her facial expression that she knew what I was thinking. "Now do you understand?" she said, motioning to the machine with her thumb.

I nodded, and turned away towards the village. There was a crowd gathering at the top of the gate, which was barred closed. They were pointing and talking amongst each other in low tones. October put on her translation gear and started to talk.

"Hello there," she said, the machine translator speaking over her voice. "We've come to ask about local dragon infestations."

The machine took a couple seconds after she stopped talking to finish. The villagers looked at each other, confused expressions on their faces. Some of them gazed at the walker with awe. Some of them laughed out loud.

One of the villagers waved his arm. He spoke loudly, but not loud enough to be picked up by the translator machine. However, his intent was clear, as soon the gates opened—just a bit—and a couple of villagers came out to meet us. They carried bows and axes, and were wary of us, as they should have been. Two people dressed in red and yellow riding a giant purple monster coming out of nowhere and visiting a medieval town was a strange occurrence indeed. If it had happened to me I wouldn't have known what to think. As it was I felt glad that we weren't attacked on sight.

October walked up to the villagers, stopping a good distance away, and began to talk. After a while I tuned her out, instead focusing on the walker, examining it. The purple dude was a blob that looked sort of like a gum-drop, only this one had arms that held a gun in typical Gundam style, along with a combat knife strapped to its ankle and several clips along a bandolier across its shoulders. The cockpit was in the cranium, tinted purple to minimize its effect on the overall look of the machine. I had seen the world clearly through the cockpit and so the tint must have only been one-way. The face looked ridiculous. I would have laughed at it if I didn't know that it was my ride, that it was the weapon we were going to fight a dragon with. This was something that I had never thought of in my wildest dreams: the purple McDonalds guy going up against a dragon. How strange life was.

October finished her talk and walked up to my side. "Tacky, isn't it?" She held her hands on her hips.

I nodded, unable to add anything else. Tacky about summed it up, though there were other words that could describe it, like stupid, overbearing, or embarrassing.

October climbed aboard the machine through a retractable ladder. I followed her. Through the entire operation the villagers watched us, some with strung bows, some with their axes held ready to swing. October waved and we started off across the plains.

"There's a mountain range some ten day's travel by foot from here," said October.

"Then we'll make it in two days," I said, doing some mental math.

"I hope the food we gave the others is enough to get them to where they need to go," said October.

"I gave them all some gold as well," I said. "Though I didn't say anything about it. I put it all in a place where they're sure to find it."

October laughed, her demeanor calm and composed despite the situation. "This is surreal. You can create as much gold as you want, for free, with no consequences. If that isn't the coolest superpower ever I don't know what is."

"Even better," I said, "I can create a hamburger whenever I want."

October shrugged. "Personally I like hot dogs better. Especially corn dogs. Those are good."

I grimaced. "I never could stomach those things. Aren't hot dogs full of animal by-products?"

"That's what makes them so good," said October. "Just like chicken nuggets, hot dogs are better because they're a mystery meat. You never know what you're getting, so it's sure to be a surprise."

"You have a radically different opinion on this matter compared to me."

"Aw, come on. Hot dogs aren't that bad."

"Hamburgers are better."

About ten hours later, night was falling, and the green nebula that filled the night sky could be seen tinting the horizon. The red moon peeked over the hills.

"We should camp for the night," I said.

October slowed down our walker until we moved at a slow jaunt. Then, she walked until we found a small depression, at which point we stopped the walker and dismounted. My legs fell asleep as soon as I got out of the walker, and I collapsed to the ground.

October looked no steadier than I was, though she managed to stay standing. We both laughed.

October sat down next to me. "So," she said, looking up at the stars. "We're alone. In the middle of the wilderness. Isn't that romantic?"

"Sure," I said, "If it wasn't for the fact that tomorrow we're probably going to be fighting the dragon."

"Don't count on me being the damsel of distress," said October, as she lay down in the grass, splaying out her limbs. "And I don't think you'd fit the description of a white knight very well."

"Was that an insult?" I said, smiling at the tease.

October laughed. "Only if you take it as one. I still think you're plenty handsome."

"Gee, thanks, that makes me feel a lot better."

"Was that sarcasm?"

I paused. "No."

We both looked up at the stars, coming out in full force now, brightly visible due to the lack of light pollution. Neither of us spoke for a very long time.

I turned over. "October?"

But she was already asleep. I materialized a blanket and placed it over her sleeping form, grabbing one for myself as well. I closed my eyes and soon everything went dark.

12

* * *

Dragon

I woke up to the sound of birds chirping. A quiet, relaxing way to start the day, not at all diminished by the fact that it was as ordinary as ordinary gets.

And then reality hit me. We were going to fight a dragon. Sure, we had fought monsters as big as dragons in the restaurant, but we were in a small, purple walker vehicle that was barely twelve feet tall with just enough room for two people and a gun turret that was pitiful compared to the awesome destructive power of the Big Mac cannon. We couldn't punch, we couldn't kick, we were basically just a snack waiting to be roasted and eaten.

And yet I knew we had to continue. We had to keep going, keep fighting for what we hoped would save the people we cared about.

Before I could get too sentimental, October woke up and tossed off her blanket. Her hair was rumpled and she looked a little bit frazzled.

"'Mornin," she said, rubbing her eyes.

We set up a simple breakfast of eggs and toast, no fire needed, not even a microwave. When we were finished I dug a pit to put the trash in and covered it up. We then boarded the walker and continued along towards the mountainous wilderness that was just now becoming visible on the horizon. Running in the walker, we made a good forty miles an hour, which was the upper limit of what we could do without jostling our bones out of shape.

When we had reached the foothills October slowed us down and we began searching for the dragon's cave, which the villagers had kindly pointed the way as well as given a few landmarks. We passed the tall tree that looked like a fox and went around the large amphitheater made out of limestone that may or may not have once been a quarry.

When we were approaching the dragon's cave, I knew it, because I could see it, and I could smell it. The air grew foul. A dank mist covered the ground. The bones of large animals poked up out of the dirt, ribcages and skulls grinning mischievously in death, some adorned with spikes, others with tusks the size of our restaurant's arms.

An opening in the rock appeared out of the fog. We approached it slowly, the footsteps of our walker echoing through the rock, bouncing off the walls.

Something shifted in the darkness. A red tail flickered out of the cavernous opening, and then a massive head arched over our cockpit, a single glaring eye hovering in front of my gaze.

The dragon spoke to us not in language, but in meaning that was instantly translated into understandable format by my mind.

Why have you come here, machine users?

October popped open the walker's hatch.

"Wait! No!" I said, holding out my hand.

October ignored me, and instead reached out with her hand, holding up a single gold coin. "We have come to purchase something from you."

The dragon made a facial expression that I somehow knew was a smirk. *It would take much to purchase anything from my hoard,* he said. *And you do not seem to have the carrying capacity to fit ten thousand gold coins, which is the price of the least of my treasures.*

"We can give you even more than that," said October, her voice reverent, measured. "We can give you whatever you ask for, be it the moon or the stars. All we ask in return is a measly two pints of your own blood."

The dragon moved its head so that its nose pointed straight at me. Fire licked the edges of the inside. *You do not speak any common tongue known to me,* he said. *Though I do understand you, and your tongue is not as barbaric as some I have encountered. You have a certain... refinement to your speech, such that I have not heard before, and as a result I am hesitant to kill you, which I surely would have in any other situation given your ridiculous request.*

"Your weight in gold," said October. "That is what we will give you in return for some of your blood."

Oh, I have gold aplenty. I do not wish to have so much that I cannot keep it all in one place. My blood is not to be measured on the scale of such paltry things as gold and silver.

"A hundred pounds of aluminum," said October.

This gave the dragon pause. It blinked once, a thin film coming over its eye, giving it a greyed-out, worn look. It was then that I knew we were dealing with a wise, crafty, and very, very dangerous creature.

Aluminum, you say? In what form would it be?

"Any you want," said October.

The dragon shifted on its perch, showing the rest of its body to us. I didn't even think about the possibility of us slaying it.

October did not look in the slightest bit shaken. "If aluminum will not suffice, then how about weapons? I can give you weapons such that this world has never seen, weapons of light that can destroy enemies from miles away, weapons that can create balls of fire large enough to level towns."

And can I use such weapons myself? For I am a dragon, and my claws are unwieldy for using such tools as humans do. Though, it may simply suffice to have weapons as you describe in my hoard, and perhaps I will find another use for them in the future.

October smiled. "Consider it."

Let me see one of these... Weapons... In action.

October motioned to me. "Make me a rocket launcher. An LAW, preferably."

I materialized on in my hand, under the watchful eye of the dragon, and tossed it to October. October set the launcher up, pointed it at the skull of a mammoth fifty feet away, and fired. The missile arced through the air and exploded in an impressive ball of fire.

I see, said the dragon, its tone thoughtful. *Very well. Give me one hundred magic wands as you have there and I shall part with a small portion of my own blood.*

October looked at me, and I materialized one hundred LAW rocket launchers, arraying them in neat rows on the ground. The dragon watched with increasing interest.

I see you have a power that I do not understand, it said. *Perhaps you can enlighten me as to its function, its usage.*

"It was a gift given by The Watcher," said October.

The dragon roared, its voice reverberating through the mountainside, shaking rocks from their foundations.

The Watcher! Ha, that old coot! Had I known he was still alive I would have sought him out long ago! Please, do tell me where he is so I can roast him alive and have him for my dinner!

October shook her head. "He only appears when time is frozen, and then only from a dimension we do not know of."

And then, The Watcher appeared, without freezing time, in his purple robe and wizard cap. He bowed, smiling slightly, standing just below the feet of our walker.

"Hello, Drax," he said. "It is nice to see that you remember me."

The dragon—Drax—roared even louder than the last time, blasting fire out of his mouth in a blazing inferno which October just barely avoided by pulling up the tempered glass canopy. My skin prickled with the heat.

Energy roared up from below, knocking aside the flame. October piloted the walker away from the conflict site, to a small depression in the mud, where she hunkered down.

The Watcher laughed, holding a magic wand that split the stream of fire in two. "You have always been a funny one," he said, his voice cast loudly enough that I could hear it through the canopy. "I have come simply to thank you for being so amiable to my dear companion here. A hundred LAW rocket launchers is a pretty price to pay for a small sample of blood, but at the same time it demeans you. I know your tendencies, and since you have already made the contract, I know you won't back away." The Watcher bowed again. "I do wish you a happy day, a happy century, a happy millennium, and may the red moon watch over you."

And then The Watcher was gone.

"What was that all about?" said October.

Drax puffed smoke from his nostrils. *I see,* he said. *I do not wish to get involved in the affairs of other dimensions, and so I must cut off contact here. You may draw a small amount of blood from my left leg, but do not take too much, as I am quick to ire.*

October knelt the walker down and popped open the canopy, jumping out onto the ground. She held out her hand. "Get me a large syringe."

I materialized on in her palm, and then another for good measure. October walked over to Drax and stuck the needle in a crack between scales. She pulled up the stopper and soon it was full of a bright green fluid that was much more viscous than human blood.

Drax did not look at all uncomfortable during the procedure. When October was finished, she bowed, backed off, and walked to the walker, which she hopped into with surprising agility. The canopy slid back over us, and October piloted us away.

I craned my neck around and watched as Drax returned to his cave. I thought I could catch the glimmer of gold from my positon, but it might have just been a trick of the light.

October held up the vial of green dragon blood. "We got it," she said.

I sighed in relief, having been tense throughout the entire encounter with Drax. It was the first time I had ever been in such close contact with a large creature like that, and it had only been accentuated by the fact that I knew the creature was older, wiser, and more intelligent than I was. We were lucky to be alive after asking for something so powerful like dragon's blood. I somehow felt that fresh dragon's blood wasn't exactly an easy thing to come by in this plane or any plane for that matter.

"We need to keep this fresh," said October, "And so we're probably going to have to use a portal."

"Why didn't we use one to get here?" I asked. "We could have saved a lot of time, and probably the health of my legs."

October piloted the walker towards a small clearing in the forest next to a small creek flowing across shallow rapids. "Because there are only a few points you can travel to in each dimension. While you can come from anywhere, you can only go to those specific points."

"Sounds needlessly complex," I said.

"Don't blame me," said October. "Get us a portal back to where we first entered this dimension."

Once the portal was set up, we stepped through, and came out right next to the restaurant. October piloted the walker back to its cove in the back of the restaurant's body. Large mechanical arms picked the walker up and hid it underneath folds of metal, and the world went dark around us before bright florescent lights flickered on. October opened up the canopy and we both stepped out into the kitchen through the cupboard that hid the entrance to the walker's compartment.

I stretched my arms and my legs. It felt as if I had been inside the cockpit for an eternity. A tingling sensation flowed down my knees and into my calves as I regained feeling in my limbs.

October opened the door to the bathroom airlock. She stopped in the portal and turned to me with a thoughtful expression on her face.

"What is it?" I asked, after a couple seconds of silence.

October turned around, shaking her head. "It's nothing."

"If you say so," I said.

October entered the airlock. I followed her. The room was a lot bigger than it had seemed when there were four extra people with us along with all their gear and weapons. I wondered how they were doing; had they retrieved the items that were needed? If they had, did they wait long?

We stepped off the boarding ramp and approached my car. I felt a wave of unease pass over me, as something touched the inside of my mind, almost as if someone was watching me. I turned around just to make certain that there was no one. There was nothing, no shadows, no movement, no object that might have aroused my suspicion, and so I decided that it was just my frayed nerves. Turning around, I walked up to the driver side door and opened it. October got in the passenger side, I got in and started the car, and then we were off down the dirt road that led back to where Red lived, the stone tower attached to the old dilapidated mansion.

Driving in my car felt a whole lot more comfortable than half-sitting, half standing in the purple walker. Still, I began to feel claustrophobic. The feeling that someone was watching me grew.

A flash of light. My side window shattered, spraying me with glass. The dashboard cracked, a new hole where there had once been a gas gauge, sparks crackling off of exposed wires. I swerved to the right, slamming on the brakes, before October grabbed the wheel and looked me in the eye. "Keep going!"

I hit the accelerator and my back pressed up against my chair. Glass flew everywhere, the wind whipped at me through the open window. Panic set into my chest, fear, a deep need to escape.

Thunder clapped, and my shoulder exploded into agony. But, in that moment, I caught sight of a pickup truck some hundred meters behind us. It was no wonder I hadn't seen it before; half of it was invisible, and the other half was only visible because of a trick of sunlight shining from my left. On top of the truck was a man with a sniper rifle just like the one I had.

"October, take the wheel," I said, getting an idea in my head that I couldn't push out. I grabbed my own rifle with my right hand. My left shoulder protested in agony, and my left arm hung limp at my side. I had no idea why I was doing this. I aimed my rifle at the truck behind us as October grabbed the wheel and held up the barrel while I sighted through the scope. Our car swerved to the right just as another bullet whizzed past to an accompanying boom.

Once my rifle was sighted, I fired, the recoil tossing my arm back against the door, broken pieces of glass scratching my skin. October leaned over me and pushed my foot off the gas pedal with her own. She was now half in my seat, half in hers, all of her stretched over the middle divider.

"This is stupid!" she yelled, over the sound of crunching gravel and rushing wind. "Let me shoot!"

I turned back to the wheel and realized what a stupid thing I had done. Why had I wanted to shoot? I should have just materialized something that would block them or maybe force them to crash. With that in mind I took the wheel again and slammed the gas pedal down to the floor while the engine groaned in agony. The back window shattered and the front windshield cracked. I materialized two RVs behind us in a pattern that blocked most of the road. Our pursuit swerved around the obstacle just in time, appearing in the rearview mirror as a fully-formed pickup truck. The cloaking was gone. I recognized the vehicle; it was one of the trucks that had come out of the outpost in the jungle in Xen and had been in the middle of the convoy in D'Yarth. Why was it here? What was its purpose?

I had no time to think before October grabbed my side. "Get me a rocket launcher!"

I materialized an LAW and tossed it to her. While I did I had to let go of the wheel which resulted in a crazy jackknife turn towards the rough pasture beside the road. We rumbled across a stony field filled with half-grown wheat as our bulk plowed a furrow in the ground.

Rocks and stones impacted against the glass of the windshield and soon the cracks that covered it widened. I swerved us back around to the road while at the same time creating several brick walls along the pathway behind us. The pickup truck blasted through them at full speed which threw up a cloud of broken bricks and red dust. They didn't even lose any speed. The shooter on top of the cab took aim with his rifle. I turned hastily to the left.

We merged onto the road right beside the truck. For a second we drove parallel before I hit the brakes hard enough to send my head flying towards the steering wheel. Our pursuit drifted in a complete circle but before they could finish I gunned the engine again and shot past them with the wheels of my car barely on the ground and my teeth clacking against each other.

The pain in my shoulder intensified and blood spattered against the seat leather. The bullet had gone straight through my flesh and yet the damage done had been extensive. I pushed the pedal straight to the floor while shifting gears madly and we were soon over the top of a hillock and down underneath where they couldn't see us. The fall left a hole in my stomach.

The road was bumpy and unpaved and because of this our car shook like all hell had broken loose. I wondered if the car could handle it while simultaneously not caring to find out whether or not going slower would do it any better.

Our pursuit rounded the top of the hillock. I concentrated on what to do next and an idea popped into my head. A skyscraper appeared in my mind. Grey concrete filled the rearview mirror and the sound of a crash reverberated through the countryside. I gripped the steering wheel with more strength than I thought was possible. October put her hand on my shoulder. "Are you okay?"

I shook my head. "No. It hurts." It really did hurt. Like hell it hurt. My entire shoulder felt as if it was on fire as an army of biting ants crawled through the ashen remnants. Pain edged the corners of my vision. I let my hand fall down from the wheel and October grabbed it just as I was about to black out. Before I went I muttered something that was only half intentional. "Don't go, October. No, don't go."

13

* * *

A Quiet Interlude

I woke up in a soft bed with next to a window with old, beaten up curtains hanging from its edges. The light of the sun came through several holes in the fabric and illuminated what was otherwise a bare room with just a couple pieces of furniture. For a moment I wasn't sure where I was, and then everything came back to me, all at once, filling my head with memories of pain. I soon realized that they weren't all memories, as my shoulder told me that something was very wrong with it. I remembered the bullet, the man on the truck, the skyscraper that was even now probably standing alone in the middle of a small country road. I wondered what the peasantry would think of that.

Getting out of bed was difficult. I managed it, though, and soon I was walking around the room with a pronounced limp. There was a knock on the door. October's voice came from behind the wood.

"Can I come in?" she asked.

"Sure," I said, walking back to the side of my bed and sitting down on the mattress. It was dusty; though not cheaply made, the fact that it wasn't a modern-day convenience was painfully clear through the presence of straw ends that pricked my skin.

October entered bearing a plate of food.

"Hey," I said, my hand moving to my shoulder. "How long was I asleep?"

"Two days," said October. Her expression was on of relief as she sat down beside me and handed me the food. "You must be hungry. While you were out we set up everything that needs to happen for the ceremony."

"I see," I said, taking a bite of the unknown meat that had been presented to me on a platter. It was juicy, good, hot, a nice meal after several days of not eating anything at all. My shoulder ached but I could still use my left arm as long as I didn't move it too fast.

"How bad was I hurt?" I asked.

October shook her head. "Bad. You almost bled out before I could get you to the mansion. Kyle had some medigel packs on him but even those weren't enough to completely heal your wound. As it is you're lucky that you're going to retain full use of your arm, at least when it heals."

I touched the bandage that covered my left shoulder. "Did you learn anything about the people who attacked us?"

"You know as much about it as I do," said October. "Though I do have some thoughts on the matter. I think they were part of the convoy that we saw back in the jungle in the dimension of Xen and on Tek in the dimension of D'Yarth."

"I agree," I said. "But do you know why? Do you know anything about what they're doing?"

October shrugged. "It's a mystery to me. I think they may be connected to the Darksiders—well, of course they are—but at the same time I don't think they're quite on the same team. They may be against us but if they were on the same team this plane would be deep underneath their armies. This place would stand no chance, not unless there was some great army of powerful magicians right around the corner. Maybe there is. Who knows."

"How about your plan?" I asked. "Do you think it will work?"

October looked away from me. "I don't know. Honestly I don't think we have that much of a chance. I've been thinking about it and probably we're in too deep for our own good."

I leaned back on the bed and let my body rest. "I don't know about that. I think we've at least got a chance."

"What gives you that impression?" asked October, as she lay down on the bed next to me.

I turned on my right side to avoid putting pressure on my left shoulder. That meant that my back was to October. "I just feel it. Call it intuition, but I think your far-fetched plan has some grain of truth to it. Maybe that's the wrong expression. But for some reason I don't feel as totally full of despair as when we first came to this dimension." I paused. "Maybe it's because of our meeting with Drax."

"The dragon?"

"Yeah, him. For some reason he gave me hope. Hope that the enemy could be defeated. Hope that we could turn the tides against them by stopping them at their source."

October laughed. "What are you, an orator?"

"Was I really that eloquent?"

October got up off the bed. "No. Get some more rest. The ceremony starts the day after tomorrow, at exactly the crack of dusk when the moon is two-quarters risen, and you should be able to join us without hindering our performance thanks to medigel. However, you probably won't be able to shoot your rifle for a couple of months. Not without hurting yourself." She paused. "That was a stupid thing you did, while we were driving. Scared me half to death." She turned away, walked to the door, and stopped. Without looking back at me, she spoke. "Don't do that again. I don't want to lose someone, not again."

Before I could think about what she meant by that, she was gone, the door closing in her wake. I stared at the ceiling. It was bare, wooden beams stretching across a slightly sloped surface with several cobwebs in the corner and a little black spider running along a thin white strand. Several flies struggled against their sticky prisons. I watched them fight for a long time before I closed my eyes again and was asleep.

When I woke up my entire body was sore. It was dark out, very much so, no stars visible and the red moon just peeking out from behind a bank of thick clouds. A small pattering of rain struck the window, which was made out of modern glass which I assumed had been brought back by Red himself, which meant that even he couldn't deal without some of Earth's conveniences. I tapped on it once, twice, three times just to hear the sound. My stomach churned. I pushed myself into sitting position and looked at the unfinished plate of cold food sitting at the foot of the bed. I got up and picked the plate off the ground. Too hungry to care about the temperature, I ate everything that was left, which didn't make me feel any less hungry. If anything, I was hungrier.

I wasn't trapped here. I could leave the room if I wanted to, maybe go outside and talk with everyone else. But only after several minutes of prompting myself was I able to do that. I got up and opened the door. There was a hallway right behind it, with doors lined up to my right and left in equal intervals. I walked down the middle of the corridor, my feet making the boards groan, and I found my way to a large spiral staircase which opened out into a grand room with a ceiling higher than the fourth floor. I judged that I was inside the round tower now. From here, I could see that the interior had been redecorated to suit the design of the mansion, and though the placement of tapestries and window glass had been skilled, it couldn't remove the air of military austerity which clouded the circular walls.

I walked down the staircase, my hand on the bannister. It was cold metal, wrought iron, forged by hand with the marks of the hammer still engraved amidst twirls of black and little thin flowers that rusted around the edges. I made it to the bottom. October was leaning against the wall in a corner with a book in her hands. When she saw me, she raised her arm.

"Hey," she said, walking up to me. She showed me the book. "Don't you think this is cool? It's like one of those books you see in a museum."

"When is the ceremony?" I asked. "Where is everyone else?"

"They're all having fun chatting in the living room," said October. "We can go join them if you'd like."

"Were you waiting for me?"

October took a moment to respond. "Yes, and no. Well I mean, I was standing here because I really don't feel like talking that much right now, but maybe just a little bit I wanted to be here when you came out. Are you okay?" She reached out and touched my shoulder where the bandages covered my skin.

A small jolt of pain ran through my body and I cringed.

"Sorry," October said, drawing her hand back.

"No, it's okay," I said. "It didn't hurt that much."

October leaned back against the wall, closing the book with a thump. She looked up at the ceiling, her expression a mix of sadness, thoughtfulness, and excitement. Her eyes sparkled. "We're going to do it," she said. "We're really going to go back in time."

"And once we're there, what's your plan?" I asked.

October placed the book gingerly down on a table and crossed her arms. "It's about time I told you my plan."

"Should we do this somewhere more comfortable?" I asked.

October nodded. "I've already told everyone else about it. They all know the drill. However, you're the one who is key to this plan. Your power is the only trump card we have—well, it's the only card we have in general—and I'm planning on using you to your full potential. The Watcher has bestowed a gift upon us and I'm planning on using it as effectively as possible."

We came into a small dressing room with couches surrounding an unlit fireplace. The red moon's light, streaming through the window, gave everything a bloody, sinister tone. October sat down in one of the chairs. A puff of dust accompanied her motion. I sat down across from her, in the center of a wide couch.

October folded her hands and leaned back, looking at the ceiling. "First," she said, "I'll tell you everything I know about the enemy. I haven't been idle while you were out. We've moved the restaurant closer to this base—you can go outside and see it if you want—and Ben was able to contact some of the Franchise remnants on Earth that are still fighting, though they're most definitely losing. They gave out some classified information after we persuaded them that our plan would work. It was a miracle anyone who knew it was still alive, and it surprised me that there was still enough structure in command for them to care. But that doesn't matter. What matters is that I know where they came from."

"Where did they come from?" I asked.

October frowned. "I was getting to that. So yes, the enemies we originally fought came from a world where Lord of the Rings met a space-age civilization based on old Soviet Russia. They fought for a little while, but eventually they realized that their goals were similar, in that both civilizations wanted to take over other dimensions. The Russians are at the head here. I don't know how they roped Sauron into following their lead, but they're definitely in charge, and they're using the mystical and fictional characters as shock troops in their conquest. Once Stalin made a pact with Sauron—in this universe Stalin happened to be uploaded to a computer bank before he died—they searched the cosmos and the multiverse for allies, building a massive army that rivals every other army ever created. Kaiju and Sith lords are only the beginning. There are zombies from all fictional universes, the Covenant and the Flood from Halo, every supervillain ever imagined, Aliens from the movie Alien--" October frowned. "It feels familiar. It's almost as if someone else has a power like..."

"Like me?" I said.

October shook her head. "We can't say that for sure. We'll have to check for ourselves before we can make any judgements. But keep that idea in mine. Anyways, back on topic. There are hundreds of other minor fictional bad guys as well, from lesser-known works. It seems that, since they all share at least some of the same goals, they're working together. For now." October adjusted her seating in her chair, pushing her bangs aside. "And I've deciphered where the source is. It's Stalin's AI. I told you Stalin was turned into a computer code, but what I haven't told you is how powerful that computer is. Skynet from Terminator doesn't even compare. Neither does Hal. AutoStalin or whatever you want to call him has power that reaches into the multiverse and can bend reality to his will. At least, that's what I've heard. And so, my plan is as such: we infiltrate the Russian government before Stalin gets turned into a computer, and we bring him down. We'll make sure that the meeting between him and Sauron never happens. We were going to use you to assassinate him, but with your shoulder..."

"I can do it," I said. "I know what the medigel looks like. I can materialize enough of the stuff to fix my wound completely."

"Are you sure?" said October. "You really aren't trained at the rifle very well."

"I'll train," I said. "We have time. We can delay the time travel ceremony for a while, right? Because it won't matter what time we come from, only what time we go to."

October shook her head, though it was a reluctant movement. "I can't say anything about that. We'd have to ask Red, and he probably can't wait to send us off. As well as this, the enemy is drawing closer every day. We can't afford to waste any time."

"So what are we going to do?"

"We're going to bust into the base the old fashioned way: with our restaurant. We'll go in, guns blazing, and hope to god that they don't have any weapons powerful enough to stop us."

"I don't think that will work," I said. "Even though it may be the sixties when we arrive, they'll still have enough big guns to take us down."

"The restaurant can handle a few tanks," said October. "All we have to do is find out where he is."

"I think we need to bring an army," I said.

October sighed. "Look. We've already decided on this plan. It may be a long shot, but it's the only shot we have."

"Do we have a way to get back?"

"We do. Red is going to summon us back as soon as we give him a signal. It's going to cost a lot more than a few tacos, but I'm sure he'll want something equally as strange, and we're not really hurting for resources. We can handle whatever he demands of us without many problems."

I stretched my arms above my head and looked at the ceiling. "Sure. I'll go along with this. I want to see where it goes. As well as that, I don't think we have any better options." My shoulder started to hurt, a little at first, and then a lot. I regretted stretching my arms, but it was a habitual motion and I couldn't have stopped myself if I had wanted to.

"You don't look so good," October said, with a concerned expression. "Do you need to go lie back down?"

"No, I'm fine," I said. "I'm fine." I let out a breath and tried to make the pain go away. It worked, somewhat. "So how is my power going to be used in this battle?" I asked.

October held up one finger. "That's where the trickery comes in. You're going to create a diversion that will be so compelling that they'll have to investigate. You can play it however you like, but in the end you'll need to pull something on a scale that you've never done before. You're going to need everything you've learned while you've been with us to make sure that you do it right."

"Do we know where Stalin will be?" I asked. "And how are we going to get to the right universe?"

"Don't worry," said October. "We've done our research, and Red will help with a lot of that stuff. All you have to do is just follow along with the plan and do your part by making a diversion. That's it. It can be anything you want it to be, even if it's just a mountain of eggs as high as Mt. Everest."

"I'll try that," I said, "But I have some fears. What if the same thing happens as happened with the map? What if they're just playing with us right now?"

October shook her head. "Not possible. We evaded the shooter on the truck, which wouldn't have happened had they been playing with us."

"I don't see where you're going with that."

"If they were playing with us, they wouldn't have attacked as openly as that."

I thought about it for a minute. It just didn't sit right with me. "I'll go along with your plan," I said, "If only because it's the only way for us to go forwards with this. If we don't go through with the plan there won't be another chance for this."

"Agreed." October drummed her fingers on the armrest of her chair.

"What did you mean by 'not again'?" I asked, though I regretted it the instant it left my mouth.

October turned aside. "You don't want to know."

"I... Okay. I'll respect your privacy."

October looked relieved. "Thanks. I may tell you later when I have the inclination."

I decided it was a very civil way to end the discussion and stood up out of my chair. "When is the ceremony happening?"

October got out of her chair and followed me to the door. "Tomorrow at dusk. Until then we can rest and train and make certain that we're ready for this."

We left the room and walked through the halls until we came to a set of double doors. October pushed them open and we walked into a large living room, where the rest of the crew and Ben were sitting around a crackling fireplace, talking and laughing. Kyle was telling story with animated arm motions, something about riding a horse and falling off of it, while the rest of the crew watched. Ben and Red were sitting next to each other engrossed in another conversation, tankards of liquor in their hands. Ben took a large draw from his tankard and slammed it down, wiping his mouth with his sleeve. He was the first to spot me, waving his hand and motioning to an empty seat.

"Here, Max," he said.

I walked over to the seat and sat down. October looked around with an awkward expression on her face; there were no more open seats. Ben laughed with just a slight tinge of alcohol in his voice. "Toby, dear, you can sit in Max's lap. I know you've been wanting to do it for a while now."

"How did you know we were going out?" asked October. "I never told you and we really haven't been showing it."

"Haven't been showing it?" said Ben, taking a draw from his tankard. "By my mother's ring you've been the most obvious couple I've ever seen. Always looking at each other out of the corner of your eyes. Youth! I wish I was young like you."

"You can still find someone," said October, her voice deadpan.

"Was that an insult veiled as a compliment?" asked Ben.

October frowned. "No." She looked at me with a slight tinge of embarrassment in her expression. "Do you mind, Max?"

I shook my head, and then thought twice. "Sorry, my shoulder probably shouldn't take too much weight."

October nodded. "Yeah, that's probably for the best."

Ben laughed with an uproarious tone. "Hah! Are you going to let that insult stick? He just called you heavy!"

October punched Ben lightly on the arm, causing him to spill some beer into his lap. Ben continued to laugh.

October sat down on the armrest of my chair opposite my wounded shoulder. "Sorry," she said, leaning close to me and whispering. "He's a real bad drunk. He'll probably regret all this later, and he's really nasty when he has a hangover."

"I know you're talking about me," said Ben, his voice even more inebriated. "Here, drink with me."

"I'm not twenty-one," I said.

Ben laughed. "Ah, who cares in this world? The American government is under the power of evil now, like they always have been, but this time it's obvious. So obvious! It's all the government's fault that we're in this mess. If they had been more aware, if the president hadn't been a damn lefty, we would have been able to fix this problem right away. Right away!"

Red, who until now I hadn't gotten a good glimpse of, looked slightly uncomfortable, but I chalked that up to the fact that he hadn't had visitors in his large home for a long time. I wondered what he thought about us freedom fighters barging in on his home and telling him to take us back in time. Though, tacos were a good reward, and I would have done some serious things for them had I been in his situation. Living in a dimension without tacos did not sound like a good thing.

October faced Red. "So, why did you leave Earth?"

Red's eyes opened in surprise, and he raised one eyebrow. "You want to know about me?"

"Yeah, you're our host," said October. "It's only natural that I would ask about you. If I'm being too pushy just tell me."

Red shook his head. "I don't talk much."

"That's obvious," said October. "But if you don't mind, I'd like to know something about you. You've been a great help to us, and we'd like to make it clear that we appreciate your assistance."

Red looked undecided. Then, he lowered his head. "I'll tell you a story. This is about a young man who discovered the multiverse through a freak accident and was branded insane. I told everyone about what I had found, but no one would listen. They gave me medications, they locked me up for weeks at a time, and even though I could bring proof of magic and other dimensions to them they refused me and only brought me pain. So that's why I left. Earth doesn't deal well with things that are different. I simply wanted to escape that."

October was silent for a long while. "I can understand. At first when I discovered the Franchises and other dimensions, I wanted to tell everyone. But every time I tried to prove something to them the Franchise military police came in and intervened, making sure that nobody found out who wasn't under contract. Eventually I got in enough trouble that I just stopped trying. That happened a while ago, and now I'm just glad to be a part of this, happy that I can have a chance to save the world, a long shot though it may be."

Red leaned back in his chair, looking a little bit more comfortable with his surroundings. "I'm glad to help. Just bring me lots of tacos. Tacos are good."

He seemed a lot less crazy and off his rocker than he had when we had first met him. Perhaps it was the beer, but he felt like an intellectual to me, someone who once had a great oratory skill and was just now rediscovering that after not interacting with people for a very long time. I was happy that we were helping the man in this way. In his previous life I could have seen him as a teacher, a professor, someone with a lot of knowledge and the penchant to share it. He was a good man on the inside. Only on the outside did he look like a crazy old hermit.

I relaxed my guard and finally started to enjoy myself. "Whatever happened to Pemex?" I asked, turning to October who still sat on the armrest beside me.

October nodded, her eyes distant. "They were the ones that supplied the codes to the pocket dimension where our base was stored," she said. "Without that, the Darksiders would have never been able to fire a nuclear missile through a wormhole, nor would they have been able to bring in so many of their biggest armies. We might have stood a chance if those traitors hadn't turned. Though, it's to be expected. Socialist ventures never really fit well with American capitalism and the Franchises that live off of it."

"But, wouldn't Mexico be destroyed because of that?"

October shook her head. "Mexico escaped the war unscathed. The Darksiders are mostly attacking America right now. The war hasn't embroiled the entire Earth yet, but I do think the Darksiders are planning on taking over everything sooner or later. It's only a matter of time before the traitors get a taste of their own medicine." She looked at me and shrugged. "Or at least that's what I think after having learned the most current situation from our sources back on Earth."

I stayed silent for a long time after that, listening to the flow of conversation around me, almost speaking several times but never really finding the words to do so. This was my crew. These were people I didn't know a week ago, but who were now closer to me than anyone else ever had. I had been through hell with these people. I had saved their lives many times.

I materialized a bag of chips and popped it open. October looked at me and held out her hand.

"What kind?" I asked.

"Anything with salt," she said.

I materialized her a bag of hot Cheetos. She smiled and popped it open, taking a big handful and crunching them between her teeth. We both watched the fire, silent, oblivious to the conversation around us. October slid down from her seat until she nestled in a small crack between me and the edge of the chair. It was a tight fit, and it put pressure on my wound, but I wouldn't have traded the situation for anything else in the world. I found my mind focusing on her. So far I had been pretty distant, as far as romance could have gone, mostly because I wasn't sure how to take everything in at once and I didn't want to go too deep into something that could consume my mind while the whole world was falling around us. But in the comfort of my surroundings I wanted nothing other than to be affectionate. How would I do that?

I had never really been good with girls. October was the first girl with whom I had shared a mutual attraction, at least one that had gotten somewhere. That in and of itself was powerful, but at the same time it meant that I didn't know what to do in many of the situations I found myself. Was I doing it right? Or was I disappointing her? What if she was too nice to tell me that I wasn't doing something the right way, or was missing my opportunities?

October leaned her head against my good shoulder and I felt her weight shift more towards me. Her body felt good pressed up against mine and I started to feel a little awkward. Willing the situation to stay as it was, I closed my eyes, and just breathed in, out, in, out. It was very relaxing. Soon I heard October snoring, just a little bit, enough to let me know that she was very much asleep.

Ben's voice rose and fell to my left. Andrew was telling a story to my right. It was a very peaceful scene, one that I hoped would last for a very long time, but which was soon about to change in a very drastic fashion.

14

* * *

Red the Wizard

I woke up with a nasty cramp in my neck and a pressure on my stomach that took me a long while to place. By the time the world came into focus I understood what it was, or rather, who: October was sprawled out over my lap in a very un-ladylike posture, drool coming out of the corner of her mouth, snoring with a sound that I couldn't help but see as cute. I didn't move for several minutes. Then, out of the corner of my eye, I caught sight of someone moving. I turned my head to look, and before I could see their full figure, they disappeared into the shadows. I surveyed the room. Andrew, George, Kyle, and Fry all sat in their respective chairs, sleeping. The fire had burned down to embers. To my right Ben lay sprawled out on the floor, having fallen from his chair during the night. Red was nowhere to be seen. I thought about getting up and looking for him, but October's weight pressed against me, and I decided against moving to avoid waking her from her sleep.

The shadow returned. This time, I could see clearly who it was: Red. The wizard inclined his head ever so slowly with a motion that was both regal and senile.

"I am sorry to do this," he said, holding his staff up above his head. "I was hoping you would all be asleep." He took a deep breath, exhaled, and closed his eyes. "This is for the tacos. Elpsum, Moris, Etian calupsithi. Halpurn mesuh caluph."

A bright light filled the room. My body froze. I couldn't move; every muscle of my body was tense, locked up tighter than if I had cramped in the pool. October's eyes flickered open, and I had just about enough time to see the surprise on her face before the world disappeared.

I awoke to a rumbling sound that could only have been a vehicle. My body bumped up and down with the sound, proving that my assumption was correct. I tried to move, but my hands and feet were bound. The world swam before my vision. What had happened? Where were we going? Who had taken us? Those were the obvious questions, ones that I knew in my gut had tough answers. For a moment my eyes lingered, unfocused, on a poster hanging on the wall. Then my eyes focused and the outline of Cyrillic characters became apparent. Russian. I knew where we were.

The trucks. The convoy that we had been chasing, unsuccessfully, to try and determine who they were and what they wanted.

"Max?"

October's voice came from my left. I couldn't turn around to look at her, but I could hear her over the sound of the truck rumbling across what must have been an unpaved road.

"I'm awake," I said. "I think we were betrayed."

"You don't say," said Kyle, who was sitting against the back of the truck. His head moved left and right with the vehicle's motion like the head of a rag doll. "It was that wizard Red, wasn't it?"

"I saw him," I said, my voice catching a little. "He didn't look too good. He said something about tacos."

"Tacos?" Kyle's face lit up with an expression that was both angry and confused. "I thought we could give him all the tacos in the world! Why would he betray us over that?"

"I don't think the man was completely sane," said George, who appeared to have just woken up. "I've seen my fair share of people in my years, and I don't think this wizard had all the marbles in his head that he started out with."

"That's probably an understatement. Any rational human from the planet Earth wouldn't side with these guys. They're evil incarnate. There's nothing to gain by siding with them."

"Except tacos, apparently," said October, from her position behind me, where I couldn't see her. "And the Pemex chain betrayed us, remember? Those guys were from Earth."

"Let me rephrase. A self-respecting American."

"Still too broad. The dark side has its allure and people join it because of what they can gain by turning against Earth. And we still don't even know why they're fighting us."

"I want to go home," said Andrew, interrupting the conversation. "I don't want to be here." He sounded on the verge of tears.

Fry's voice comforted him. "Hey man, it's going to be okay. Keep it together."

Kyle looked around the interior of the truck. "Ben? Is Ben here?"

No response.

"Hey, can everyone look around themselves? If you see Ben give a holler."

"Nope," said October.

"No," said Andrew.

"Can't see him," I said.

"Nobody here matches his description," said Fry.

"I'm the only one I can see," said George.

"Anyone else?" said Kyle.

There was no response. I felt a chill go down my spine. We were in trouble. Big trouble. Ben was the one who knew how to relate to the wizard, he was the one who we were depending on to hold everything together. If he was gone we would be put into a bad situation, worse than the one we were in at the moment.

I needed to get us out of this mess. I had an obligation, with my power, to save us from whatever problems we might encounter, this one included. I wondered if I could do it. What would I materialize? How would I escape my bonds?

I decided to start with a simple idea: a knife. I materialized a blade between my hands and started rubbing the rope against it. After several minutes without feeling any change in resistance, I checked. No good. The rope was untouched; it must have been made of some special material that couldn't be cut by metal; that wasn't a far-fetched idea for a space-age civilization. Maybe it was something along the lines of Kevlar. I hadn't expected it to be that easy anyways, since they knew of my power.

Maybe I could materialize something outside, a barrier for the truck to crash into, or maybe a car that we could somehow control. But no, that wouldn't change the basic fact that we were bound and captive. Any attempt to stop the vehicle would only be countered and we had no way to prevent that.

"Does anyone have any ideas about how to get out of this mess?" I asked. "Anything I can materialize?"

"Have you tried a knife?" said Kyle.

"Yeah," I said, "But the ropes are made of some super tough material. I can't cut them."

"Try acid," said Andrew.

"I don't know enough chemistry. Besides, I wouldn't be able to apply it without burning myself."

The room was silent except for the rumbling of the vehicle.

"How about an acetylene torch?" said October. "Have you ever seen one?"

"As a matter of fact I have," I said, calling to mind an image of the object.

An acetylene torch was a device that produced an extremely hot flame by burning acetylene. Just being close could give third-degree burns in fractions of a second, and melt flesh in seconds. It would be dangerous, especially with how my mobility was impaired, but as I thought about it more I came to the conclusion that it might work if two people were to work together on it.

"I'll operate the torch," I said, "Unless someone else has experience using it."

No one spoke. I shrugged, materialized the torch, and struggled my way over to the closest person, Kyle. I held the torch in my bound hands and aimed it at the ropes that bound Kyle's wrists. Kyle nodded. "Do it."

"Someone turn on the gas," I said.

Metal creaked, and wind started to come out of the torch's nozzle. I lit it with the sparker at the tip and blue flame illuminated the desolate room. With the motion of the car, I was barely able to hold the torch straight, and yet I knew that I had to or else I would risk giving Kyle a permanent wound that would give us some serious trouble.

"It's hot," said Kyle, as I moved the torch closer to where the binds restricted his hands.

"Sorry," I said. "Hold on. I'm moving closer." I inched the torch towards the binds. When the flame touched the rope, it sparked, sizzled, and the rope began to melt. For several minutes I concentrated on holding the flame steady. The cut moved with agonizing slowness, but it was working.

The rope snapped. Kyle fell to the side. The flame petered out, as someone turned the gas off.

Kyle brushed off his hands and flexed his fingers. "That was uncomfortable. I think my hands are burned."

"At least your flesh hasn't melted," said October. "I'm next."

At that instant I was hit with the universe club in a very familiar fashion. We were going through a portal. Everything went black for a second, and when I came to, I was on my back with my eyes focused on the ceiling.

Kyle positioned himself with his feet closest to me. "Hurry up. We don't have that much time."

I grabbed the torch and pointed it at the binds. Someone behind me turned on the gas and I lit the flame. Time was running out. If we didn't get free soon, we would stay prisoners. I had the gut feeling that we were in for some serious trouble if my plan didn't work.

After about ten minutes Kyle was free. He took the torch from my hands. "Even if I have no training, I'll be better than you with your hands bound."

I didn't argue as Kyle proceeded to remove my binds. Before Kyle could move on, the truck slowed to a stop, and the sound of voices came from outside. Kyle and I looked at each other and came to the same conclusion. We would pretend to be bound and go along with them until we saw our chance. I materialized a knife and a gun and tossed them to Kyle, who hid them in his shirt. I gave myself a dagger about six inches long, hiding beneath my belt. If they tried to search me I would give them hell.

The truck's doors opened and several people came in. They lifted us up without ceremony and pushed us out the back. Those of us who were still bound had trouble walking, and so I mimicked them to avoid arousing suspicion. It must have worked, because they paid no attention to me, leading me through a snowy landscape towards a large, grey building that reminded me of everything that surrounded old Soviet style. The bleak walls, the receded windows with less-than-clear glass, the dirty snow. There was no doubt about it; this was a Russian facility. A gulag.

We were led through a dark doorway and into a sparse, empty room with a bank of computers along one side and prison cells along the other. There was no one else in the area besides us and our captors.

The captors spoke Russian to each other and then left us in the room, locking the door behind us. Two of them stayed inside, guarding the entrance. Without knowing what to do, I walked towards the bank of computers, which looked like the innards of a space ship from 1950's sci-fi television, all vacuum tubes and levers and small, curved television screens with pre-DOS command-line interfaces. However, though they looked old-fashioned, these computers were not weak by any means. I sensed a futuristic bent to their functionality, the same kind of aura that the Franchise restaurant had, the same kind of feeling that I had felt on the hovercraft on Tek, multiplied by a factor of ten. This was not a computer to take lightly.

I stepped up towards the center of the room. When I walked into a circle engraved in the floor, the computer bank booted up. Tape reels spun, dot matrix printers churned, lines of code flowed upwards on the tiny, hard to make out screens.

"Welcome, child of The Watcher," said a mechanical voice that reminded me of Hal in more ways than one. "I see that you have managed to escape your binds."

I moved my hands behind my back without thinking. But it was too late; if the AI could notice that, he could notice everything else. Whatever being was inside that computer bank lived.

A force field surrounded me. October spoke something, but I couldn't hear her, only aware of a faint buzzing around my body. I looked at the bank of computers.

"Why have you brought me here? Who are you?"

"I am a simple corrections machine," said the computer. "I do not have the authority to tell you such things. I have brought you here to make you an offer. Your skills are powerful. We have been gathering all those with powerful skills to our side for many ages now, and we have found you to be among the most powerful of them all. We would be delighted to have you with us."

"What is your goal?" I said, deciding to play along with this machine.

"Our goal is nothing short of total domination of all the planes in the multiverse," said the machine. "Transitioning them into glorious people's republics, of course, for the good of the common man."

"You mean turning them into communist despotisms," I said.

The machine laughed. "Oh, that is such a capitalist way to describe them. I see you have fallen prey to their nasty propaganda. You shouldn't believe everything you see on television, young man."

"And I shouldn't believe everything a computer who tried to capture me and my friends says."

"You have me there. What, then, can I do to make you trust me?"

As I talked, I saw out of the corner of my eye Kyle inching towards the computer bank. Without looking at him directly, I waited until he was ready, and then I materialized a rocket launcher in his hands.

Kyle pointed, fired, but before the rocket could reach the computer a force field surrounded it, neutralizing it. The missile exploded in silence.

"You can't defeat me like that," said the computer, its voice sounding amused despite the lack of human feeling. I was reminded of GLaDOS from Portal. "You still have a long way to go before you become the most powerful among our ranks, but I will admit that I see much potential in you. You could become a great warrior and a great assassin. Both options will be open to you should you choose to join us in our quest for glory and control. I hope you don't mind staying here, because until you do decide, that's where you're going to be."

In the corner of my vision, October made some hand gestures that I interpreted as "Stall."

So that's what I did. "Why did the map that I took from the trucks on Tek turn out to be a fake? Were you the one who planned it?"

"Map? I don't know what you mean. If you're talking about you materializing some sort of equipment that was originally attached to one of our research vehicles, it would be obvious what your problem was. The vehicles have a protection against magical, aetheric, and supernatural phenomena that extends to your ability as much as anything else. You're not really *that* powerful. You may think your power gives you an advantage, but as you've probably seen, there are many forces in this world that are more powerful than you are. The map may have just been the spells playing a trick on you because they were bored—they're sentient, in a way, and they're very mischievous."

October gestured with her hands in the corner of my vision. I couldn't tell what she was asking for; she was making a wave with her arms and pointing to the computer. It was a motley movement restricted by her bonds and I tried my best to interpret it and failed.

Then Fry spoke. "Magnets."

"Ah," I said, and then I materialized a rare Earth magnet as close to the computer's data banks as possible. Hundreds more followed in quick succession. When the computer tried to throw up force fields, they failed, the magnets falling through and sticking to the banks of processors. The force field around me failed and I ran up to the bank of computers, magnet in hand, and ran it across the monitors and wherever I thought needed to be broken. The computer spat out sizzling noises before it exploded into smoke. A little piece of ticker tape ejected out of a printer.

You won't get away, it said.

I ran for the door and tried to open it. It was locked. Fry pulled me back. "Materialize a truck as far from the door as possible. A big one. A really big one."

I did so, and Fry ran to it and leaped inside. I tossed him the keys. Fry jumped in, followed by Andrew, George, Kyle, and October. I got on last, holding onto the side through an open door. Fry gunned the engine and got the car going at about twenty miles per hour, towards the door. We slammed into it, crashing, smashing our way through the concrete and coming through into another room.

This room was large, high-ceilinged, with a number of aircraft stored underneath its canopy. I crawled through the hole made with the car and stood up, brushing myself off.

October came through after me. "Make us a robot."

I complied, and a shadow appeared over my head. The McDonalds robot was back in all of its red and yellow glory. October ran for the boarding ramp as alarm bells went off and a number of guards rushed into the room bearing automatic weapons. I created several buckets of oil above their heads and dumped them on the floor, causing most of them to slip and fall. In the intervening time, the entire crew got on, the airlock door closing behind us.

When we entered the kitchen, October went straight for the captain's chair. "Prepare us for an operation!" She spun around and began pressing buttons on her dashboard.

The rest of the crew returned to their stations amidst the food preparation equipment and beeping computers. Dozens of guards came out through doors all along the sides of the hangar. October piloted us over an airplane, crushing its wings. Sparks jumped from the wreckage and set the oil on the ground ablaze. The smoke rose through the air, obscuring our vision until October turned on an infrared scope. Even with that, the fire filled most of the screen, the bodies of the guards only just visible amidst the heat.

We blasted through the outer door and crushed several low-lying buildings. The air cleared. Several tanks rounded the corner of a building to our left and took aim.

"Load Big Mac round!" commanded October, pointing the robot's missile arm towards the enemy. She turned to me. "Max, man the antipersonnel turret."

I nodded and made my way to the small bubble where the turret was mounted. I had wondered where the playground that was in the back of the McDonalds had gone and now I knew: the turret bubble was made out of red plastic reinforced with bars of steel covered in blue foam. I saw the world through a scratched-up plastic window. However, I knew just by looking at the setup that it was at the very least bulletproof and most likely far more than that.

I grabbed the machinegun and vowed to never let my kids play in a fast food restaurant playground. A belt of ammunition was stored in the area behind the ball turret above the triangle-filled tower which you climbed to get to the upper levels; this was information that had come with my automatic training. I grabbed enough ammunition to fill the gun and climbed back down, loading the gun in a couple of seconds. I fired off quick, short bursts like I had been trained. The bullets were huge, aircraft cannon size. The gun was more like an autocannon than a machinegun to be honest. The recoil shook me to my spine and the noise forced me to materialize some ear protection before I lost my hearing for good. I fired without aiming, spraying every spot where I thought there was an enemy with an RPG. Several streaks of smoke told me where to shoot next. There was a medium-sized building with a row of windows that I shot out in a line. Several soldiers fell out of the broken glass. A tank exploded to my left.

The low roar of an airplane caused me to look at the sky. There, flying towards us, was a helicopter that looked oddly familiar. After a few seconds, I managed to recognize the distinctive green on red coloring: it was a Pemex helicopter. Several missiles hung on little stubby winglets at its side. I aimed my cannon at it and fired off several bursts, which weren't enough to bring it down but were enough to destabilize it. A missile streaked through the air and impacted our robot in the leg. The world tilted to the right.

"Max!" came October's voice, through the intercom. "Defend us from the missiles!"

I got creative and materialized a mountain of water inside the helicopter, which sent it spinning out of control while I sprayed it with my autocannon. My body began to grow numb from the recoil and even with my ear protection I heard a loud ringing in my head. The gun chattered away as I pressed the trigger, next shooting down a squadron of men running at us from the runway, then blowing up what must have been an ammunition depot with the fire from my tracer rounds. The explosion sent a wave of energy that shook my ball turret back and forth like a tree in a hurricane.

We reached the edge of the compound. October stomped through the three layers of fences and barbed wire, knocking down a watchtower in the process.

Several Pemex planes flew in at a low altitude. I fired my autocannon upwards at them, but they were moving too fast. Several missiles detached from their wings, and they opened up with cannons that sounded like a continuous tearing of the air. With just enough time left before the impact, I materialized an aircraft hangar around us, and the walls exploded into light. I was starting to feel a little bit of fatigue. The Watcher had implied that I wouldn't have to use energy for my power, but I was starting to doubt that I would be able to keep this up.

And I was also doubting that we could get out alive. Even with my power I knew that it was only a matter of time before a huge army overpowered us. And so, we had to do something, fast. We had to run. And we had to do it here.

"Max!" said October. "Portal to Telroth. Now!"

I created the portal without a second thought—it was simple to connect it to Telroth in this state—and we jumped through. The world hit me on the head with a club, and everything went black. I recovered to see our restaurant kneeling in front of me. It took me a while before I realized that this was one of the restaurants that I had materialized and left behind. It looked forlorn, abandoned, unhappy to be replaced without so much as a second thought.

A gigantic creature too big to make out landed right next to us, crushing the restaurant I was looking at, flames spewing from a mouth filled with teeth the size of a human. I looked the creature in the eye and recognized it. Drax, the dragon we had traded with. Our restaurant raised its arm to shoot, but I knew that we were gone—if Drax wanted to destroy us. But the look in his eye was different.

I scrambled back into the kitchen. "Stop! October, don't shoot!"

October lowered the arm. Apparently she too had noticed Drax's expression.

Drax lowered his head so that he looked right into the view screen. *I see you have brought trouble to this land.*

October keyed in the outside microphone. "What do you want with us, Drax?"

"You know this dragon?" said Kyle, his voice full of surprise.

"Yeah," I said. "We made a deal with him for his blood."

I learned that you need to go back in time, he said.

And then I saw him, beneath Drax's feet. Ben. He was standing between two of Drax's claws, folding his arms and smiling. "I heard you needed some help," he yelled.

"What happened to Red?" asked October.

He was a tasty treat, said Drax, licking his fiery red lips. *I followed you through the plains to see what you would do with my blood. It made me curious to no end. I wished to see what you would do with such a request, and I am not disappointed. To travel back in time to save the multiverse is an honorable use of such regal liquid.*

It was clear that Drax held himself in very high regard, if only from his tone of voice, or whatever it was that he used to speak into my head.

Drax took a stance around the portal we had entered through. *They are coming. This world is no longer safe. I can perform the ceremony to take you back in time, but I will need at least half an hour.*

"Until dusk, right?" October said.

Until dusk.

The sun was already low in the sky, just a little bit above the horizon, and dusk was soon approaching. I guess we were lucky in that regard.

Drax began to draw in the dirt with his tail, making first a circle and then a series of complicated patterns in the center. It was some distance away from the portal, which October soon destroyed. However, more portals appeared, and a number of Russian tanks charged through. October took a fighting stance. One fast food restaurant versus the might of the Soviet army. We wouldn't know who would win until it was over.

15

* * *

A Turn for the Crazy

"Communist magic?" I said, watching the wind blow drifts of snow at high speeds past the view screens.

Ben nodded, shivering, his entire body covered in ice. We had just picked him up during the firefight, which had devolved into a snowstorm, us with our vision impaired, our instruments frosted over, and an army of Russian tanks at our heels. We had all but lost sight of Drax.

Ben coughed, covering his mouth with a frost-covered hand. "Marxism mixed with Leninism mixed with a dose of traditional Russian winter. They can see through the storm. We can't. We need to get out of here."

"General Winter," said George, as he played with a number of dials underneath a screen showing nothing but static. "The friend and ally of Soviet Russia. They brought him along, it seems."

Inside the restaurant, it was starting to get cold. The heating system fought to keep the temperature stable, but even I could feel the change in environment. If top-of-the-line equipment couldn't keep the cold out, I didn't know what could.

"Where's Drax?" asked October, as she piloted the restaurant through the storm.

"He should be fine," said Ben. "Dragons have an innate resistance to cold. They're creatures of fire, after all. The snow should melt upon contact with his skin, and his internal temperature is regulated by magic."

"Looks like we'll have to postpone our adventure back in time."

"No," said Ben. "We can do it. Let's find Drax and continue with the ceremony."

"Even though we can't see the sunset?"

"Yes. I think we can do it. If this magic doesn't abate we'll have to do it."

October clenched the controls. "We'll do it. Overlay thermal imaging."

Kyle shook his head. "The processor can't handle—"

October cut him off. "Then do something about it!"

Fry typed in a line of commands at his terminal. "I can manipulate the ley lines tapped by this storm of magic and divert them around a small point."

"Er, say what?" I said, not understanding what was going on.

"Do it," said October.

Fry continued to input commands. "Done. The cameras should be cleared at any moment."

I sat back and watched the proceedings without saying anything. The best thing I could do was to stay quiet and keep my head clear. We were in for a tough ride, that was certain, but if I lost my cool I would be doing more harm than good.

It was only a couple of minutes after the Russians came out of their portal. At first we had an easy time dispatching the tanks, with our Big Mac cannon and our turrets, but after a short period of time the wind picked up, clouds covered the sky, and the temperature dropped fifty degrees. We were trapped in the middle of a snowstorm.

Russian magic was a beast.

A cannon round impacted the side of our restaurant, tearing a hole in the wall and ripping apart our left shoulder. Another round crashed through the sensor array at the robot's head. Half of the view screens went blank. The cold seeped in through the cracks, through the twisted metal and burning oil that seeped out of the ruined deep fryer. I hit the floor with my hands over my head as the entire restaurant shook. The light fixtures swung. Sparks jetted out of a broken power main.

"Do something about this!" said October, turning to me for just a second.

"What do you want me to do?" I asked, my mind blank, panicking.

"Anything!"

Another round hit the side of the restaurant and fire exploded out of the airlock. Fry flew backwards and slammed against the wall, slumping down to the floor with blood on his clothes.

I grabbed a med kit and scrambled over to his body. My shoulder wound flared up and I cringed in pain, stopping for a moment.

Fry grabbed my arm. "Don't worry about me. You have to save her. Save October."

I took hold of Fry's hand. "I'll get us out of this." The med kit opened with a click and a roll of bandages tumbled out, followed by a medigel injector and several other medical tools. I tore Fry's clothing and injected the medigel into the wound in his side, which was seeping blood enough to cover my hands. The gel foamed up with a red hue and the bleeding stopped.

The restaurant shook. Cold blasted in through the hole in the wall. The other half of the view screens went dark.

A box labeled "Hambugers" flew out of the freezer and smashed open against a griddle, spilling autocannon rounds onto the linoleum tile, the metal clanking and clinging as it spread across the floor. The grease fire around the deep fryer moved closer to the pile of ammunition.

I materialized a fire extinguisher and put out the flames before they could reach the volatile ammunition. My hands shook. I tossed the extinguisher aside and leaned against a wall. I couldn't think. Panic overtook me. I thought, agonizing, about what I could do—and then it came to me.

Like that, the blizzard stopped. The snow disappeared. The temperature in the room rose several degrees.

Kyle connected a power cord and an emergency view screen fired up. We stood in the center of a domed football stadium, in a cavern of cool, open air, with a number of Russian tanks surrounding us. October pumped her fist in the air.

"That's what I'm talking about!" she yelled.

I materialized a flood of random objects to block the Russian tanks as October ordered a round loaded, fired, loaded, fired. The restaurant recoiled with each blast of the cannon, and with each report a Russian tank exploded. I hadn't expected to come out of the situation alive; I now had a healthy respect for the limitation of only being able to create objects that I had seen before. A football stadium was huge, sure, but the time it took me to realize that I had seen one before was too long.

The last of the tanks that had been caught in the stadium exploded in a ball of orange fire. October let her hands fall from the restaurant's controls. No one spoke for a long moment. Then, Fry laughed, his voice filled with pain and half delirious; he sounded like he had been pushed over the edge. October joined in with him. Soon everyone was laughing, including me, even though I really didn't see what was so funny. It was contagious.

I stood up from where I had been sitting—I hadn't even realized it, but I had sat down at some point during the battle, my attention too focused on the proceedings to care that I now had a coating of Fry's blood on my pants.

Fry looked to be okay, though, and even though there was a lot of blood it didn't seem like he was going to die. His laughter was a good sign. The fact that he was conscious was also a good sign. In fact, everything was a good sign, now that I was alive.

The stadium rumbled as Drax crashed his way through the player's grand entrance on the far side of the field. Concrete tore off around his scales and cracks ran through the wall. The dragon stepped inside, unfurling his wings, and opened his mouth wide—he appeared to be yawning.

It's warm in here. His voice was broadcast for everyone to hear. *And it looks like we'll be safe, for now. No more enemies have come through the magic portal. Are they from the same universe as you people?*

"Sort of," said October, through the microphone that was usually used for calling orders for people outside—it had a tinny, cheap sound to it I half expected October to finish with "and a side of fries."

But she didn't. This was serious business, no time to be fooling around, and so I didn't mention my thoughts.

Drax began drawing on the grass once more, his tail tracing through half-melted snow, digging through the AstroTurf without any resistance as if it was regular grass. The shape of a circle appeared, though it was much more complicated than any figure I had ever seen in geometry class. Angles rebounded off the inner and outer walls, circling in spiral patterns, creating thin, stilted scripts in several different languages, several different styles. When Drax was finished he stepped back and stretched out his wings.

Good luck to you. Step into the center of the circle and we shall be off with you. Ben has given me the materials, which I have prepared and inserted into the blood-ink used to create this moniker.

"Thank you for helping us," said October.

It's my pleasure. It's not often that a dragon gets to assist travelers from another dimension.

October piloted our restaurant into the middle of the circle. Drax craned his neck and began to hum, a deep, bass sound that reverberated through the walls and caused exposed wiring to sparkle with incandescent light. Our restaurant was pretty beat-up but it still functioned, and if necessary I could always create a new one—we were ready to go as we were. We could handle anything the Russians threw at us, I was sure of it. I had my power. We had weapons. We had a plan.

Drax inclined his head, and then the world disappeared into a flaming white ball of fiery brilliance.

We came out the other end in the middle of a sea of nondescript grey buildings, covered in metal pipelines, a long row of factory tanks stretching into the horizon on both sides. Catwalks filled the spaces in between. We crushed several walls as we landed, throwing up a cloud of dust and debris. Several human workers ran out from buildings and pointed excitedly at us. I could just barely hear them—they were speaking Russian.

"What era is this?" asked October, looking around the view screens.

"We could ask," said George, as he typed in commands at his terminal. "Permission to begin unloading sequence?"

"Permission denied. We don't know if they're hostile or not."

"They don't look hostile," said Ben, crossing his arms. "And we have someone who can speak Russian with us." He looked at George.

George shook his head. "Use the translation device. I'm no good at conversation."

Ben shrugged.

"We're in no position to go about searching right now," said October, as she began to pilot the restaurant towards the edge of the compound. "We need to rest, recuperate, and repair. We're not going to be able to achieve our goal if we aren't in the best possible shape."

"I agree with October," said Kyle. "We can't do this as we are now. We need to come up with a viable plan, a viable solution, and we need to do some reconnaissance. The enemy probably won't know who we are or why we're here—we're back in time, after all—and so we have to use that to our advantage."

"Don't worry about the specifics," said October. "I've got everything planned out." She glanced at Ben.

Ben nodded. "Just trust her. We'll get everything done, we'll make sure Stalin never becomes an AI, we'll make sure that this Russia doesn't win the Cold War."

We made it to the edge of the compound. The plains stretched to the horizon, unbroken by trees, just open earth for miles and miles, bare emptiness where the only thing moving was us and the flickering emergency view screen.

A thought came to me. "How are we going to get back?"

"We'll warp," said October. "Dimensions exist independent of time. Normally we can't get the coordinates for dimensions in a different time frame from us, which locks us into one linear "time" shared between connected dimensions, but since we have the keys to our own dimension at our own time we should just be able to jump back like normal."

"I see," I said, only half understanding. At least it made sense. At least we weren't stuck. If we didn't die, that was.

We walked through the wilderness until the factory complex was just a smoke stain in the distance. Once we were far enough, October stopped the restaurant, and we settled down into a resting position. October got out of her seat and stretched her back.

"Hah!" She said, closing her eyes and making a funny face. "That was tough. Let's not do that again."

Fry chuckled. "We may not have a choice."

October frowned. "You're probably right, but let's not think like that. Let's be optimistic."

"Sure thing, boss," said Fry, as he coughed and clutched his side. Some blood came up in his spit. He wiped it off with his wrist, stared at it for a moment, and then flicked it off. Then he closed his eyes and leaned against the wall.

My own shoulder wound ached. I had been unaware of it thanks to the tense situation but now it was starting to hurt again. Even the advanced technology of medigel couldn't instantly heal a wound like the one I had, or Fry had. I wished it were easier but that was life. I would have to deal with the pain.

I reflected on how far I had come since being initiated into all this. It was far. I had learned about the Franchises, AI Stalin, Dragons, superweapon non-sequitur magic bequeathed by a purple-robed, time-traveling old man. It was no time to be dying, no time to give up. We had a mission and we were going to complete it no matter what—we were going to save the world.

Hah, save the world. Since when had my ambitions gotten so large? The Franchises, with all their armies, couldn't hold a candle to the power that wanted to take over the multiverse. Who were we, six people in a beat-up restaurant, to challenge them?

And yet I still held on to some form of hope, just the idea that everything would be okay as soon as this was over. We would all live. We would save the world. We would become heroes.

I clenched my fist. I was the ace player here, I needed to be in top shape.

"What next?" I asked, looking around at the now-silent kitchen.

"We search," said October, resuming her posture in the captain's seat. "We look for our enemy, and if we're lucky, we'll find him."

A shadow eclipsed the sun. The plains lit up with a bright light, the sky tore open, and purple energy swirled in a massive hurricane in the center of the tear. A starship of immense size flew out of the energy void at high speed and headed straight for our position. October clutched the controls and faced off against the ship, but it was too big—our restaurant was dwarfed. The shape of the ship looked familiar, though I couldn't place its source.

October dodged a blast of energy with a complicated maneuver. "Fire antiradar nuggets!"

The entire restaurant shook. The emergency view screens flickered, fuzzed, flashed on and off underneath a barrage of blinking lights. Fry flipped a comically large switch built into the McFlurry machine and a pop like the sound of a firecracker echoed through the kitchen. We dove to the right. A screen of white pasty nuggets spread through the air. Strangely enough, the stuff dispersed with the wind instead of falling to the ground.

Before I could wonder what they were made of, we turned and ran, our restaurant shaking back and forth with violent abandon as we put distance between us and the giant spaceship.

October looked grim. "We might have been too late."

"I don't think that's what we think it is," said Ben, standing solid in the middle of the kitchen. "We might still have hope."

"You can say whatever you want," said October, "But that doesn't change the fact that it's shooting at us!"

Another blast of green energy tore a crater in the ground to our right. The screen of pasty material was working. In our current damaged state, there really wasn't anything we could do, but at the very least we had some countermeasures.

I had to help. I summoned several large retaining walls like the ones I had seen around the California freeway, in layers, which exploded into bits of brick and mortar as the gigantic spaceship continued to bombard us with lasers.

A dust cloud picked up in the distance. Soon the shapes of several trucks resolved into solid form. They were covered in mud, dirt, grime, green camo and scratched paint and canvas stretched over wire. They approached at high speed, made a U-turn right behind us, and then began driving alongside our restaurant. A man stood up out of the top of one of the trucks and began waving.

We were moving at maybe sixty miles per hour. The restaurant took huge, leaping steps, and the trucks were barely able to keep up on the rough terrain of the plains.

On closer inspection, the trucks resembled the convoy that had been plaguing us our entire journey. However, there was something different about these trucks. They were a little too dirty, a little to modern-looking. These weren't the same trucks that we had been chasing. However, they looked similar.

The man began signaling with a flashlight.

"Does anyone know how to read mores code?" said October.

"No," said Ben. "I wish I did."

Fry pushed himself across the kitchen and made it to the radio. "I can fix it. They have to have a radio."

"Don't worry about that," said October. "You'll hurt yourself. I don't want you to die any more than the next person, but at this rate, you will."

Fry ignored October and continued to mess with the destroyed radio. The man in the truck stopped signaling with his flashlight and disappeared back into the body of his vehicle. The trucks peeled off and accelerated until they formed a line in front of us. Then, one of the trucks turned around and zoomed the other way. It passed with a swish.

"I think they want us to turn around," said October.

"Do it, then!' said Ben. "I have a feeling this is for our benefit!"

October gripped the controls, her knuckles turning white. "I don't know. How are we supposed to fight that thing behind us?"

"I can handle it," I said. "I can make this thing go away, somehow. If I can't destroy it."

October seemed to be thinking. Then, she nodded. "I trust you. Full stop! Turn around! Set our reactor at ninety percent output! Bearing north-northwest, engage cooking oil procedures!"

All of the crew, including Fry, scrambled to follow October's commands. We pulled a drop-kick turn, blasting up a wall of dirt, while at the same time ejecting a cloud of pasty white chicken filler—which is what I had determined that stuff to be. We dug a furrow in the ground with our legs. The spaceship headed straight for us, guns blazing. The earth around us split, crackling with green and blue energy blasts. Our restaurant dove for the ground. We went prone, aimed up, and fired. I summoned a suburban house over our heads, the roof of which exploded into splinters as wave after wave of laser energy tore it to shreds. Furniture flew in all directions. It was the house of a friend from the neighborhood, a fact that I reflected on as his graduation photo flew past the view screen, blazing with green fire. We rolled away, crashing through a wall, lasers burning up our backside. October got us back on our feet.

"Do something!" She yelled at me.

"I'm trying!" I said. I summoned a tank, several of them. They sat there, not shooting. Why had I confidently said that I could handle the spaceship when I didn't have a plan?

And then I did have a plan. I summoned a jumbo jet flying at high speed right next to the spaceship. In an eerily poignant moment, it smashed into the side of the spaceship, sending it reeling. I summoned another plane. This time, an explosion of red fire lit up the sky.

The radio crackled.

"I got it!" said Fry.

A voice echoed through the comm system, distorted, crackling, filled with tension.

"Get your ass out of here!" it said.

We booked it for the hills. Though, the world was flat where we were, so that expression doesn't really fit. The spaceship behind us headed straight for the ground, and then I really understood how large it was. Its shadow engulfed the entire sky. I had thought it much closer than it really was.

It was huge. Enormous. It was like a giant cumulonimbus cloud bearing straight down on our position while it crackled with lighting, ready to strike at any moment. A skyscraper in the sky.

Laser beams dug trenches to our right. A piece of burning debris smashed a crater the size of my house to our left. Behind us, the ground rose up as the backside of the spaceship impacted first. The front side closed in. We dove forwards, out of the shadow, just as the last bit of the spaceship bit the dust. Our restaurant performed an agile roll that was surprising considering how big we were.

The trucks in front of us swerved to a stop. The voice over the radio spoke again.

"Let's get out of here."

I couldn't have agreed more. We followed the trucks across the plain until the spaceship receded into the distance. A forest sprung up around us. Snow capped the trees, covered the ground in undisturbed drifts which the trucks kicked up underneath their wheels and which we left gigantic footprints in. Once we were deep enough into the woods, the trucks stopped.

The voice came over the radio. "You guys were stupid, trying to change the past like that."

"You know who that spaceship belonged to?" asked October.

"Yeah," said the voice. "The time management bureau. They make sure that people don't try to do what you do and change the past. They must have been really pissed to send a capital ship at you."

"We needed to go back in time to save our planet."

"Everyone says that. They all say that some form of evil went supernova or some bull like that and now their entire universe is under the cover of darkness. That's a pretty common occurrence here in the multiverse."

"Who are you?"

"Me? I'm just a trucker."

"Why are you here? Why did you help us?"

"Because we don't like the time management bureau any more than you do. If the world would be divided between good, bad, and neutral, we'd be neutral. But we do have an interest in keeping you alive. There's a certain someone with a power given to them by The Watcher with you, right? We have an interest in preserving him."

"What do you want with me?" I asked.

"Nothing, other than that you stay alive. You see, The Watcher doesn't just give his prey powers. He changes their entire destiny in a way that causes them to become way, way too important to the fabric of reality."

"Prey?"

"Ignore that. You are a special case even among the special cases. We've been chasing after you, trying to get you before our competition did. Looks like we made it."

"Your competition?"

"Never mind that. We have to get you somewhere safe. You can't be journeying around the multiverse and the space-time continuum without a care in the world like you have been doing. Because, if you were to die, bad things would happen."

"I can't do that," I said. "My world needs saving."

"That's what they all say, kid. Their world needs saving, they need to avenge their dead parents, there's a real bad baddy guy that they have to kill. A fight with the boogieman. Look, you're not special—well, you are special, but you're not. At the same time. Do you get what I'm saying to you?"

"No, not really," I said. "I can't accept this. Stalin is going to take over my world. Pemex is going to betray us. Orcs are going to go into space suits and Skynet is going to become communist."

"You don't really believe any of that, do you? Look, your enemies are the same enemies that all of us face. It's just a different skin that they wear. You're nothing special. However, you do have an important part to play in the flow of the universe. And so, we can't have you traveling through time and picking up the ire of the Time Management Bureau, or whatever big baddy that you absolutely have to beat. We have to get you back where you belong before our competition gets you."

"I think your competition is working with our enemy. I saw their trucks. They looked just like yours."

"There are a lot of different factions in the world of truckers, kid. You don't know if they're the ones we're up against. Besides, it's none of your business. Let us handle taking down the bad guys. It's in our best interest to make sure that one side doesn't get all the glory, and we have to say your enemy in particular is getting a little bit too much stage time. However, you're not the one to be fighting them."

October clenched her fist. "Max is coming with us. We're fighting our enemy, we're saving our world, and we're making sure that none of this ever happens. And besides, how can we trust you? How do we know that you aren't playing a trick on us and are planning to take us down as soon as we turned our back?"

"Look, lady, if we wanted to kill you we would have done so already. Or we could have just left the Time Management Bureau take you down and been done with it. But we need Max here alive, along with all his friends who have become causally related. We want the whole group of heroes to save the world. Let some contractors clean up your mess."

"Contractors?" said October.

"Yeah, guys who get paid to remove evil overlords from dimensions. They're real cheap, I've heard. I wonder why no one's suggested that to you before? You really don't need to go about playing hero when you have someone who can do the job for a couple hundred thousand multiverse credits."

"A couple hundred ... thousand ..."

"What, is that a lot to you guys? Where I come from that's chump change. Your dimension must have a real big trade deficit."

"We don't really do much interdimensional trade where I come from ..."

"Really? We have a bunch of kids from the boonies here! Wow, I can't believe you guys actually made it back in time without having your heads lopped off by an interdimensional dragonfly. Look, traveling the multiverse is dangerous if you don't know what you're doing. The ball of yarn is tightly woven, and if you cut one place, you can destabilize a whole lot of others. One of the jobs of contractors is to make sure that doesn't happen."

"Can you help us find some contractors?"

"As a matter of fact, I can. I have some connections. But first we need to get you somewhere safe."

The trucks formed a circle around us, reminding me of those old Indian movies where the wagons formed a fort and the Indians were surrounding then, hollering and shooting arrows. Though no one was shooting arrows now. It was all serious. We were in some trouble, that much was obvious.

Light sparked into existence in the center of the circle. Our restaurant shook, shimmered, shivered, and then I got hit in the head with the universe's galactic punch. When I came to, we were in the middle of a massive, vast city, with roads that looked perfectly tuned to fit our hulking monstrosity of a restaurant. All around us machines of similar size to our own marched past. Though, they all looked very different from what we looked like. Even so, we weren't out of place. Everything in the city was so garish, so sci-fi and yet steampunk and yet at the same time fantasy-looking, that I couldn't place one single idea about how everything fit together.

There, an inn that looked straight out of a Final Fantasy game. Here, a galactic cantina, there, an artifact skyscraper, over yonder a pulsing mess of insectoid flesh that must have been a hive. Everything moved. Everything buzzed.

Where were we?

No one in the kitchen spoke. Everyone looked amazed, blown away, as if they were witnessing something unimaginable.

"I thought it was a myth ..." October let go of the controls.

"It looks like it's real," said Ben. "The real deal. We really were sent back in time, that's for sure."

"How can anything be amazing in a universe like this?" I said. "Look, in the past few days I've experienced more crazy stuff than anyone deserves in their lifetime. I don't think you guys have a right to be stunned."

"There's amazing," said Fry, "And then there's *amazing*. This is *amazing*."

"It's like the holy grail of every dimensional explorer. The place where every piece of fiction interacts with every piece of non-fiction. The melting pot of the universe, the center of the multiverse. We've found it."

"Basically we entered a black hole and came out the other side," said Ben, crossing his arms and leaning against a griddle.

"So, this place, is, like, Atlantis," I said.

"Yeah, about right," said Ben. "We're in a place as legendary as that. You might not have heard about it since you're new to the whole multiverse thing, but the legend is that there's a place where every multiverse collides. The streets there are paved with pure idea, and everything you can imagine lives there. Here. Which is where we are."

"I see," I said, not really getting the amazingness part of the whole shebang. It looked to me like we just entered a slightly crazy artist's impression of the internet. Though everything did look very real.

"So what do we do now?" I said.

"Find some contractors," said October. "The truckers had some good ideas. We'll find a way to make money with your power and then we'll hire some people to clean up for us without, you know, ruining the ball of yarn or whatever." She paused. "At the very least, it's less of a long shot than us defeating AI Stalin and the entire Russian military, as well as the Time Management Bureau. Those truckers must have been really good guys."

"What about the plan you had?" I asked.

October sighed. "It was going to be a tough challenge anyways. I wasn't very confident that it would work in the first place. It's no use going over it now. We're at where we're at, and now we have to deal with the cards we've been dealt."

"So how are we going to go about earning money?" I asked.

Ben smiled. "Trying that." He pointed to a large electronic billboard that was covered in advertisements for alien technology, alien porn, and surprisingly, Coca Cola. In a small corner of the board was a descriptor in twelve different languages—including English—advertising for a tournament. The pay was in the millions of, well, what I assumed were multiverse credits. The sign was like those holographic corners of rare trading cards—or those stickers on the back of credit cards. It was very shiny. I kind of liked it; it reminded me of money more than the dollar sign did. It also reminded me of when I was really into Magic the Gathering.

Did people play that here? I wondered.

Then I ended that train of though and clenched my fists. "I can handle it. We can do this. We can win that tournament."

October laughed, which was surprising in its ability to relieve the tension in the kitchen. Everyone relaxed. Even Fry, who still looked like he was dealing with his wound in the worst way possible.

"If you're that confident, then I'm confident too," said October, letting her hands fall to her side. "We just have to figure out how to enter. We're not fighting in this beat-up old machine, are we?"

"I'll make us another restaurant."

"But first," I said, "I have to ask. Why aren't you guys thinking of me using my power to create something we could sell? I've seen gold coins before, I can create a whole bunch of them and we could just sell them and get the cash."

"That would be ..." said October.

"Too easy," finished Ben. "You forget where we are. The streets aren't paved with gold, but here the laws of object permanence don't apply. There's so much dimensional driftwood around here that nothing is in short supply. It's ideas that are the currency here. When pretty much everyone has a molecular printer at home that can make whatever they want, objects aren't worth anything anymore."

"You seem to know a lot about this place," I said. "Have you been studying it?"

"Are you kidding me? Every dimensional traveler knows of the Core. It's like a bedtime story, like Santa Claus for the multiverse. Just as unbelievable, too."

"I imagine what we're all feeling right now is the same that you would feel if you were to suddenly find yourself in the North Pole with Santa's Elves everywhere making toys," said Kyle.

"I've never heard of the place," said Andrew.

October shrugged. "Some people haven't. I don't know. I thought it was a lot more well-known than that."

"Enough talk," I said. "Let's figure out how to enter this contest."

October nodded, and we piloted our machine through the streets, looking for something that resembled familiarity. We passed round, domed buildings topped with neon blue, floating bubbles filled with fish, too many towers disappearing into the sky to count. It was like going down the Vegas Strip times ten plus aliens and every fantasy steampunk visual trope in existence. Brass piping, Xenon blue, smokestacks, flying cars that looked like they were taken straight out of Back to the Future right next to Star-Wars-esque speeders. Dragons, pterodactyls and an eighteen-wheeler with the Taco Bell logo emblazoned on its side.

Finally we made it to a quarter where there were some recognizable signs hanging above the buildings. Some were in Chinese, some in Arabic, but they were unmistakably from Earth. I wondered why there was a community here when this place was so legendary, but I figured anything went at this point.

We stopped at a parking structure that was as tall as any of the nearby skyscrapers. A massive mechanical arm reached out and grabbed our restaurant, lifting it into the air like it was a toy, and then we were slid into a recession in the center of a round, open room that went from the bottom of the building to the top.

Thousands of other vehicles were parked in other recessions. They were as crazy and out-of-this-world as everything else in the city. I was reminded of The Hitchhiker's Guide to the Galaxy; that was the kind of vibe I was picking up. It was as if Douglas Adams himself had stepped out of his grave and designed a world. If he was crossed with a semi-sentient AI that spat out random bits from every known piece of fiction.

"The air here is breathable," said Kyle, typing in several commands at his station. "But it looks like there's some sort of magical effect that keeps that in place. The actual atmospheric composition is pretty crazy, twelve percent Argon, with a healthy point-five percent Radon gas. Somehow the rad count is normal, though. We'll live."

October got out of her seat. "Grab the translator. We're going to find out as much as we can, and then we're going to enter that contest and win our way to saving our planet."

"I wonder why the Franchises couldn't have done this on their own," I said. "Why did they have to put up a fight when they could have just hired someone?"

"They didn't go time-stepping like we did," said October. "The only reason we're in the bigger multiverse here is because we did something stupid. Even the Franchises in all their power can't rival what we've done. Now, are you done asking questions?"

I nodded. "Let's get this over with." I created a translation machine, strapped it to my back, and we left the kitchen through the bathroom airlock. It was broken, halfway caved in, and yet the door still worked enough that we were able to exit.

When I stepped outside I was immediately bombarded with a world of smells. The hint of cinnamon wafted above machine oil and the smell of Chinese cooking. It was definitely like stepping onto the surface of a foreign world, though at the same time it was strangely home-like, almost as if I was stepping through a portal that took Earth and spat it through a hashing algorithm. It was an experience that was both comforting and off-putting.

October led the way. We walked to a bank of elevators built into the side of the tower, stepped inside, and were whisked downwards at an incredible speed. I was surprised when we didn't go weightless, but after a few seconds I lost the feeling. I was done being surprised by what I encountered.

The ride was silent. We stood, weapons resting in their holsters, watching the world fly past. I carried my sniper rifle in pieces in a case strapped to my back, right next to the translation machine. I figured that since this world was already crazy that carrying around dangerous weapons would be a small deal.

I was right. The citizens of this place were armed to the teeth. I wondered what kind of government this place had, and then decided that there must not be any to allow this sort of crazy society to exist. It was the perfect libertarian ideal. Though what that amounted to was unknowable at this point.

We walked through a crowded street and passed every manner of alien being, as well as a few distinctly human characters. Everyone looked like they had a mission of their own. October led us to a section of the city where the signs were in what I deemed to be Japanese.

Something clicked inside my head. "Is this ... Akihabara?"

"Akihaba ... what?" said October.

But it wasn't. It only reminded me of the place. Because, the whole place was themed around anime. And then, I got a better look at the buildings. They were colorful, strangely detailed, a little distorted to my vision.

"We must be entering a divide between a three-dimensional world and a two-dimensional one," said October, slowing down. "What is this? Cartoons?"

"Anime," I said. "This is ... Real life anime."

The buildings evolved, and soon the boundary between reality and the twisted version of Japanese cartoons became fuzzy. This really was a legendary place, after all. Everything gathered here.

The people became more colorful, turning into classically styled characters.

It wasn't just anime. It was everything. Cartoons, comics, from sources other than Earth as well. It was just the Earth comics I noticed first.

Ben chuckled. "Anime style isn't unique to Earth," he said. "I see your eyes boggling. Earth is just one of the many outposts anime has come to through its conquest of the multiverse."

"I see," I said, looking at the colorfulness of my own hands. "So where are we, exactly? Have we become two-dimensional?"

"Not exactly," October said, "Though there looks to be some magic in place that allows our interaction with this plane. Hey, you like anime, don't you? Can you communicate with some of these people? They look like they speak Japanese."

"Don't we have the translator for that?" I said. "Besides, I'm really not that good at Japanese. In fact, I'm horrible at it. George is probably better at Russian than I am at Japanese."

"Whatever you say," said October. "Though the translator will be cumbersome."

We entered a bar with a mix of steampunk and Japanese style, brass piping over a sign that read "Ramen" in several different languages, including English.

The inside was steamy and smelled of noodles. People from both the two-dimensional world and the three-dimensional world mingled like it was nothing new. The sound of voices in every language drifted on the sweet odor of soy sauce and the tingle of monosodium glutamate.

It felt nice. I finally relaxed, after being tense the entire walk. We walked up to the bar and found ourselves some seats in between the other patrons. They were strangely non-solid, the seats, and I felt odd with my legs half in and half out of the three-dimensional world.

October fired up the translator and spoke into it. "Hey, can you serve us seven ramen sets?"

The translator did its job. The bartender, a robot that was oddly familiar looking, gave us a dirty look, or a look as dirty as a robot could give. "You don't have to use that piece of junk. I am fluent in over eight million different forms of communication."

"Oh, god," I said, recognizing where the robot was from. Star Wars. This was great, just great. I decided to take it in stride.

"Sorry," said October, powering off the translator. "Can we have seven ramen sets?"

"We have brax tongue, waffalo, or minced bullet crab," said the bot. "Those are today's specials."

"Then let's have the minced bullet crab."

"A good choice."

"Hey," said October. "Do you know where we can find out about the fighting tournament that's happening in town?"

The robot went quiet. "Why do you want to know?"

"We need the money."

"That place isn't where newcomers to the Core like you should tread. You must be careful here, no matter what power you possess. I sense some great energy coming from that boy over there, but it takes more than power to survive the Ring."

"The Ring? That's what it's called? I think we can handle it. We have no other choice."

"If you say so." The robot served us up some noodles—they were completely free, as they came out the back end of some sort of synthesizer machine—and we took our meals and ate. The stuff was good. Very good.

I wondered what kind of place this was. If everything was free, what did people do with their time? What kind of entertainment did they watch? Or did they even watch it? Because, here, it seemed like the line between entertainment and entertained was blurred, the line between reality and fiction no longer as distinct as it was back in the real world.

I wanted to thank those truckers for bringing us to this place. At the very least they had showed us some kindness—it was shaping up that way, anyways.

There was finally an end in sight. All we could do was hope that the end would be the one we wanted.

16

* * *

Dreamworld

The registration office was grand, voluminous, all sumptuous leather and red velvet and floating holographic screens displaying the latest battles. Dozens of individuals from all manner of species walked around the center room or waited in line or clustered around the view screens. It gave the room an air of festivity, one that was well-deserved.

There was another bot similar to the one in the restaurant who took our ticket and registered us. He spoke in a fast, watery tongue to the person in front of us, and in a rough, Germanic-sounding language to the person after us. The robot's voice was well-balanced and didn't sound so robotic, more regulated than piecemeal like the robots in many sci-fi movies talked.

After we got our ticket, we were told to wait in the middle of a vast arena while we were evaluated. Each member of our staff was scanned by a large machine, and then we were split up into different stations where our measurements were taken and weird looking headbands were given to us. Little drones buzzed about constantly, taking pictures and operating the testing machinery.

I demonstrated my power by summoning a car. The few people who were watching us clapped, though the sound was more cursory than appreciative. The concept of a golf clap came to mind. The Core must really be a wonderful place for my power to have received only that much excitement. Maybe people like me were a dime a dozen or grew on trees or some other stupid metaphor like that. What was I to know?

Still, I was confident. My skills, though very new, had been refined through the fire of live combat. Playing in a simple game would be a cakewalk.

Hopefully.

We finished our examination and the examiner robot handed us our ticket, which was a black metallic orb that glowed in blues and reds and greens like a science fiction galaxy map without the map part. October tossed it up into the air and caught it with her other hand.

"We're in the second category," she said. "Not quite the major leagues, but still passable. I guess that's the best we can hope for."

The team gathered around her. We were a battered group, tired-looking, about ready to collapse from the pressure we had been under. But still, there was an air of confidence about us that hadn't existed just a day ago. Having a clear goal must have contributed some small amount to that, but the biggest thing was simply that we were in the last stretch.

We left the testing building and walked down the city streets, which were layered on top of each other like catwalks and which shot to and from between the tall buildings, angling up and down and twisting and turning into elevator platforms that could fit a hundred individuals. We rode up one of those platforms on our way to the staging ground.

The arena was massive. A domed building visible from miles away, covered with bright searchlights and fluttering pendants. After a good amount of walking we made it to the entrance. October presented her ticket at the gate and the gateman let us through without a word. We came into a hangar with a ceiling high enough to be foggy and indistinct, filled with vehicles of every size and shape. People walked on the ground in between. On the walls screens played videos of the currently airing battles, with commentary in several different languages both spoken and written.

We found our empty staging spot, and I summoned a restaurant in its loading bay. The restaurant was in its eatery mode, a mode which I hadn't seen in a while. The McDonalds sign lit up with neon color, powered by the restaurant's reactor.

Andrew ran his hand along the stucco exterior. "It's good to be back," he said.

George leaned against the wall and crossed his arms. "What are we doing here?"

October opened the door and leaned in. "What do you think we're doing? We're going to win, that's what."

"That's obvious," said George. "What I wanted to know is our plan. How are we going to win? We don't know anything about our competition. We could be in way over our heads. I was just advocating for some preparedness, is all."

"You don't have to get all mad," said October. "I was planning on doing that. In fact, let's do that now. We're going to the arena. George and Andrew, you guys visit the level three field. Ben and Kyle, you guys visit the level two field. Me and Max will go to the level one field. Fry, you stay here and guard the ship."

"Sir," said Fry.

The seven of us parted. I walked with October through the massive hangar, towards a door in the wall that shone with a sign that must have read "Exit," though I couldn't understand the script. It looked kind of like Klingon to me, though it probably wasn't.

We stepped through the door and into a wide hallway filled with people. Screens floated unbound at about twice head level, which was about head level for a couple of very tall individuals with long, giraffe-like necks.

October stopped at an entrance to the arena. Then, she turned around and faced me, her hands behind her back. "Since we're finally alone together, do you want to do something special?"

That was right. October and I were ... I don't know what we were, but I was hopeful. At least now that things had calmed down some we could get back to what normal, everyday high schoolers were supposed to do.

October tilted her head. "What do you want to do?"

"I want to watch the arena," I said, for a lack of better things.

October smiled. "Then let's do that." She took my hand. We walked through the entrance and into a massive domed room lit by floodlights and laser beams. The middle battleground was a city of obstacles the size of buildings. Some of them were buildings, derelict monoliths that had probably once served as offices or apartments. People gathered in the seats around us, trickling in through the entrance ways, chattering in a dozen different languages and a hundred different accents. There was a special place on the other side of the stadium that was for people from the two-dimensional plane, and right next to it was a place I assumed as for people from the fourth dimension. There, the walls curved up in impossible ways, moving back and forth, appearing and disappearing Mobius style while being all one surface.

October took a seat in the middle of the bleachers. I sat down next to her. The seat was hard, cold, metal that wasn't exactly the color of copper but wasn't the color of steel or aluminum either. It was more purple than red, more yellow than orange. It felt smooth to the touch like a gossamer curtain and was surprising in the way that it made my back feel comfortable. I relaxed. This was going to be interesting. In this world where everything existed at once, I was going to watch something spectacular, a battle between powers that I could only guess at.

The lights dimmed. The stage lit up with bright contrast. In the left corner, a gate opened and a mammoth beast the size of a school bus with six legs lumbered out. On the other side, a tiny door opened and a single figure stepped through, holding a gun twice her size, wearing armor that sprouted wings at her back. Jet fire coming from a backpack caused the air around her waist to shimmer.

A bell sounded. The six-legged beast roared, shaking the stadium, and the single girl took off spiraling into the air. She flipped backwards, sideways, dodged a rock thrown at high speeds, swirled around a blast of acidic spit, dove under a snap of the monster's jaw and landed on its head. The monster tried to shake her off. The girl pressed her gun against the monster's skin. The monster rolled over, almost crushing the girl against an obstacle. The girl just barely managed to jump away before being trapped. The monster snatched her out of the air and held her in its claws.

The girl pulled a lever on her suit and an explosion ripped the monster's hand apart. The monster reeled in shock, and the girl flew up and fired several laser blasts at the monster's eyes. The monster stumbled, blinded, and then the girl ended its life with a shot to the cranium.

The crowd cheered. It had been a short battle, and now it was over. The girl was victorious. I wondered who she was; would we be fighting her?

The next act came on. I noticed October leaning against me, but I didn't do anything about it. This was the time for me to be taking notes. The six-legged monster had been a formidable enemy. I wasn't sure if even our restaurant would have been able to take it on.

However, the girl had been even more powerful. If that was the level of combat that we would be experiencing, I wondered how I would be able to handle it.

The next battle started once the carcass was cleared out of the arena. This time, a blob of liquid the size of a house battled against a shape-shifting demon from the fourth dimension.

The demon flickered in and out of existence while the blob of sentient liquid separated into parts, froze itself, turned itself into steam, and maneuvered around the field with an agility that shouldn't have been possible. The crowd cheered with wild abandon. Cameras floated through the air, mounted on drones, recording every hit and every explosion.

The demon from the fourth dimension was eventually trapped inside of a well-laid snare and its skin was boiled off until it collapsed into a hole in the fabric of the universe.

It hit me that this game would be dangerous. We weren't playing till first blood. We were going all out; the battle would be until one side couldn't fight anymore.

What a gruesome, harsh scenario. Maybe the Core wasn't as utopian as I had first assumed. Or, perhaps, there was something that made death irrelevant. If that was the case, we were at a disadvantage. I continued taking notes in my head about how the contestants fought, about what sort of rules it looked like the game had. Well, it wasn't a game. Not when the contestants died if they lost, or at least had a chance of dying. It wouldn't be a game to us.

We continued to watch the fights. There was an endless flow of contestants, an endless number of people coming and going from the stands and the bleachers. Robots hovered back and forth offering refreshments. Cheers filled the air.

My whole body tensed up; I could sense someone watching me. I looked around but there were too many people to single out any one particular individual. Who was it?

October didn't seem to notice. She was sitting still, watching the games as they played out in front of her. Her face was scrunched up in concentration.

I stood up. "I have to go to the bathroom."

"Sure," said October. "Come back safe. Don't get yourself into any trouble."

"I won't," I said, as I left through the aisle and entered the outer ring of the arena which led in a circle around the stands. I searched for something resembling a bathroom—it wasn't that I needed to go. I was searching for a place where I could confront the person watching me, following me. Because I could still feel it. Whoever had an interest with me wasn't peeling away.

If I was lucky I could catch them off-guard and get them to spill the beans as to why they were watching me. However, I wasn't so optimistic to believe I could win in a fight against someone with a considerable amount of power. I had to rely on my luck and my instinct for this.

Not that there was much of that to begin with. I walked into what looked like the restrooms.

I was wrong. What I saw was a sort of food vending area, with techno-thriller vending machines covered in pipes and gears but at the same time possessing the style of an Apple product. What I had mistaken for a bathroom sign was really something else.

And it was a dead end. I turned around. There, in the doorway, was The Watcher. He leaned against the doorframe with his arms crossed.

"What are you doing?" I asked, relieved to know that the person watching me wasn't trying to kill me. At least, I assumed so.

The Watcher shook his head. "This isn't the way to go, my child."

"What do you mean?" I asked. "You haven't said anything but cryptic riddles. How are we supposed to work when we have people like the Time Management Bureau up against us?"

The Watcher frowned. "I did not give you your power so that you could get someone else to do your heroics for you. You were meant to save your own world."

A sudden burst of anger ran through me. "What do you know? Your gift has saved us several times, sure, but why are you expecting so much from me? I can't do this! I'm not a superhero! I'm just a random high school kid who happened to get sucked into something crazy!"

The Watcher walked up to me and put his hand on my shoulder. "I'll be watching you. Just know that whatever path you take, make sure you feel it to be the right way. I can't tell you more because I don't know more. I'm not an all-powerful figure. However, I do have wisdom, and I do have experience. With that I can tell when something will succeed. And, your plan has a high chance of failure."

"So what do you suggest we do?" I asked. "Go back and fight AI Stalin? Battle the Time Management Bureau? We can't do something like that! We have to get someone else to do it!"

"You've taken on something huge," said The Watcher. "Maybe you should reconsider your position as the hero. Maybe you weren't meant to be who you think you were meant to be. Maybe ... Maybe you could return to a time when none of this was real."

"None of this was ... real?"

"Yes. Back when you were ignorant. Could you give this all up? Could you take back what you had before, exchange what you have now for it? Could you accept the fact that none of this is real?"

"What do you mean? I ..."

"Think on that choice. When you are ready to answer it, call me. I will show you the way out."

"The way out ..."

The Watcher flickered, his image turning into a projection, then a flat image, then a person-shaped mist. I let my hands fall to my side. What did The Watcher mean? Was this real? Or was this a dream? I suddenly doubted everything. What was going on? Why had this idea suddenly come into my head?

And who was I to say any of this was real, anyways?

"Max?" October leaned into the door. "Max! I found you. You were taking a long time." She paused. "Hey, this isn't the bathroom."

"I made that mistake too," I said. Then, I gave an awkward grin. "Let's get back to our information gathering session."

October took my hand. "You don't look too good."

"Sorry," I said. "It's just that I'm a little scared about what is to come."

October sighed. "I am too. Don't worry. We'll get through this with our lives, our world, and we'll be heroes. Or at least, we'll be the people responsible for cleaning up this mess."

"Right," I said. "That's what I thought."

October tilted her head. "You look like you're thinking about something."

"I ..." I decided not to tell her. Mostly because I feared what would happen if I did. What if none of this was real? What if everything was just one big dream? Would talking to October about this turn it into a reality?

I decided not to talk about it. "I'm fine," I said. "I'm just a little worried, is all. What we're doing feels really dangerous."

October sighed. "Yeah, I know. But do you know of any better options?"

Good, she didn't suspect me.

October led me back to the stands where a hundred thousand other people milled around us. We sat down in our seats and continued to watch the battle progress. Several more contestants duked it out while we watched, though there was nothing spectacular. When we were done, when we had enough information, we left the arena and walked through the streets of the city. Everything was awash in color. Bright neon lights advertised movies and entertainment, though there was nothing resembling food or products. Of course. Everything physical in this world was free, after all.

Such an interesting concept. One that was bound to cause us some trouble.

Were there other people like me out there? I wondered. Maybe that was why this place was the way it was. If one person had my power—me—then other people should have it as well.

Not that any of it mattered. October and I walked through the busy streets, looking at the passerby, not talking. Nothing needed to be said. We came to a shadowy alcove in the road where a couple of trees hugged a wall next to a bench. The trees were supported by a hydroponics system—there was no soil. In the background the hum of electricity droned on, ever so slightly fluctuating in a regular cycle.

We sat down on the bench. October leaned back and put her hands behind her head. "This place is nice," she said, her voice wistful. "I wish we could live here."

"So do I," I said, "But we don't. This place is foreign to us. We don't belong here."

"You're right. We belong on Earth." October sat up straight. "Let's go report back to the restaurant."

Our little moment of peace was gone.

Back at the restaurant, we met up with the rest of the crew. None of them looked hopeful, and, as we shared what we had found, the situation started to look pretty grim. Our opponents would be powerful. The winnings wouldn't be enough after only one or two battles. We wouldn't be able to fight every single day; there was a waiting list for contestants.

As the bad news piled on, the only thing that I could do was hope that something good would come along and ease our tension. But, in the end, nothing came. We were stuck with what we had at the moment. Was there another way to earn money? Was there something else that we could do?

The situation was starting to get desperate. October sat down on the kitchen floor and folded her arms, an intense expression of concentration on her face.

"We have to do this," she said. "There's no other option."

No one responded. Everyone looked around, their eyes darting, not a single person without some form of tension in their body language. Fry tapped his foot nervously on the ground. Andrew chewed on his lip. George paced back and forth between the deep fryer and the radar console.

Ben held up his hands in a placating motion. "Should we just go home?"

October shook her head. "No. We can't abandon everyone, and besides, there's no home to return to." She paused. "What gave you that idea?"

"Well, since we traveled back in time or whatever, couldn't we just go to a time when everything was good and warn the Franchises about the coming war?'

October looked thoughtful for a long while. Nobody said anything. Silence hung heavy over my head. I felt suffocated, claustrophobic, as if the kitchen walls would close in on me at any moment, swallowing me whole without any chance of escape. I wanted out. I wanted something to drink.

Maybe a soda would calm my nerves. I walked out the employee door and took a soda cup from the stack next to the targeting computer and the napkins, below the dual cash register and hydraulics control station. I filled my cup with Diet Coke and took a long swig.

It tasted good. I didn't want to lose something like this. If I died, would they have Diet Coke on the other side? I idly contemplated the depths of that question while staring at the bubbling, popping liquid inside of the paper cup I held in my hands.

October walked over to me and put her hand on my shoulder. "Cheer up. We can do this."

I shook my head, taking another long drink of soda. "It's not that. I'm afraid. I'm afraid that this is going to be our last battle."

"Then let's go out with a bang," said October. "Everyone, time to get going. We have our first match to fight."

17

***

Resolving the Core

The harsh stadium lights shone bright even when put through the view screen's filter. The crowd was quiet, not rowdy, without the impressionistic mob mentality that I had seen at the other battles. Perhaps it was because we were unknown. Perhaps it was because our restaurant did not look as threatening as our opponent—maybe they thought this would be an easy win for the other side.

The enemy was a dragon. Not like Drax, more like a serpent, more Chinese than western in its stylings, though it did not entirely resemble one of the props from Chinese New Year's. This dragon had a long beard that ran in two strings down its left and right side. Its scales were gold and green, with hints of ruby red in streaks spiraling around its joints. It opened its mouth and smoke poured out from between its jaws. Small jets of flame roasted the air.

I mentally readied myself. This was going to be a battle to the death, or until whichever side could not continue to fight. I planned on going all the way. I wouldn't be taken down so easily that the game would end before I pulled my trump card.

The strategy was to hide my power until the right moment. Right now, surprise was on our side. The enemy probably didn't expect us to have something other than our robot to support us. This was to our advantage. If we could get the dragon into a position where I would be able to take it down by summoning something, then we would be able to take the lead or even win outright. That was the plan, at least. One that we needed to execute on, one that could go wrong at any moment. One that could cause our deaths.

The gong went off. The dragon swirled through the sky, wings furling, swiping at the air, claws outstretched. Fire blasted from its mouth and its nostrils. October dove for the ground, sending our restaurant rolling, until we turned around and landed a drop kick vertically on the dragon's chest. The dragon pulled back. October blasted the dragon with Big Mac rounds. Fry and Andrew operated the playground ball turrets. Bullets and tracers flickered through the sky, impacting the force field that separated the crowd and the arena. The dragon easily dodged most of the machinegun fire and had an even easier time absorbing the ones that did hit.

Claws impacted our right side. The dragon's face filled up the view screens. The jaws opened, wide, teeth the size of kitchen knives ripping through our metal hide.

Now. With the dragon's internals exposed through its mouth. I materialized a flood of gasoline and poured it down the dragon's throat. The dragon choked, spat fire from its mouth, and the gasoline exploded with a blast that cooked the outside of our restaurant. We rolled backwards and out of the range of the flailing dragon's claws.

The dragon roared, flame splashing out from its mouth in fountains. So it hadn't been killed by the blast. However, we had injured it.

The dragon only became more enraged, more aggressive. It body-slammed our restaurant, enough to send us tumbling to the ground. We were pinned. October fired the cannon into the dragon's hide point-blank, once, twice, three times, to no effect. The dragon tore off our right arm and threw it across the arena, where it landed with a skittering slide and bumped to a stop against the arena walls. October whipped our remaining arm around and punched the dragon in the face. The dragon reeled. October pushed our robot onto its feet and curb-stomped the dragon's head into the side of a building. The building collapsed. Debris buried the dragon's head while its backside undulated with a ferocious frenzy. October stomped on the dragon's head again, again, and again, until a crack rang out through the arena that split my ears. The dragon shivered once, and then was silent.

The crowd didn't cheer. Nothing happened. Were they disappointed? Did they not like how the battle had ended up?

And then a voice came over the intercom. "Hello, my dear adversaries."

It was in heavily-accented English, stereotypical Russian with a hint of vodka and bears and cold, icy Siberia. I knew who it was on the second word.

AI Stalin. He had found us. How I knew this, I didn't know, but what I did know was that our days of having fun trying to save the world were over.

The crowd looked as confused as we were. The doors burst open. Rows upon rows of orcs in space suits with laser rifles marched through, coming from every direction.

October leapt our restaurant into the air, landing in the bleachers after a sizzling break through the force fields surrounding the arena. The crowd scattered. Laser blasts fired from all directions. It seemed like the crowd was becoming a part of this battle too. Everyone carried a weapon in this society, and they were making great use of that fact. An explosion rocked the foundation of the arena. October piloted us out into the streets, where fire burned in multiple buildings, where several skyscrapers billowed smoke and looked as if they were about to collapse.

It was clear what had happened. AI Stalin had come to take over the Core. People ran in all directions, orcs in amongst them, shooting, looting, screaming and using magic like no tomorrow. A blue whale appeared out of nowhere and slammed into the side of a building. Several animated school buses flew through the air only to collide with a rubber Godzilla, leading to an explosion of candy technicolor filled with raining mushrooms. October took us through the chaos as both of our playground machineguns fired on full-auto, ripping through orcs and citizens alike. I hated the fact that everything was so chaotic that we couldn't aim, and I knew that we would regret our actions later, but now wasn't the time to be reflecting on what was right and what was wrong.

We were in danger. AI Stalin was about to come and bring his retribution to us. We were going to lose.

Several dragons like the one we had fought and killed in the arena were engaged in a dogfight with Pemex helicopters and flying mechas. One Pemex station exploded in a bright ball of gasoline-powered light before its pieces spiraled into the side of the tallest skyscraper in the local area. Then, two seconds later, that skyscraper collapsed in on itself, bringing with it a cloud of ash and smoke that covered our visual radius. It was all flashes and crushes and explosions and screams.

Sweat poured down October's face. "Max! Open us a portal to somewhere. Anywhere!"

"Will do!" I said. I created a portal right in front of us—and the portal collapsed instantly.

October slammed her fist down on the dashboard. "They're jamming us!"

A projectile hit the side of our restaurant, sending us reeling. The view screens shorted out, to be replaced by the emergency lookout monitors a couple seconds later. We viewed the foggy, ash-filled air around us through low-resolution cameras as October did her best to keep us alive amidst the chaos. Everything was being destroyed. Another building toppled, then another, further thickening the atmosphere. We stumbled through the streets blind, without any idea of where we were going, only hoping to make it out of the mess alive.

And then everything went quiet. The air became still, the ash settled. And above us, around us, on top of the buildings and in the air, were the Franchises. Burger King. Wendy's. Kentucky Fried Chicken. Popeye's. McDonald's. Hundreds upon hundreds of Franchise restaurants spread through the city, dropping from the sky, from gigantic floating advertisement blimps that had "Goodyear" scrawled across their sides in cheesy ticker-tape. There must have been a thousand of them.

A fierce battle ensued, one more crazy than any other one I had ever experienced. There was no understanding it, explosions everywhere, smoke covering everything, but eventually I understood the outcome. The orcs were beat back. The city was liberated. Our enemies retreated back through the portal from which they had come.

A single restaurant rocketed down right next to us. A view screen turned on in our kitchen, and a familiar face showed itself.

"King!" October said.

It was King. He wore a grin that was bigger than it had ever been, and he looked to be the proudest person in existence.

"Didn't think we'd come back for you, did you now?" said King.

October looked like she was about top cry. "How!? How are you still alive?"

King looked both thankful and gloating at the same time. "You saved us. When you went back in time, you opened a dimensional rift that allowed us to slip through the cracks in the multiverse. It was you who warned us about the coming doom. Probably a future you, to be honest, but I'll thank you in past-advance for what you've done for us."

October gripped the controls of our restaurant. "Then ... We did it. Somehow, we managed to save the world. In the future."

"Right, in the past," said King. He laughed. "You'll be fine. You don't have to do anything else, we'll take everything from here."

We marched through the city until all the orcs, all the enemies, were purged. The Franchises surrounded us. I hadn't had to use my power after all.

I remembered what The Watcher had said. Had I listened to him in my heart? Was that why everything was changing now? Had he even had anything to do with this?

What if it was all a dream? One that I would wake up from, not remembering half of it?

* * *

And then I woke up. In my bed, in my room. Nothing had been real. It was all gone. The memories of what had happened those few days—had they been days? They were slowly fading away.

I was in my bed. In my room. A McDonald's sign was visible from my window, the McDonalds that I had fought in for so long. Or had I?

I got out of bed, went to the bathroom, and brushed my teeth. There was lots of gummy stuff in my mouth that felt great to get rid of. I rotated my shoulder and it felt stiff, like it had been wounded recently—but there was no scar. Perhaps I had merely slept on it wrong and imagined it to be a wound in my dream.

I rode my bike down the street to school. October was waiting for me at the gates. "Hey, Max," she said, smiling. She walked up to me and gave me a hug. "How are you doing?"

I thought for a moment. "Good. Hey, listen. I had the craziest dream last night."

October looked tense for a moment, and during that second I almost had the feeling that everything had been real. But then October relaxed and that moment went away.

"Hah," she said. "What was it about?"

"You won't believe this," I said, "But I dreamed that McDonald's was really a giant robot army fighting against AI Stalin and space-age Lord of the Rings Orcs."

October laughed. "That's the craziest dream I've ever heard."

I laughed with her, though inside, I felt a little ... Strange. Like I had forgotten something important.

Very, very important.

* * *

October

"Do you think he'll be okay?"

"Yes. He'll keep the things he's learned. He'll stay a better person for this, keeping with him the lessons that were taught to him through trial, through fire and battle."

"Why did you have to delete his memories?"

"He was too powerful. If he had stayed with us, he would have upset the balance of the multiverse. He already did it enough by opening a time-rift between several universes. Normally, there are safeguards in place, and there's the Time Management Bureau to worry about. But with his power everything became a moot point."

"Why couldn't he have stayed with us? What was wrong with him?"

"Nothing. He did save our planet, after all. But, sometimes the fate of a planet is a small deal compared to the fate of the multiverse. Because of him, the Core was almost conquered by a rouge agent. Because of him, multiverses that were not supposed to interact, interacted. We needed to stop that."

"I still think you should have let him keep everything. Including his memories."

"Would you want to be responsible for the fiasco that happened?"

"No. Are you saying he is?"

"He's the reason why we lost. He's the reason why we won. He's the reason for everything that happened. He was the catalyst. When a person with his imagination enters the impressionable dimensions, lots of things turn loose that shouldn't be turned loose. His imagination caused the war. And it's his imagination that should remain imagination. Don't worry. He has gained a whole lot from his experience, and has come out a much, much better person. You'll figure this out for yourself eventually."

"I ... Yes, sir."

* * *

I leaned back in my seat, sitting next to October in math class. It had been a month since we started going out, and in that time I felt like I had changed, a lot. I was a lot calmer in tense situations. I felt like I could analyze data and make decisions that were lucid when others wouldn't have been able to. I felt in control of my life. Why was that? Was it October?

It had to be her. She was the reason why I had changed. She was a positive influence in my life. Now, all I had to do was play my cards straight.

Then I would end up a happy person. Yep, that was it.

But that dream ... That dream stayed with me, for as long as I can remember. Was it real? Or was it fake? I still don't know to this day. Everything has a dream-like tone to it. Is reality a dream?

But that stuff has been hashed until it doesn't even resemble hash browns anymore. I'm interested in more interesting stuff. Like a sandwich.

I'm kinda hungry right now. I think I'll go make one.

Epilogue

Joseph Stalin stood in front of an army of Terminator robots, T-34s behind him, men saluting in their top hatches. A DOS-style computer screen stood in front of him, green text scrolling across its surface.

You are my successor. You are the one who I have been looking for. Together, we shall rule this world. We shall conquer dimensions that we never would have imagined before this encounter.

A white wizard with white hair and a white beard, white staff in hand, walked up to the meeting. "Greetings. My master is interested in this pact as well."

Saruman, said Skynet. *You do not have a history of loyalty. What makes you think we believe you are here in your master's stead?*

Saruman held up his staff. "I have seen the eye. Anyone who walks away with his life will be forever branded. I cannot resist no more than you can resist the temptation that is controlling all of humanity."

Skynet laughed, though it was hard to interpret as such—it was robotic, not human at all, cold, alien. *Then we shall see.*

Joseph Stalin held out his hand. "Let us—"

A Pemex fighter hovercraft sped into the negotiation zone.

"They're coming!"

"Who?" said Stalin.

"The Franchises! They came out of nowhere!" The hovercraft turned around, and in a blast of light exploded into molten metal. Pieces of green-painted steel rained down from above.

Joseph Stalin dove for the ground. Skynet cut off communications with its terminal. Saruman began to speak, his voice low, magic energy radiating from his white cloak.

A Burger King battle bot landed in the center of the meeting, guns blazing, dancing around the blasts coming from the Terminator robots and T-34 tanks. Joseph Stalin's head exploded in a blast of red. Saruman tripped, fell, and smashed his face on the skull of a dead orc.

A virus the magnitude of which had never been seen before entered Skynet through the terminal, infecting it, bringing it down and with it its network of battle robots. The world became a frenzy of fire. Pemex planes crashed in droves. A nuclear explosion rocked the horizon, as the One Ring dissolved in hydrogen-powered atomic fire, much more powerful than the fires of Mt. Doom.

A poster of Joseph Stalin's face rippled over the battlefield, torn, covered in dirt, as the Franchises cheered in victory, stepping back through the time portal from which they had entered.

The last to leave was a dragon, red-skinned, and as he stepped through the portal of his own making he smiled, puffing smoke out of his nostrils.

Reminds me of how Red tasted. Kind of like ... Tacos.

Made in the USA
Middletown, DE
08 May 2022

65494572R00129